CONTENTS

The Serendipity Shop

Dorita Fairlie Bruce

Girls Gone By Publishers

COMPLETE AND UNABRIDGED

Published by

Girls Gone By Publishers
4 Rock Terrace
Coleford
Bath
Somerset
BA3 5NF

First published by Oxford University Press 1947
This edition published 2009

Typeset in England by AJF
Printed in England by CPI Antony Rowe

ISBN 978-1-84745-062-3

THE LOCATIONS OF *THE SERENDIPITY SHOP*

Dorita Fairlie Bruce used the north-west Ayrshire coast, the Firth of Clyde, and its surroundings, as the location of *The Serendipity Shop*, the first of the 'modern' Colmskirk books. This was where DFB had spent part of her childhood, and, after moving to Ealing, returned for many holidays, finally going back to live there again. Eva M Löfgren writes in her *Schoolmates of the Long-Ago* (p163) that 'Colmskirk is Largs', and explains that 'the parish church of Largs was always dedicated to St Columba'. I visited the area twice, together with other enthusiastic readers of DFB's books, and, following in her footsteps, found that some of the places and streets in this book are real, and many of them are still there.

DFB begins her story by describing the Serendipity Shop:

> It stood in the corner of the little grey square just behind the sea-front at Colmskirk, and, unlike any of the other shops, it had a window that looked two ways—into Gallowgate Square where it properly belonged, and round the corner into the little short street, only a few yards long, that led up to the square from the Esplanade. And this queerly shaped window was filled with the most astonishing and delightful things. At least, so little Merran Lendrum thought, though there were other people who described them … as "so much junk."
>
> (p33)

Whilst waiting in the shop for her doctor father, Merran asks Mr Roberton the owner what his beads are made of and from where he gets them. He says, on page 37, "Made of? … Why, chuckie-stanes maistly—the sort ye pick up ony day oot yonder

Gallowgate Square

on the shore. But ye's require to pick up the richt yins, ye ken. It's no' ilka chuckie that'll polish up into a bonnie bead." This last sentence causes problems for Merran later in the book, when she has inherited the shop, and, with her younger sister, Julia, gone back to live in Colmskirk.

Merran and Julia arrive at Colmskirk station one evening, 'as the shadows were creeping down on the green hills behind Colmskirk' (p50), to be met by Sandy Lamond, their lawyer, who drives them to his home, 'that old house on Robin Water, just below the railway bridge' (p44), from the station car park into Main Street, where Julia says, 'Merran, there's Robin Water … and there's the ferry-steamer coming over from Inchmore.' (p52). Gogo Water is the real name of Robin Water; and Inchmore, shown on any road gazetteer as Great Cumbrae, is the island opposite Largs. I was able to follow this, almost as DFB describes it, as many of her descriptions of the scenery help to confirm the various locations.

I was pleased to find that Gallowgate Street ran along the sea front, just behind the harbour, and also, at the end, Gallowgate Square—but now, sadly, with two of its sides missing—opened up at the front, so that, if you stood with your back to the sea, you were looking at the row of shops and houses that, in the story, Mr Bartle had bought, and was intending to demolish—along with Merran's newly owned shop, that he hoped to buy from her. However, if you look in the top left-hand corner there is a building that has the 'window that looked two ways—into Gallowgate Square …'

Merran and Julia have lunch at Macrae's on their first day back in Largs, and DFB writes that 'they managed to secure a table in the window of the restaurant above the big baker's shop' (p71). Thomas Mackay and Son's Bakery and Tea Rooms in Main Street, which has been identified as the model for Macrae's, no longer exists, but a photocopy of an advertisement in an official guide to Largs which includes a photograph of the tea rooms, found by Eva, shows them in the building now occupied by a branch of the Royal Bank of Scotland.

A historical landmark in Largs can still be seen, though not quite as the sisters first see it from their bathroom window above the shop when they move in. 'For immediately opposite her the backs of the Main Street shops were completely concealed, by a conical grassy mound, which rose to the level of their sloping slates' and Merran says, '"Gallowgate Square—that means 'the square on the way to the gallows.' I believe this must be the old gallows-mound of Colmskirk."' (p57); and later in the book Sandy tells Julia that it is known as 'the monument' and is 'the original cairn where they piled the Norwegian dead after the big battle on the shore in the days of King Alexander … just outside the kirkyard wall' (p187). A visit to Skelmorlie Aisle, with a walk through the archway behind it, enables one to look over the kirkyard wall to see the remains of the mound, now very much smaller.

I was interested to find that there is a Boyd Street in Largs, which leads into Brisbane Road and then Brisbane Glen Road, the area called 'Glenbruie' by DFB, and where she placed Drumbruie House, the home of Perry Boyd's family. Boyd Street intrigues me: did DFB take the Boyd family name from it? The original of Drumbruie House was Brisbane House, which was demolished in 1942. Lizbeth Bartle, Julia's schoolfriend, drives Julia up Glenbruie for a picnic, where they meet Perry Boyd, and Julia tells him that Merran thinks she can remember him at parties as a small child.

Merran and Julia take a holiday one Wednesday afternoon, and take the boat to Rothesay; from there, Merran says they might 'find a steamer going through the Kyles, and get some tea at

Above: the ferry crosses from Largs to Great Cumbrae
Below: the north coast of Largs

Above: yachts moored beyond the quay at Tighnabruiach
Below: the Kyles of Bute

Tighnabruiach' (p125). Julia points out rhododrendrons among the trees along Loch Riddon, and white yachts in the Narrows of the Kyles. We also went to Tighnabruiach, by the ferry from Largs, and I have a photograph of rhododrendrons, also in flower on the shore; we, too, saw white yachts but no red-sailed *Fiammetta*, the yacht owned by Perry Boyd.

DFB also used Glasgow, by name, as the main town in the area, to which Merran goes by train to meet the managing director of the firm which orders work from her.

Mr Bartle lives in a large house on the Broomieknowes, behind the sea front, which is where Julia has been collecting the 'chuckie-stanes' from which Merran makes her jewellery. The Broomieknowes are the present Broomfield Street, which is to the south of Gogo Water, and there was 'a grey, rambling house with big rounded windows' that we think could have been used

The quay of Tighnabruiach

by DFB for Mr Bartle's house. In the story, Merran is warned by Sandy that Mr Bartle owns that part of the beach, and objects to her collecting from it. So she decides to take a boat over to Inchmore, and 'investigate the beach there, immediately opposite the Broomieknowes. It's just possible it might hold the same kind of stones' (p152). I took my car on the ferry over to Great Crumbrae (Inchmore), and we drove along the coast, and walked on to the red sand of the beach (which reminded me of Devon) to pick up pebbles and stones, but, unlike Merran, we did not find any dull yellow ones. Leaving on the ferry from Largs, I could see the green hills behind the town, just as DFB described it when the sisters first arrived.

I found that researching the location of *The Serendipity Shop* was rewarding, and very satisfying, as so much of it was more easily identifiable, than usual, especially with DFB's use of the actual place names; and her descriptions of the countryside showed her love of Scotland, which I share with her.

Chris Keyes, with thanks to Eva M Löfgren, Doreen Litchfield, Stella Waring and all who joined us.

THE COLMSKIRK NOVELS

The nine Colmskirk novels, set on the west coast of Scotland in an area overlooking the Firth of Clyde and published over a period of twenty-five years, consist of stories linked by characters and events. They reflect the changes in political and social history over a period of three hundred years, from the 1650s to the 1950s, but they also reflect the way in which books for young people were written from 1930 to the mid 1950s, and throw light on the way in which Dorita Fairlie Bruce developed as a writer.

However, they were never conceived or marketed as a linked sequence; they came from three different publishers, and by the time the later, 'modern' books were published, the earliest had long been out of print. I had read some of them as a schoolgirl in the 1940s and the later ones as a librarian, but I had never thought about them as a series until I met Eva Löfgren, author of *Schoolmates of the Long-Ago* (Stockholm, 1993) in the 1980s and she talked of them as 'the Colmskirk novels'.

They are set in an area much loved by DFB, stretching along the Scottish coast to the south-west of Glasgow from Wemyss Bay in the north to West Kilbride in the south. Although she spent much of her life in England, this is where her roots lay, where she spent many holidays and to where she eventually retired in 1949. Largs, which lies at the centre of the area, is called both Redchurch (in the first two Colmskirk novels and in the school stories about Springdale and St. Bride's) and Colmskirk. DFB's choice of names is appropriate, as Largs Church is red and dedicated to St Columba. The anomaly of Primula, a former pupil at Springdale, returning in the last Colmskirk novel, *The Bartle Bequest*, to be Curator of the new museum is completely ignored.

The stories are linked through the important families of the area—the Mellishes of Braidburn, the Boyds of Drumbruie, the Hunters of Garth and the Raesides of Windylands, who intermarry. Family fortunes rise and fall in turn, in keeping with political and economic conditions. Less prominent families also appear throughout the series. Generations of Beiths provide lawyers and solicitors, eventually taking the Lamonds as partners. Sandy Lamond appears in all the modern Colmskirk novels; possibly DFB had him in mind as a suitable husband for one of her strong-minded female characters. At a lower social level, the Gibbie Ritchie of Portarlie who appears in *Wild Goose Quest* is surely a descendant of Janet Ritchie and her son Gibbie, who play an important role in *Mistress Mariner*.

Even before *The King's Curate* was published in 1930, DFB had already used in three short stories the plots that she later developed in *The King's Curate* and the following book, *Mistress Mariner* (1932). 'The King's Curate', which had appeared in *The British Girl's Annual* in 1917, is a shortened version of the book of the same name and uses slightly different names for the characters. 'Captain Betsy' (*Mrs. Strang's Annual for Girls*, 1926) and 'The Smugglers of Portincross' (*The Oxford Annual for Girls*, 1929) both appear, again in slightly changed form, in *Mistress Mariner*. 'Captain Betsy' was a fictional account of a real person, Betsy Miller, who captained a ship and became a legendary figure in the area.

The King's Curate and *Mistress Mariner* were both published by John Murray. They may have been written and published with an adult audience in mind as there are no illustrations and the novels that are advertised at the back of them seem to be family books rather than books for young people. They were published just before Geoffrey Trease's *Bows Against the Barons* (1934), which radically changed the way of writing historical novels for the young. In the use of archaic language, DFB's books hark back to Henty, the popular writer for boys, and seem closer in style to those of Georgette Heyer, Jane Lane and Jean Plaidy, all of whom began to publish historical fiction in the 1920s and became middle-brow best-selling authors for the next fifty years.

Unfortunately DFB did not, like them, use historical periods and events likely to be familiar to most of her readers, old or young. An understanding of the plot of *The King's Curate* depends on a reasonable knowledge of Scottish history in the 1640s, the period of the English Civil War. English readers would know about Roundheads and Cavaliers but probably not about the Scottish Covenanters, the Presbyterians who, in the National Covenant of 1638, swore to maintain their own form of worship, and in 1643 promised military help to the English Parliamentarians in return for the establishment of Presbyterianism in England. (Although Scotland and England had the same king, the Act of Union between the two countries was not signed until 1701.) At the Restoration in 1660, Charles II restored the episcopacy in Scotland, and resisting ministers were dismissed from their livings. The reader really needs to know this to appreciate the romance of Patrick Mellish and Anne Carstairs, and the relationship that develops between Patrick's sister, Alison, and Ebenezer Baldie. Patrick Mellish is the King's Curate sent to replace Ebenezer Baldie, the Presbyterian minister.

The background to *The King's Curate*, the use of Scottish words and phrases (although the meaning of many of these can be deduced from the context and there is the occasional footnote) plus the Heyer-style period language make the book difficult to read. (People educated in Scotland would presumably have had a better grasp of the historical situation.)

Mistress Mariner is slightly easier to read, partly because it is set at the end of the 18th century so the French wars and trade with America, which form the background to the plot, are likely to be more familiar to the reader than the doings of the Covenanters. The heroine is Philithea Mellish, a descendant of Patrick, an attractive young woman and a contrast to her friend and cousin, Gillis Boyd, who is very feminine and dreams of romance, while Philithea's ambition is to follow in her father's footsteps and captain a ship herself. Together they travel south to Furze Hill in Gloucestershire to visit Guy Catteral and his parents, an incident which reminds me very much of Catherine Morland's visit to Northanger Abbey, while the villainous Guy is reminiscent of George Wickham in *Pride and Prejudice*.

A Laverock Lilting (1945) seems to be set in about 1820—the book can be dated from the fact that Sir Walter Scott and his family are firmly settled at Abbotsford to which they moved in 1812—but time has telescoped a little. Fergus Boyd, who courts and marries Jentie Crawford, is a grandson of Hugh Boyd, a contemporary of Philithea. This book was published by the Oxford University Press, who had published DFB's school stories, and is illustrated by Margaret Horder, one of the finest illustrators of girls' stories in the 1940s. It is clearly intended for a young readership, girls who were moving on from school stories and hoping for a little mild romance. Jentie is a delightful Cinderella character who, through her talent, hard work and a certain amount of luck, pursues a successful singing career. (Both Anne Carstairs and Philithea enjoyed inherited wealth.) *A Laverock Lilting* introduces real historical people—apart from Sir Walter Scott, Sir Henry Raeburn, the portrait painter, appears and Fergus's father is based on Sir Thomas Brisbane (1773–1860) who was born at Brisbane House near Largs, distinguished himself as an astronomer and soldier, and became governor of New South Wales. It is a novel which seemed appropriate for the young people's book market in 1945 and was reprinted, hence the number of copies still around.

The next book in reading order, *The Bees on Drumwhinnie* (1952), which was also published by the OUP and illustrated by Margaret Horder, is set in the 1840s, when the railway has just reached Westharbour, the port south of Kirkarlie (West Kilbride). Felicity Brown arrives by train to live with her aunts, the Misses Hunter, who, together with Felicity's mother, their younger sister, have been brought up at Garth, one of the local big houses, but who are now living in penury as the house has had to be sold to pay off their father's debts. The Browns know that Eliza and Mia have been forced to leave Garth but are unaware of how little money has been left for them to live on. Felicity is shocked but, being a very practical young woman, insists on carrying out her plan of living with them and solving their financial problems by paying board and keep for herself and her younger sister. She soon conceives the idea of keeping bees and selling the honey to make a little extra.

Did the OUP insist on certain changes to make the book appealing to girls of 12 or 13? The younger sister, Deborah, who arrives by sea ten days later, seems to be introduced almost as an afterthought, a bright and articulate schoolgirl of 13, with whom younger readers can emphathise. By the late 1940s, public libraries were developing fast in the post-war world, and increasing emphasis was being placed on services to young people. Libraries provided an assured market for their products, so publishers began to take note of what librarians wanted. Girls were maturing earlier in their reading tastes and enjoyed the books of Georgette Heyer and Jean Plaidy rather than pale imitations of them. As teenage fiction, the Colmskirk novels were ahead of their time.

Felicity meets the young laird, Simon Raeside of Windylands, in the first chapter almost as soon as she arrives at Westhharbour, and in the last chapter accepts his proposal of marriage. In between come her successful attempts at beekeeping, despite the efforts of a villainous local tenant farmer, family mysteries, the financial saving of both the Hunters and the Raesides, friendships and romances. It is a well-constructed plot, characteristic of DFB.

Meanwhile *Wild Goose Quest*, the next in reading order and the oddest book of the nine, had been published by the Lutterworth Press in 1945. This looks like an attempt to break into the adult market and might well have been written some time before it was published. With a plot based on a treasure hunt, sparked off by a letter and map left by Philithea, that takes Katharine Raeside and her friends across Scotland to Easterbraes, it could have suggested itself to DFB soon after the completion of *Mistress Mariner*. All the characters are adult and belong to the world of the 1930s—bright young things, a bit of do-gooding, private aeroplanes, flying lessons, the great families falling on hard times. When the mystery girl, April/Ailsa is scared by a passing aircraft, it is suggested that she was perhaps born during an air raid in the First World War. The good works in which Katharine, a direct descendant of Felicity and Simon, assists Agatha Spence are typical of the social movements of the 1930s, and although Agatha never actually appears in the book, she sounds rather like one of the do-gooders with whom Richmal Crompton's William gets involved in the earlier 'William' books. There is no question of Katharine looking for a real paid job, despite the reduced circumstances of the Raesides, although she mentions the possibilities of keeping bees and says that it has been done before. Perhaps both *The Bees on Drumwhinnie* and *Wild Goose Quest* were written some time before they appeared in print.

The last four books in the series were all published by OUP soon after they were written, and are clearly intended for the young reader. *The Serendipity Shop* (1947) is rightly described as the first of the 'modern' Colmskirk novels. It is firmly set in the post-war world, when life was changing and career novels for girls were emerging. These were written for schoolgirls about young women earning their living, pursuing careers and usually getting their man as well. Although it is Merran Lendrum who inherits the shop, develops her skills as a carver of local stones and gets her man, Perry Boyd of Drumbruie, it is her younger sister, Julia, who is the stronger character of the two. Still a schoolgirl in this book, she is a major character in all the last four Colmskirk novels. Although the Lendrum sisters have been living in London with relations after the death of their parents in a railway accident, they return to their roots in Colmskirk, where their father had been the doctor, confident that they will meet people that they know. Their arrival in Colmskirk introduces the reader to the town as it appears in the remaining three books. The letter telling Merran of her inheritance comes from the long-established law firm of Beith and Lamond. Sam Bartle is a new character, an example of the successful business man who emerged in the post-war period. At first he is a source of conflict but Lisbeth, his daughter, and Juliet make friends quite early in the story and in the end he becomes a good friend.

Triffeny (1950) is another career novel. Triffeny Blair must be one of the most quickly reformed teenagers in fiction, her desire to study art, preferably in Paris but certainly in London, successfully channelled into working at the pottery run by her great aunt, Tryphena Blair, in Craigs, just north of Colmskirk, where she has been brought up by her aunts, who are Beiths and the elder sisters of her dead mother. This time the villains are her cousin Phena and Phena's accomplice, Habbie Tewson. Julia Lendrum, who is now Sam Bartle's secretary, provides a role model for Triffeny. This must have been a very special book for DFB as the Blairhill pottery and the adjoining house are based on the house called Triffeny where she lived from 1949 until her death.

In *The Debatable Mound* (1953) Susan Crawford's successful pursuit of a career in fruit-growing is a central theme, but the book is also a holiday adventure story. The Crawford family, consisting of father, Lalage (19), Susan (16), Keith (13) and Cubbie (12), move from Ealing to St Ringan's, north of Colmskirk, where Professor Crawford, an archaeologist, had spent many boyhood holidays and where he now wants to explore a mound in the grounds of the house he has bought. The boys, Keith and Cubbie, are delighted to find they now have a boat. By the early 1950s, publishers and libraries were in search of books that would appeal to both sexes, and holiday adventure stories were ideal for this purpose. Stories about children and boats had been popular since the 1930s, thanks to Ransome. In the 1950s archaeology became a popular topic because of the television programmes of Sir Mortimer Wheeler. The mound is the cause of a feud between Professor Crawford and his neighbour, Admiral Majendie. Susan's interest in fruit-growing leads her to work for Perry Boyd and eventually to an agricultural college in Easterbraes. There is romance for Lalage. However, one can't help feeling that the element that appealed most to DFB in this book is the romance between Cousin Pen, who moves to a nearby bungalow to 'keep an eye on them', and her two suitors.

Cousin Pen, now Mrs Crawford, plays an important part in the final Colmskirk novel, *The Bartle Bequest* (1955), which is most notable for the reappearance of Primula Mary Beton, who is appointed Curator at the new museum in Colmskirk. However, mindful of the need to provide a young character and the fact that Primula and her friend Julia Lendrum are now both successful career women in their mid twenties, even though the reader may have first met them as schoolgirls, the story begins with Bethia Fairgreave, aged 16, who, on the death of her step-father, is obliged to leave school find a job and somewhere to live immediately. At a domestic employment agency she meets Primula, who works at the Scottish History Museum in Edinburgh and is in search of a cook-housekeeper. They take an immediate liking to each other, and Bethia is at the centre of another of DFB's skilfully constructed plots. Julia visits Primula—Mr. Bartle, by now a well-established character in the modern Colmskirk novels, has donated and endowed a museum to the Burgh of Colmskirk, and Julia, Mr. Bartle's efficient secretary, feels Primula will be the ideal Curator. Her only rival for the post is a young man, Tim Nisbet, a friend of the Crawfords, and they both submit applications. There is no interview but Primula wins the day and Tim becomes the manager of the nearby Serendipity Shop now that Merran is married to Perry Boyd. Once again, there is a villain and a mystery to be solved, not to mention a romance, and the book makes a fitting conclusion to the Colmskirk series. *The Bartle Bequest* reflects life in the early 1950s as I remember it (one character travels around selling nylons to village shops—they were still a novelty) but also recalls a life-style that was beginning to disappear: I paid someone to clean my bed-sit once a week but Primula needs a full-time housekeeper, and I think that Colmskirk Burgh Council would certainly have interviewed her and her rival before making an appointment.

Although the nine Colmskirk novels represent various kinds of writing and lack the coherence of DFB's other series, they share common elements. They all feature determined and able young women—Anne Carstairs, Philithea Mellish, Jentie Crawford, Felicity Brown, Katharine Raeside, Julia Lendrum, Triffeny Blair, Susan Crawford and Bethia Fairgreave, who all have clear ideas about what they want to do with their lives. Their strength seemed to be enhanced by their lack of mothers—and sometimes fathers as well. Jentie, Felicity, Katharine, Julia, Triffeny and Bethia are all orphans, while Philithea and the

Crawfords have only a doting father. (Primula's parents are kept firmly off stage.) Most of them marry—only Philithea and Julia, and those who are still young at the end of the series, do not—and who is Sandy Lamond going to marry? Many of the girls in the later books come back to their roots in Colmskirk—this is true of Felicity, Katharine, the Lendrums, the Crawfords and, in a way, Primula, although her previous links with the area are ignored. Another recurring motif is the use of dogs or cats as Greek chorus commentators on the action. Jentie's Birkie, the Lendrum cat, William of Orange, Triffeny's dog, Muffins, the Crawfords' dog, Geoff, and cat, Lorenzo, and, most of all, Mr Tiddlewinks, who adopts Primula and Bethia shortly before they leave Edinburgh, are good examples of this.

There are many links between the books and with other series by DFB. Primula promises to introduce Bethia to Dimsie and Anne in *The Bartle Bequest*. The treasure hunt in *Wild Goose Quest* begins with the discovery of a letter left by Philithea to a young Raeside cousin. The crystal necklace that Fergus gives to Jentie in *A Laverock Lilting* is lost and then found again in *The Serendipity Shop*. Katharine refers back to Felicity's beekeeping. Is Professor Crawford related to Jentie Crawford's family? Is Nancy Caird's husband Angus Macrae related to the minister of the same name who occupies the Manse at Easterbraes in *Wild Goose Quest*? Julia is confident that the Patersons will take Merran in if she's stranded on Inchmore when the fog rolls in—are these the Patersons of the Nancy books? There are probably many more links but these are a bonus. Each of the Colmskirk novels stands alone as a satisfying and enjoyable story.

Sheila Ray

THE COLMSKIRK NOVELS IN READING ORDER

The King's Curate, John Murray, 1930. A longer and slightly changed version of 'The King's Curate', published in *The British Girl's Annual*, 1917

Mistress Mariner, John Murray, 1932. The short stories, 'Captain Betsy' (*Mrs. Strang's Annual*, 1926) and 'The Smugglers of Portincross' (*The Oxford Annual for Girls*, 1929), are both adapted for the plot.

A Laverock Lilting, OUP, 1945, illustrated by Margaret Horder

The Bees on Drumwhinnie, OUP, 1952, illustrated by Margaret Horder

Wild Goose Quest, Lutterworth Press, 1945

The Serendipity Shop, OUP, 1947, illustrated by Margaret Horder

Triffeny, OUP, 1950, illustrated by Margaret Horder

The Debatable Mound, OUP, 1953, illustrated by Patricia M Lambe

The Bartle Bequest, OUP, 1955, illustrated by Sylvia Green

PUBLISHING HISTORY

The Serendipity Shop was first published in hardcover by Oxford University Press in 1947, with a wrap-around dustwrapper and black-and-white illustrations by Margaret Horder. We have used the full dustwrapper on this Girls Gone By edition. To the best of my knowledge, there have been no further editions until this one.

Adrianne Fitzpatrick

NOTE ON THE TEXT

For this Girls Gone By edition of *The Serendipity Shop* we have used the text of the first edition. In the Appendix we explain what we have done about the few typographical errors that we found in the original. We hope that we have not introduced any new ones.

Some words ('shop-keeping' for example) appeared only when broken at the ends of lines, so we have had to make our own decisions about whether or not they should have hyphens.

We have reproduced the chapter titles in our Table of Contents just as they appear on the first edition's Contents page, despite the fact that some of them differ slightly from the versions in the chapter headings.

The running heads for Chapter I were shortened in the first edition to 'MERRAN REALIZES AN AMBITION'. This appears to have been done for reasons of space; since our design allows room for the entire chapter title, we have used it in full.

Since the original book contained no List of Illustrations, and most of the illustrations have no captions, we have not attempted to produce a list for this edition.

Sarah Woodall

SERENDIPITY

The faculty of making happy and unexpected discoveries by accident.

OXFORD ENGLISH DICTIONARY.

Here used as the name of a shop full of fascinating bits and pieces, from carved necklaces to antique lanterns. The very shop that all of us would love to explore.

THE SERENDIPITY SHOP

DORITA FAIRLIE BRUCE

Illustrated by

MARGARET HORDER

To C. M. M.

CONTENTS

CHAPTER I

MERRAN LENDRUM REALIZES AN AMBITION

IT stood in the corner of the little grey square just behind the sea-front at Colmskirk, and, unlike any of the other shops, it had a window that looked two ways—into Gallowgate Square where it properly belonged, and round the corner into the little short street, only a few yards long, that led up to the square from the Esplanade. And this queerly shaped window was filled with the most astonishing and delightful things. At least, so little Merran Lendrum thought, though there were other people who described them simply and tersely as "so much junk."

Merran stood in her scarlet coat and tammy, with her nose pressed against the cold pane, and her eyes fixed on the wise-faced grandfather clock, the dark cupboard with the brass handles that might contain anything, the spinning-wheel, which looked as though it had come straight out of a fairy-book—and might have done, for all she knew—and, best of all, the black tray inlaid with mother-of-pearl on which were heaped chains of the most wonderful many-coloured beads, which were, she felt sure, worth a king's ransom, however much that might be.

Merran was waiting for her father, whose car stood outside one of the whitewashed cottages on the north side of the square. To-day it was her treat to go on his afternoon rounds with him, for it was a half-holiday and there were no lessons to prepare. Actually it had been Julia's turn, but Julia, being only six, had not yet been promoted to afternoon school, so was free to go with Daddy at any time when he could take her. She was usually tenacious of her rights, and Merran had been afraid of a dispute, but it so happened that Julia had other fish to fry to-day, so had given in without a struggle. Julia, though no one knew it, meant to run away in search of adventures; she did this from time to time, and though always discovered and brought back before any adventures could happen, she was never discouraged, and always set out again at regular intervals. Julia was like that—quite different from her ten-year-old sister. But then, to be sure, ten is a responsible age, or Merran felt it so.

She glanced round wistfully at the car, and wondered how long Daddy was going to be, and whether she had time to slip inside for a few minutes and ask old Jeems to let her see the beads at closer range. She had always longed to hold them in her hands and let their gay gleaming colours run through her fingers, but so far she had never summoned up courage to suggest this to Jeems, though he was a kindly old man, and always nodded and beamed on the doctor's children when they went into his shop. Merran knew very well that if Julia had wanted to hold the beads in her hands she would have said so without hesitation, and her desire would probably have been fulfilled at once; but, then, Julia never did hesitate. It must be nice, Merran reflected, not for the first time, to be as un-shy as Julia.

Her father was coming out of the cottage. Merran skipped back and prepared to get into her seat; but suddenly, round the corner from the Esplanade, came a little barefoot laddie running at breathless speed, waving a bit of dirty twisted paper, which he pushed into the doctor's hand.

"It's wee Teenie!" he panted. "She's no' weel—her throat. Mither sent me to find ye."

Dr. Lendrum knitted his thick brows over the shaky scrawl

and growled, "It's her throat, is it? I'll come at once. And you, my man—don't you be going home till I've discovered what's the matter with Teenie, for it might be something infectious. Away to your Grannie's, and stay there till you get word to go back. As for you, Merran—" he paused and gazed down at his daughter, while the ragged urchin disappeared into a lane which ran out of the Square near its head—"I'm sorry to disappoint you, lassie, very sorry, but I daren't take you round by Coronation Cottages if there are throats about."

"Oh, but Daddy, you won't be all the afternoon at Coronation Cottages. If you're going there now, couldn't you leave me somewhere and pick me up as you come back? Couldn't I—couldn't I wait for you at the Serendipity Shop?"

This was Daddy's own name for old Jeems Roberton's place, and Merran loved to roll it off her tongue, though she had not the least idea what it meant. He glanced across at it now a little doubtfully, and said, "You won't make a nuisance of yourself, will you? The old chap may be busy cutting his beads, and not keen on having a kid thrust in upon him uninvited."

"I'll be as good as it's possible to be," promised Merran recklessly; "—better, if you like! Oh, Daddy, you don't know how I've pined to spend a really long time in there and look at everything thoroughly. This will be the most marvellous opportunity!"

The doctor laughed good-naturedly. "Run along then, and ask him very politely if I may park you there for half an hour or so. I shan't be longer than I can help, for I've got a bad burn waiting to be dressed up at Faraway Farm—unless Nurse has managed to get there before me. You didn't happen to see her go past on her bike, did you?"

"No," answered Merran, and ran back across the cobbles, pausing at the door of the Serendipity Shop to wave him farewell.

Then she lifted the heavy latch, which was rather stiff for small hands to manage, and stepped down into the crowded, queer-shaped room below.

"Good afternoon, Mr. Roberton," she said, with a politeness quite beyond praise. "I hope you will forgive me for being thrust upon you uninvited, but, you see, Daddy has got to go to Coronation Cottages, where there are throats about, so he can't take me. And he says, if I'm not a nuisance, may he park me here for a little, and fetch me on his way back?"

Old Jeems came out of the shadows in the rear, looking rather like an outsize gnome in his green baize apron and ruffled white hair. He always wore two pairs of spectacles, one on his nose and the other pushed up on his forehead, which Merran considered most intriguing. He had round, apple cheeks and a little grizzly moustache, and his face beamed with grandfatherly kindness.

"Why, surely, missie dear, surely!" he said in his hearty pipe. "Come and sit ye doon in this wee patch of sunshine, for ye're welcome as the flooers in May—which are far enough awa' the noo, guid kens! Just let's see what we can find to amuse you," and he looked about his crowded treasure-house, uncertain what, among all its contents, might be likely to appeal to a visitor aged ten.

"Please don't bother to amuse me, Mr. Roberton," said Merran earnestly. "I mustn't be a nuisance if you're kind enough to let me stay. Whatever you were doing when I came in, just go on doing it. What were you doing, by the way?"

"Why, I was cutting and polishing, missie, cutting and polishing I was. Now I wonder, would ye care, mebbe, to see how the beads are made, that lie on yon tray when they're finished, for folk to buy that hae a fancy for them?"

Merran clasped her hands together.

"Oh," she exclaimed, "there's nothing I'd like better—except one thing. When Daddy said you might be busy making beads, I hoped you'd say I might watch."

"Weel, weel, that's a hope easy fulfilled," chuckled the old man in amusement. "Come awa' ben to my workroom, whaur there's a better licht to see by—and what was the one thing ye'd like better than to see me cut my beads? Mind the step."

Merran followed him between carved chairs and inlaid tables, through a curtain of knotted string into a bright little room at the back, where, under the wide window, stood a bench and a battered deal table littered with tools. A box filled with ordinary-looking stones stood on one end of the bench, and other pebbles were strewn among the implements on the table.

"Is this where you make them?" she asked in awed tones. "But what are they made of?"

She knew very well that she was much too old to believe in magic—even Julia had begun to be a bit doubtful about fairies—but anything might be true in a place like this, and certainly old Jeems looked more gnomish than ever with his big ears sticking out beyond the little red smoking-cap he wore at all times.

"Made of?" he echoed, dusting a three-legged wooden stool as he drew it forward for her. "Why, chuckie-stanes maistly—the sort ye pick up ony day oot yonder on the shore. But ye's require to pick up the richt yins, ye ken. It's no' ilka chuckie that'll polish up into a bonnie bead."

Merran stared, round-eyed, from her perch, as he settled himself again on the bench and, selecting a stone from the box at his side, picked a curious-looking weapon from the assortment before him.

"But that's just a common stone," she objected. "How can it ever make a beautiful bead like those on the tray in the window?"

He laughed again as he turned the pebble this way and that, holding it in a small vice.

"No sae common as ye'd think, missie. Watch a meenit and ye'll see."

He worked away at the stone, chipping tiny flakes off its surface, then suddenly plunged it into a basin of liquid that stood at his elbow.

"See to that, noo!" he exclaimed, holding it towards her on the palm of his hand; and the child saw, fascinated, that the erstwhile dull surface was now wet and glowing with deep shades of ruby and rose. "Ay, it's as bonnie a bit o' cornelian as ever I've seen, when ye ken what to dae wi't."

For a moment Merran was dumbfounded by this miracle; then, as he drew back his hand and began to work on the stone again, she asked breathlessly, "But are they all like that inside—all the dull plain chuckies that lie about on the beach for anyone to find?"

He shook his head, and the tarnished tassel on his cap swung with the movement.

"I wouldna say just that. There's chuckies and chuckies, ye ken, and they're no' a' by-ordinar. But there's mair than ye'd think gin ye didna ken what to look for. But ye havena telt me yet what it was ye wanted maist of a' tae be daein'."

"It was only this," Merran answered shyly. "I've wanted it for a very long time, but I didn't feel I knew you quite well enough before, Mr. Roberton. Now that we're properly friends, though—it was just—if I might hold some of your beads in my very own hands and feel the feel of them in my fingers."

At that he threw back his head and laughed outright, while the tassel danced more fascinatingly than ever.

"Why, surely, surely! Pit your wee haund intil this wooden bowl and tak' oot a' ye want. There's a wheen o' the feenished article in there just waiting to be strung."

He pushed the bowl towards her, and Merran joyfully plunged her fingers in among the shining, glittering, many-coloured gems that filled it, gathering them up and letting them stream down again gently before she drew out another handful.

"Oh, the bonnie, bonnie things!" she cried gleefully. "Don't you love making them, Mr. Roberton?"

"Ay," said old Jeems soberly, "I'll no' say it isna a pleesure to see sae muckle beauty come oot o' a plain-lookin' stane at my ain command, sae to speak. I jalouse, Miss Merran, ye've got the feeling for the work yoursel'. Hoo would ye like gin I was to learn ye some o' the simpler processes? There's tools ye could haundle, and a wee machine here that rins sae easy ye could ca' it withoot ony deefficulty whatever."

"Oh, Mr. Roberton, would you really teach me?" cried Merran, starry-eyed with excitement. "Could I make beads my very own self?"

"I'm no' sayin' ye could dae the whole thing withoot a bit help—no' just yet, onyway—but ye could mak' a beginning—mebbe on Saturday or when ye get your holidays frae the school."

"It's far, far too good of you!" she told him fervently. "I don't know how I can ever thank you for being so kind."

He looked at her with a look half-sad, half-affectionate, which she could not quite understand.

"Eh, bairn," he answered, "ye've nae need tae be thankin' me. What the doctor's done for me and mine naebuddy kens but me and the guid Lord Himsel', and gin I could repay even the least wee bittie o't I'd be gey and prood. He's a graund mon, your faither, as a' Colmskirk kens weel, but he hasna a patient that kens it better than auld Jeems Roberton, an' it's no' muckle I wouldna dae for him. There's his car coming into the square the noo, sae I'll hae tae bid ye good-bye—but mind, it's settled. Whenever ye've got the time to spare, and your mither's willing, ye'll come alang here, and learn tae mak' beads wi' the best."

CHAPTER II

MERRAN'S LEGACY

JULIA LENDRUM ran upstairs two steps at a time, and turned left along a short passage that led to the schoolroom, a square, isolated room furnished in shabby comfort, and set apart for the younger members of this big suburban household. A bright fire burned in the grate, and on the hearthrug, washing his toes before it, sat a large yellow cat. The only other occupant, a brown-haired girl of twenty, was busy at the table with an electric iron, and she looked up as her younger sister entered.

"Hullo, Judy, you're home early this afternoon."

Julia slipped the strap of her satchel over her shoulder and flung it down on the broken-springed sofa, followed by her school hat; then, shaking her dark curls loose, she sank down on the hearthrug and clasped the cat to her in an ecstatic embrace.

"I know," she said. "The maths. mistress let us out on the stroke, and I had no particular reasons for hanging about. School isn't the same place this term with Jacynth gone. I suppose in time—such is life—I'll pal up with somebody else, but at present I look round the form and wonder who on earth it's going to be. They're a pretty dull crowd in the Upper Fifth just now."

Merran ran the tip of her iron carefully into the corners of a dainty embroidered handkerchief.

"Perhaps," she suggested, "they've got hidden possibilities."

Julia lifted her tip-tilted nose and sniffed disdainfully as she rocked the cat to and fro in her arms.

"They may have," she said, "but if so, they're extremely well hidden. I am coming slowly to the conclusion that there isn't much scope for me in Slingsby nowadays, either at school or at home. Where are Polly and Marion, by the way?"

"Gone into town with Aunt Elsie. And Pearl is roller-skating over at Richmond. She asked me to go too, but I had a strong suspicion amounting to a certainty that she's got a date with Tony Davies, so I discreetly declined."

"Very wise of you," said Julia approvingly. "Pearl's a kind-hearted girl, but she hasn't much personality, and you'd soon cut her out with Tony Davies if he saw too much of you. Which would be a pity, as you've no use for him, and she has."

"Julia!" exclaimed Merran, shocked by this display of precocity. "I wish you wouldn't be so—so vulgar. It's appalling when you're only sixteen."

"I may be sixteen in years," rejoined her sister modestly, "but I'm much older than you, Merran, in common sense and *savoir faire*. It all comes of living in a house with an aunt and three grown-up cousins. I don't count you because I never can regard you as being properly grown-up at all. I feel like a mother to you half the time."

"Thank you!"

"Well, you know, there's something so fresh and simple about you—a sort of arrested development. Not mental, of course, and certainly not bodily, but—oh, you know what I mean!"

"I certainly do not. It sounds as though I were completely batty, and I haven't got quite that length yet, though I very soon shall if I don't manage to find some kind of job—or at least discover what I am capable of doing."

"The trouble with you," remarked Julia sagely, "is that your education was never specialized. You hadn't any strong bent, so Daddy and Mummy, bless their hearts, hoped they might keep you at home till you married. They couldn't foresee the railway accident—and that home, after that, would be with kind relations in a London suburb, and only enough money to keep us in clothes and educate me."

"Oh, don't, Judy!" exclaimed Merran in a stifled voice, driving her iron blindly over a blue spun-silk slip. "I'll find something somehow, and meanwhile let's be thankful that the relations really are kind. Aunt Elsie grudges nothing, and the girls are ready to let us in on all their amusements."

Julia continued to rock the cat tenderly in her arms while she replied, "Yes, I know. And it isn't their fault that their sort of amusements don't amuse us frightfully. I suppose it's because we were born and brought up in a Scottish seaside town where everything's so different. I felt a pig to be so ungrateful last summer when Polly took me to Hampton Court on a river-boat; but all the time I was thinking of our lovely Clyde steamers—even the ferry from Craigs Bay to Inchmore would look like an ocean-liner beside those Thames tubs; but I took care not to show my ingratitude."

"I should hope so, indeed," retorted Merran severely. "Quite apart from the fact that the smallest of our boats would be altogether unsuitable on a narrow river like the Thames and would probably burst its banks. It was extremely kind of Polly. She gave up an afternoon's tennis to take you."

"I know. I thanked her most warmly. Look at William of Orange going to sleep in my arms like a baby. He really is a most adorable cat.

> "Hush-a-bye, Billy, on the tree-top!
> When the wind blows—"

But here the adorable cat, coming to an end of his patience, gave a violent wriggle, clawed at her wildly, and landed right side up on the carpet, where, having removed himself to a safe distance, he sat down to repair the damage to his toilet.

"Little beast!" exclaimed Julia, sucking the back of one hand, while with the other she dived into her coat pocket in search of a handkerchief. "Oh, hullo!—I nearly forgot this letter for you, Merran. I took it from the postman just now as I came in."

"A letter for me?" Merran regarded it with languid interest as she switched off her iron and proceeded to coil the flex. "It doesn't look very interesting in that narrow typed envelope. Those are your hankies, dear, and if you're going up to get tidy for tea you might take my things along too, and lay them on my bed."

"I don't know," responded Julia, picking up the little pile of garments, "that I need bother about getting tidy if you're the only one who'll be in for tea, but I'll take them along all the same. Aren't you going to open that letter, Merran? After all, it's stamped 'Beith and Lamond, Colmskirk' on the back, and even a forgotten bill from Colmskirk would be like a breath of the sea."

"Beith and Lamond," repeated Merran, glancing down at it. "Why, it's not a bill—those are the lawyers. Surely you haven't forgotten Sandy Lamond, who used to come to our birthday-parties years ago? They lived in that old house on Robin Water, just below the railway bridge. What can they want with me?"

"Open it and see," suggested Julia as she left the room.

When she returned ten minutes later it was to find her sister standing by the window with dazed eyes, reading and re-reading the closely typed sheet.

"Look at this, Julia," she said in a voice as dazed as her expression. "I can't quite take it in, but it seems—"

Julia advanced briskly and took the letter from her.

"Why," she asked, "has somebody died and left you a fortune?"

"Not exactly, but you're getting warm. Somebody has died and left me—a shop—the Serendipity Shop in Gallowgate Square! You remember old Jeems Roberton, who was so devoted to Daddy because he cured his wife of something quite incurable—I don't know what?"

"Of course I remember, though I never knew him as well as you did. He taught you to make beads, didn't he? You were always going round there in the holidays, and you spent hours working with his tools; it was your favourite pastime."

"He seems to have remembered that, poor old dear," said Merran. "I believe he was rather fond of me, but it was mostly on Daddy's account. He says something like that in the extract from his will that the lawyers have enclosed with their letter—'Having no kin of my own, and my wife having predeceased me, I wish to benefit, as far as lies in my power, the family of the late Dr. Julian Lendrum of Colmskirk. Therefore I do will and bequeath my shop in Gallowgate Square, with all it contains of tools and stock-in-trade, to Miss Marion Margaret Lendrum, daughter of the said Dr. Julian Lendrum, in the hope that she may derive some good therefrom.' … Wasn't it *decent* of the poor old soul?"

"Humph! No mention of dear little Julia, I notice!" interjected that young lady. "Never mind, Merran! I have a great and magnanimous spirit and can grudge you nothing—not a single warming-pan or needleworked footstool!"

"Don't be such a goose!" cried Merran, laughing rather shakily. "You know—and I expect old Jeems did, too—that whatever I get is shared with you. See! he said he wished to benefit the family, which means you. I fancy he thought I'd know better what to do with the beads and the instruments connected with them."

"And what *are* you going to do?" enquired Julia with deep

interest. "Look here—the lawyers say they await your instructions, and that they are forwarding you an estimate of the property as soon as they can get it valued. Probably they expect you to sell it and realize the capital—whatever that amounts to."

"I don't suppose it would mean a very great deal," said Merran slowly. "I don't know—I'll have to think. This has come upon me so suddenly that I feel a trifle stunned. The beads were lovely, you know, Judy."

"Well, I suppose they'll let you keep what you want of them. But you can show the letter to Uncle Basil when he comes back from the office. He is a sound business man and he'll give you good advice. Meanwhile, there's the gong, and I'm ravenous!"

Messrs. Beith and Lamond's letter and enclosures caused a good deal of excitement at the dinner-table that evening, when the family had got back from its varied business and pleasures, and heard what the post had brought for Merran.

"My dear girl, I'm delighted!" cried Uncle Basil heartily between spoonfuls of soup. "It may not amount to much—we can go into that later with this chap, Lamond—but at least it will mean a few more pennies in your pocket than were there before, and every little helps."

"If properly invested, of course," added Aunt Elsie; "but your uncle will be able to advise you about that. Dear me, girls, we little thought, when we went out this afternoon that we should come back to find Merran an heiress!"

"The least she can do," declared Polly, "is to fit us all out with bead necklaces before she sells up the stock."

"Was the old johnnie a lapidarian, Merran?" asked her cousin Harry. "Was his stuff worth while?"

"I don't know," replied Merran uncertainly. "He made some lovely things out of the plainest-looking pebbles. When I was a child I regarded him as a cross between a magician and a conjuror;

but I know people liked his work and bought it—especially the summer visitors."

Her uncle drew a leather diary from his pocket as they waited for the next course, and fluttered over its pages rapidly.

"I'm just wondering," he said, "if I can spare time to run up to Scotland myself and give this legacy of yours the once-over before the lawyer chaps start to sell it up. Wouldn't do to let 'em think you'd no one to protect your interests. There might be more in this than meets the eye, apart from the shop and its contents. Seaside property at a popular resort fetches a good price nowadays. You can't let it go for an old song, my dear."

"I don't know," said Merran suddenly, "that I want to let it go at all. I'm still rather bewildered about the whole thing, but it's beginning to dawn upon me that I might like to keep it. The old johnnie, as Harry calls him, taught me a lot about his trade, and I believe, with a little practice, I could make those beads myself, and sell them at a profit. You see, I've wanted a job so badly, but there seemed to be nothing I could do—and this looks like the answer—though it isn't exactly what I was picturing."

"Good gracious, no, I should think not!" ejaculated Aunt Elsie, the first to recover her breath. "Have you entirely taken leave of your senses, my dear?"

But Julia, who up till now had been assuaging the pangs of hunger in perfect silence, laid down knife and fork and clapped her hands delightedly.

"Not she, Auntie. She's only just come to them. Bravo, Merran, old bean! You stick to your Serendipity Shop and I'll join you. Between us we'll make the fortunes of the house of Lendrum—see if we don't, everybody!"

CHAPTER III

BACK TO COLMSKIRK

It was difficult for Merran's relatives to grasp at first that she was serious in her intentions, but having once realized, though slowly, that she did indeed propose not only to retain her legacy but to live on and by it, the storm broke. Uncle Basil argued from the business point of view—"A piece of very risky speculation, my dear girl, since you haven't the remotest idea how to run a business of any sort." Aunt Elsie took the social line—"Do you understand, dear, that you will become a small-town tradesman, and cut yourself off completely from your own circle?" Harry said, "You'll tie yourself up hand and foot, old thing, and have no time left for the lighter side of life." Her namesake, Marion, said, "It may seem fun while the novelty lasts, but, believe me, you'll get awfully sick of it after a bit." And Pearl and Polly bewailed the idea of any attractive girl of twenty burying herself for good among beads and bric-à-brac.

But Merran was ready with an answer for each and all.

"It won't really be such a speculation as you think, Uncle, because I know quite a lot about beads and how to make them. That information is no use to me here in London, but at Colmskirk there is a demand for such things, and I believe I might make it pay. And I don't see why I should be cut off from all my old friends, Aunt Elsie, because I do a job of work; everybody does nowadays, and quite a lot of people keep shops. But if I've got to lose my old friends, I must make new ones, that's all. I expect I shall get as much time off for amusement, Harry, as most girls do who work; there's nothing so boring as having an incessant good time. I should soon get sick of that, if you like, Marion. Of course I'll get fed-up sometimes—who doesn't?—but I don't mean to bury myself, I can tell you, girls!"

"No," put in Julia placidly, "I'll see she doesn't."

"You!" exclaimed her family in chorus, and the arguments started all over again on different lines; but Julia was even better prepared than her sister.

"It won't interfere with my education in the very least," she maintained firmly, "because there's an excellent day-school at Westharbour, only three stations up the line, where Merran was to have gone at thirteen, and you know quite well, Uncle, that education in Scotland is cheaper and better than it is anywhere else. And it isn't like going to some strange place either—don't forget that we were born and brought up at Colmskirk and have heaps of friends among Daddy's old patients; so there will be far more people there for us to marry, if that's what you're thinking of, than there are in Slingsby. Well, I'm sorry, Aunt Elsie, but you know you do approve of girls getting married; you always say it should be a really womanly woman's ultimate ambition."

"My dear Julia," protested her aunt plaintively, "you need not be so vulgarly literal. Of course I think there can be no happier lot for a girl than a suitable marriage, but it has to be suitable, and I hardly think—"

"Oh, but that's because you don't know the place or the people. Anyhow, Merran may do what she likes, certainly, but it isn't my ultimate ambition. I mean to train as a super-secretary—the sort that M.Ps. employ—because I feel that I might do something in politics eventually."

Merran always maintained that Julia's grand manner, and high-vaulting aims, invariably left the relations too much flattened out for further argument. Since she, at least, was not of age, they could quite easily have foiled her plans for going back with her sister; but this they made no attempt to do when they found that she, as Uncle Basil put it, refused to listen to reason. The truth was that they regarded Julia as "a peculiar girl," and Aunt Elsie was more than a little relieved to find herself free from the responsibility of a problem niece; though the poor lady would undoubtedly have done her best for her, accordingly to her lights, had Providence not disposed otherwise.

So it came to pass, one evening in late April, as the shadows were creeping down on the green hills behind Colmskirk, where spring was coming over the banked woods like the bloom on a red grape, that the two Lendrum girls found themselves on the familiar platform, surrounded by all their worldly possessions, including a large yellow cat in a capacious basket, a cat who had sunk into a coma of utter exhaustion, having expended all the language he knew during the first part of the long, weary journey and found it of no avail.

"Poor darling, he's worn out," exclaimed Julia sympathetically. "It's the first time in his life he has failed to get his own way in the end by patience and persistence. I can quite understand how he feels, can't you? Hullo! Who's this coming, Merran? I remember his face somehow."

"So you might," replied Merran, turning with a feeling of relief to greet the staid-looking young man who had just hurried into the station. "That's Sandy Lamond, and I expect the firm have sent him to meet us, since they have got the keys and everything else we require. Oh, Sandy, I am pleased to see you! I was just wondering how we should get into the shop to-night with all our luggage."

"Good evening, Merran; it's awfully jolly to see you back

again. My word, Julia, how you've grown! But you're not going to the shop to-night. The luggage may go—that is, what you don't require. I'll come back and see about that later. But I've got the car outside, and Mother says I'm to bring you both back to stay with us as long as you may wish. There's nothing ready for you at Gallowgate Square yet—not even beds—we couldn't get going till you were here in person to direct us."

"But, Sandy—it's frightfully good of Mrs. Lamond, but—well, two of us are too much—and anyway, why should she?"

Sandy favoured her with a faint grin as he seized a suitcase in either hand.

"You must have forgotten Mother," he said, "to ask a question like that. Seven years since you left, isn't it? Well, well! Come along now, or the steak-pie will be cold. Mother remembered you always chose a steak-pie from Macrae's for your birthday dinner, so she got one in on purpose. Tickets all right? We'll go in to the shop and everything else to-morrow."

He led the way towards the entrance, sending a porter to see to the heavy luggage until he himself could return and take it round to Gallowgate Square. A few people were still coming away from the train, among them a heavy, square-faced man with a thick watch-chain decorating his waistcoat, and a pretty, fair-haired girl in a school hat hanging on to his arm.

"Who's that?" demanded Julia instantly. "He looks as though he were going somewhere and meant to get there. But the watch-chain's incredible!"

Sandy Lamond glanced over his shoulder as he pushed the cases into the car and turned to help the girls in after them.

"Oh, he's going somewhere all right! Whether he gets there is another matter. That's old Bartle of Bartle's Wholesale Stores and Emporium, our biggest innovation since you left Colmskirk. Sure that's all you want to bring along with you just now? Hand me that basket, Julia, and I'll sling it up behind. It's too heavy for you to hold on your knee."

"Thank you very much, but I couldn't let it out of my own hands," replied Julia firmly. "That hamper contains William of Orange, and though he is completely exhausted now, he might come to and start swearing again if he thought I'd abandoned him. Ordinarily he's a most gentlemanly cat, but this journey has been a revelation to me. I can't imagine where he learned it all."

"I do hope," said Merran anxiously, as Sandy let in the clutch, "Mrs. Lamond won't mind us bringing him with us, but I don't see what else we can do."

"Certainly not," said Sandy reassuringly, guiding the car into the wide Main Street, empty just now, since all the shops were closed. "I told you you'd forgotten Mother, but you must be able to recall that our house is always full of animals. Another more or less makes no difference, and we just let 'em fight it out between them."

"Oh, Bill's a pacifist," retorted Julia cheerfully. "He stirs up wars and leaves other people to take the consequences. Merran, there's Robin Water, as strong and turbulent as ever. And there's the ferry-steamer coming over from Inchmore. Everything's exactly as we left it, all those years ago."

"Not quite," Sandy told her. "Old Bartle has seen to that; but he hasn't done much harm so far—nothing to what he will do if he can only get himself on to the Town Council. Here we are, and there's Mother waiting for you on the doorstep. Welcome back to Colmskirk!"

There was no doubt about that welcome, as the two Lendrum girls were to find in the days that followed. The doctor had been greatly beloved, and his tragic death, when he and his wife had perished together in a railway accident, had helped to impress his memory on the patients who had lost him so suddenly. The odd story of his elder daughter's inheritance, which had brought her back to the town with her sister, had interested all the Colmskirk people—still more so when they learnt that she did not mean to dispose of her legacy, but was going to live there and carry on old Jeems Roberton's business herself.

"It's an experiment certainly," remarked Mrs. Lamond, shaking her head dubiously as they discussed it, that first morning, at the breakfast table. "Girls do queer things nowadays, but I've never heard of one doing anything quite like this before."

"I know," admitted Merran, "but I'd like to try. I've got all sorts of bright ideas on the subject, and Julia will help me to get them going during the Easter holidays, before she starts at the Westharbour Academy."

"And, of course," said Mrs. Lamond, brightening a little, "you will have Dave Nisbet. He'll be a help."

"Dave Nisbet?"

"Yes. Don't you remember him? A lame man—I think he was wounded in the first war—who used to do a lot of work in the background for old Jeems."

"I believe I do," said Merran hesitantly, "but he was never much about when I went there for my lessons. Do you think he'll want to work for me?"

"He hasn't a doubt about it himself," Sandy assured her drily. "When he heard you were coming back to take over, he came round to us for the keys—said he must get the tools cleaned up and the machines oiled, as he supposed you'd want to begin at once with the summer season coming along."

"So I shall," replied Merran gaily. "I'm dying to begin. But first of all I must get the house set in order so that Julia and I can move in as soon as possible, and not be a burden on you."

"You know very well you're nothing of the kind," cried Mrs. Lamond indignantly. "And really, my dear, I don't quite see how you can live in that poky wee place. You may find it better to let it—except the shop and workroom—and take rooms elsewhere for yourselves. I know of a nice woman across the burn there, in Water Street, who would make you extremely comfortable."

"I should like to live under my own roof if I can," said Merran. "I know it's small, but for only two of us it might not be so bad, and I think I recall there was one story above the shop."

"It possesses a certain luxury," remarked Sandy, "which is not to be found in many of the old Gallowgate houses, and that's a small but modern bathroom with hot and cold. Roberton had it put in as a present for his wife not long before the old lady died. I believe he'd saved up for years to do it, poor old chap, and now you'll reap the benefit."

"That's a load off my mind, anyhow!" declared Julia. "I don't object to leading the simple life if only it includes a bathroom. I said nothing to damp Merran's ardour, but I was terribly afraid it mightn't."

"You needn't have been," said Merran calmly, "because I knew about the bathroom all the time. I remember it being put in, and the excitement over it; I believe the old pair felt they had reached the summit of all earthly ambition. Sandy, we shall be quite ready, when you are, to go round and take possession. There must be so much to arrange and settle that the sooner we begin upon it the better."

CHAPTER IV

TAKING POSSESSION

THE Serendipity Shop, when they had let themselves in and taken down the old-fashioned shutters, looked very much as it had done in Merran's childhood. It seemed that Mrs. Nisbet had been in the habit of going there now and again, with the lawyers' permission, to dust and polish, so that everything was in apple-pie order. The same ancient grandfather clock stood in its old place, and though the spinning-wheel had been sold, the brass-handled press was still there along with many other things new or familiar.

"It's amazing to think it's all mine!" said Merran in awe-struck tones as she stood looking about her. "If this had been foretold to me ten years ago it would have felt like living in a fairy-tale. But the beads—where are they? Or aren't there any?"

"Plenty," replied Sandy Lamond, jingling the keys on his forefinger, "but they're all locked up in a deed-box in the back room. They may not be valuable, but they looked it, and I wasn't taking any risks."

"I must find the inlaid papier-maché tray," Merran declared, "and pile them up in the window again where the sun will catch them and bring out their colours. Come on, Judy, let's go through the house and see what we can do about it. Don't let us keep you, Sandy, wasting your time here, for I'm sure you must be very busy in the office. It was very good of you to come round with us, but now we shall be able to manage quite well."

Thus gracefully dismissed, Sandy had no excuse to linger, but he turned at the door to explain.

"You won't find much furniture upstairs, I'm afraid. Old Jeems left all his more personal possessions—like his bedroom suite and things—to the Nisbets. You must just let us know if there's anything we can lend you. And you know where the office is, if you get in a jam of any sort and need me? At the top end of Main Street, near the station."

"Thanks awfully," responded Merran. "We'll certainly appeal to you if in doubt. *Au revoir* in the meantime!"

"That's better," declared Julia, with a sigh of relief, as the door closed behind him to a jangling of bells. "Sandy Lamond is all right, but we couldn't do with him underfoot all morning. Now we can really begin. Where does this lead to?"

"Mind the step," said Merran mechanically. "The workshop is through there, but we'll look at that presently. The first thing we have got to discover is where we are going to live, and how. This other door on the right is into the kitchen. You see, the shop, being on the corner, is L-shaped, so it has two rooms behind it, and the kitchen fits into the angle, with a good scullery beyond."

"But—how do we get up to the bedrooms? Where are the stairs?"

Merran laughed as she led the way into the kitchen, and opened a door in the wall beside the old-fashioned range.

"There you are," she said. "They're rather steep because they're built into the thickness of the wall. I shouldn't have known where they were myself, only I remember seeing the door standing open one day when I came in here to see Mrs. Roberton. As to what it's like upstairs, Julia, I know no more than you, for I've never been there. Isn't this exciting! Let's go up and explore."

The two girls hurried up the narrow wooden stairs and found themselves at the end of a short passage off which opened four doors. The first of these led them into the famous bathroom, which had evidently been contrived by sacrificing a bedroom above the scullery, and proved to be all that even Julia's fastidious heart could desire; the very window was filled in with some remarkable stained glass which, Merran was inclined to think, might be good, though she admitted she knew nothing about the subject.

"I remember it was some that old Jeems bought at a sale, and it used to stand in the shop. But he decided that no one would want to buy it loose, so to speak, and he thought he might as well add it to the beauties of the bathroom."

"I suppose he wanted to shut out the view of Main Street 'backs,'" suggested Julia, throwing up the sash and leaning out. "Why, Merran, what on earth is that, and how did it come there?"

For immediately opposite her the backs of the Main Street shops were completely concealed, by a conical grassy mound, which rose to the level of their sloping slates and blocked out a good deal of the morning sunshine.

"Good gracious!" exclaimed Merran, staring at it in astonishment. "It isn't a natural hillock, but it must be frightfully old—older than the square or the houses along the front, for it could hardly have been put up in that angle after they were built."

"Of course not," exclaimed Julia impatiently. "Who would want to throw up such an earthwork at their back windows? It must be most frightfully ancient, but I never heard of anything like that in the very middle of the town, did you?"

"Never!" replied her sister. "But then we left before we were old enough to take an interest in the local antiquities. Unless—why, Julia!—Gallowgate Square—that means 'the square on the way to the gallows.' I believe this must be the old gallows-mound of Colmskirk."

Julia hung farther out and regarded it with round-eyed fascination.

"Do you mean where they used to hang all the criminals? Glory be! But what a heavenly thing to have outside one's bathroom! We might even get a ghost from it. I *am* glad old Jeems left you this place!"

"So am I," agreed Merran, "but not because of the gallows-mound. I did know there was one somewhere about, but I always thought of it—if I thought of it at all—as being outside the town, somewhere at the back. Come on, Julia; you can gaze your fill at it any time, but we've got three other rooms to explore."

Julia drew in her head reluctantly, and followed her sister on her further investigations. There were two bedrooms, both small and looking into the square, and a third, larger room over the shop, with a sideways view down the little short street leading to the Esplanade.

"This must be our sitting-room," decided Merran, "and we'll have our meals in the kitchen for convenience. Shades of Aunt Elsie! But it's only common sense."

"Besides being the height of the fashion in these days," declared Julia briskly. "Aunt Elsie's ideas are quite outmoded—and a lot can be done with that kitchen. I like those two old wooden chairs with the round backs; if we made cushions for them they would be very comfortable."

"And did you notice the geraniums on the window-sills?" asked Merran. "Mrs. Nisbet must have been looking after them. Mrs. Roberton used to be famous for her geraniums. She watered them with cold tea."

"We might move a few of them up here," suggested Julia. "That's what this tin-topped table is for, isn't it—the round one in the window? But there isn't much else in here except the low book-shelves on either side of the fireplace. We may as well face it soon as late, Merran—what are we going to do about furniture? Because we can't afford to buy it."

"Nor borrow," agreed Merran, adding recklessly, "But we can steal—from the shop. Don't you see? It's all mine, and if I choose to use it for ourselves instead of selling it, no one can interfere. Besides, the place is crammed so that one can hardly move; there should be plenty left for stock."

Julia seized her round the waist and danced her over the worn boards.

"Splendid! Let's go down and start rummaging at once. Couldn't the grandfather clock stand in the kitchen beside the staircase door? And that press would do beautifully in your bedroom to hold your clothes."

"The room that contained that press would be furnished if there was nothing else in it," maintained Merran, laughing. "But it probably hasn't occurred to you that we must have beds, and I didn't see anything like that in the shop."

Julia halted in dismay at the head of the staircase.

"I hadn't thought of them," she confessed ruefully. "What on earth are we to do? You don't seem as perturbed as I should have expected."

"I'm not," retorted Merran, still laughing. "You've forgotten that cheque Uncle Basil slipped into my hand as a parting gift."

"I haven't. I thought it was particularly generous of the old boy, considering we're flying full in the face of all his prejudices by coming up here. But he said it was to be kept for an emergency."

"Isn't it a big enough emergency to find ourselves completely without beds?"

"I think he meant illness," said Julia doubtfully.

"Oh, but we're not going to be ill in our glorious native air, with sea breezes blowing in upon us all day long."

"Not with t.b., perhaps, or goitre, or rheumatoid arthritis; but you can break your leg or have appendicitis anywhere."

"You don't if you take reasonable precautions—and anyhow, we shall have made a lot of money before then. If you're going to be so painfully pessimistic, Julia, I'll tell you what we can do—I'll tax all our takings for an appendicitis fund. Put so much out of every sale into a money-box—we can settle the percentage later; but beds we must have at once."

"All right," said Julia, "since you say so. And we shall have all Mother's household linen and blankets. What a mercy they were stored up here. They're all at Gregor's, aren't they, round in Cochran Street?"

"Yes. Uncle said at the time that it would be cheaper to store them here till we needed them again. We'll go round to Gregor's and see about all that after lunch. We may be able to buy our beds there. I told Mrs. Lamond we'd have lunch at Macrae's, Judy—so as not to impose too much."

"Quite right," called back Julia, descending. "Though Mrs. Lamond lives to be imposed upon—nothing makes her so happy. In the name of Mike, what's that?"

For a violent cannonade of knocks sounded from the shop door, causing Merran to tumble hurriedly downstairs behind her.

"It can't be a customer already—we aren't open. Sandy said I wasn't to sell a thing till I'd gone over some sort of inventory with him. Wait a minute, Julia!"

She darted across the kitchen, pushing the younger girl aside; then paused uncertainly among the furniture in the shop beyond. If this importunate person proved indeed to be a customer, how in the world did one sell things—important things like antiques? Merran suddenly felt terribly inexperienced.

But the knocking started again, more emphatically than ever, and with a burst of resolution she walked quickly across to the door, slipped the bolt and opened it.

"I'm very sorry," she said firmly, "but I can't possibly let you buy anything at the moment. I know I took the shutters down, but that was because we needed light to see our way about, not because we meant to begin selling. We're not open yet, and I'm not quite sure when we shall be."

"You see," added Julia helpfully, coming forward, "we might sell something we needed ourselves if we started now, before we've had time to settle in. Couldn't you come back the day after to-morrow? We should have had time to turn round by then."

But the person in the doorway stepped determinedly down into the shop, and the girls recognized him as the stocky, square-jawed man whom they had seen in the station the previous evening.

"Day after to-morrow won't do," he stated positively. "I'm Samuel Bartle of Bartle's Stores (Edinburgh, Glasgow, Aberdeen and Dundee), and I want to buy the whole thing as it stands, lock, stock and barrel. So you won't be needing time to turn round or settle in."

CHAPTER V

INTRODUCES MR. BARTLE

MERRAN fell back in astonishment, gripping the edge of a table behind her with both hands.

"I simply don't know what you are talking about," she stammered.

"Perhaps you don't. But I'm willing to make the proposal in proper form to your legal advisers, and a thundering good offer it will be, too! I'm not a mean man—not a skinflint in any sense of the word. I'm out to benefit Colmskirk now that I've come to live in it, and I shan't grudge any expense."

Here Julia stepped in front of her sister and took over the situation, for it was plain that Merran was completely flummoxed.

"I'm quite sure you won't," she told him soothingly, "and I feel certain Colmskirk will be most frightfully grateful; but what my sister can't understand—and neither can I, to be candid—is what we've got to do with it, or our legal advisers either."

Mr. Bartle glared down at her suspiciously.

"H'm!" he snorted. "Why, sell me your place here, of course! Not that Colmskirk will be grateful—isn't in 'em—but that shan't stop me from doing the right thing by 'em."

"But I wish you'd explain," persisted Julia patiently, "how the town is to benefit by your buying my sister's shop? Not that you're going to, of course, but we'd like to know."

"I haven't the faintest intention of selling the shop," affirmed

Merran, beginning to recover a little from the first shock. “Why on earth should I? It has only just been left to me.”

“I know that. That’s why I’m here,” retorted Mr. Bartle. “Came straight round directly I knew you’d arrived. I’m a chap who never beats about the bush. Been waiting for this ever since I heard you’d inherited. Couldn’t do anything with Roberton—obstinate old fool who didn’t know which side his bread was buttered! Couldn’t see he’d be much better off in a cosy bungalow at the back of the town, with every modern convenience. But you’re different—you’re a couple of educated girls with no use for a tumble-down old junk-shop.”

“It isn’t tumble-down!” denied Julia indignantly, “and it isn’t junk. As for being educated, Merran may be, but I’ve still got a good year to go—and anyhow, it’s her legacy, not mine.”

“And I mean to keep it,” reiterated Merran. “If it’s in such poor condition, why do you want it? What are you going to do with it?”

“Pull it down,” replied Mr. Bartle promptly. “Pull down the whole square, and rebuild it as a large up-to-date store. Got a place now on the end site of Main Street, up by the station, that gives me no scope at all. Shops alongside won’t sell. But I’ve bought up this side of Gallowgate Square, all except this corner, and when I’ve got that I can start in and build. Think of the advantage to the town—think of the trade it’ll bring! Why, we’ll double the number of summer visitors when they know their food and all they want will be secure, and at half the price. Yachts, too—they’ll put into the bay there in droves just to fetch off stores at a reasonable price, and the whole place will profit. Not to mention families in the outlying countryside, who’ll shop at Colmskirk and find it much more convenient than sending into Glasgow for every whipstitch they need.”

“Do you mean to say,” asked Merran in a dazed voice, “that

you're going to pull down Gallowgate Square? All the little thatched cottages that have been here for hundreds of years?"

"That's it," he responded cheerfully. "Just as soon as I've got the title-deeds of this corner in my hands. You can see for yourself the scheme would be nothing without it. Couldn't finish off the block properly with this old place left as an eyesore to spoil its appearance for everyone turning up from the sea-front. Must make a good impression at first glance—half the battle in business."

"Well," said Merran slowly, "I don't know much about business yet, but I mean to learn, for I'm going to stick to this shop, since it's mine, and make a success of it, too. And one thing I do know. If you pull down this little old square and put up a garish modern building in its place, you'll destroy part of the character of Colmskirk. You'll do away with something that can never be replaced."

Mr. Bartle bristled.

"Sentimental nonsense!" he cried fiercely. "Time the character of the place was destroyed if it consists of a lot of fishers' cottages. What the west coast of Scotland needs is a few rattling good towns like they have by the sea in England, but you can't get that without enterprise. Now, I'm a man of enterprise, and will let nothing stand in my way when it's for the public benefit. That's why I'm prepared to offer a thumping good price for this corner of yours."

"It seems almost impossible to convince you," exclaimed Merran in exasperation, "that I'm—not—prepared—to sell. I was born in Colmskirk and I love every stone of it, and I haven't the slightest desire to see it converted into a cheap copy of Brighton or Margate, so none of your arguments carry any weight with me. And now, as we are exceedingly busy trying to settle in, perhaps you will excuse us if we ask you to go just now. There really is a great deal to be done here."

Merran

"But—but," stuttered Bartle, growing a delicate purple, "you don't appear to take my meaning—you—"

Julia stepped in again, edging him while she spoke gradually nearer to the door.

"I assure you we do understand—we understand perfectly," she said, reverting to the soothing tones she had adopted first of all; "but it isn't a bit of use trying to get my sister to sell, so I shouldn't waste any more time over it if I were you. Try to think out some other way of benefiting Colmskirk. What about a hospital? We haven't got one, and you could go all modern over anything like that. It could be built out at the back of the town there, and you could call it 'The Bartle Memorial.' It really would be a public benefaction."

Somehow or other, and entirely against his own intentions, Mr. Bartle found himself out on the pavement with the door gradually closing behind him.

"'Bartle Memorial,' indeed!" he snarled. "I'm not dead yet, young woman, and I'm not done, either! Imagine I'm going to throw away the whole of Gallowgate Square because your sister chooses to be a damned obstructionist! If so, you'd better—"

"I don't think," interrupted Julia in shocked tones, "you ought to swear at a young girl of my age, however annoyed you may be feeling. You wouldn't like it, would you, if a man were to use such words to your own daughter? Good morning, Mr. Bartle. I am sorry—very sorry—that you should have forgotten yourself so far," and the door was closed finally with the sound of a bolt shooting into its place.

"Well, I'm blest!" ejaculated Mr. Bartle, staring back at it. But he rammed his hat violently on to his head and stumped off towards the Esplanade without further demonstration; and late that evening, when he was smoking his after-supper pipe in his big rambling house on the Broomieknowes, he growled aloud, *à propos* of nothing at all, "Bartle Memorial, indeed! And me just going on sixty-two! But she's got something there, all the same. A hospital would certainly add to the amenities of Colmskirk—no denying it!"

The girls, meanwhile, had gone back to their interrupted task of sorting out furniture from the stock which they thought might be useful to them. Merran was ruffled and irate over their visitor's blustering ways, but Julia, conscious of having got the last word, was inclined to regard the whole incident as a huge joke.

"He can't make you sell if you don't want to," she pointed out, "but you, by holding on, can prevent him from messing up Gallowgate Square. Think of the advantage to the town!" and she chuckled again as she copied Mr. Bartle's pompous voice. "Can I have that sweet little chest-of-drawers for my bedroom, Merran? If I stand this swing-mirror on the top it will make a splendid dressing-table."

"It's Georgian, and it's called a low-boy," said Merran. "Yes—have it by all means! It's a bit battered and shabby, but you could polish it up. What a blessing that, with the very superior bathroom, we shan't need wash-stands. I am going to carry up these two ladder-back chairs now, then I shan't require anything more in my room, to begin with."

"Let's go round to Gregor's and buy beds," proposed Julia. "Then we can have lunch, for I'm getting quite hungry. We'd better know for certain when Gregor is likely to send the beds and our linen-boxes, because we could get his men to carry up the heavy things for us."

Gregor, a fatherly little man with a pointed beard, was delighted to see the doctor's bairns again, and eager to give them any help he could. He promised to get their property out of store and send it round "this verra afternoon." He also offered to come over himself after closing time and go through Merran's inventory of stock with her.

"It's no' that I ken aboot antiques, Miss Merran, but I'm a furniture-dealer and I can jalouse pretty weel what ye ocht to ask for the maist o' your pieces; and the things that are extry special can mebbe be valued by an expert. Ay, I would advise that, for it would pay ye in the end. Auld Jeems, gin ye follow me, was a wee thing vague aboot his prices, and whiles he was cheated—I ken that fine—so I wouldna like ye to start oot wi' hauf your stock undervalued—no' if I can help to pit ye straicht. He was a graun' haund at the beads and geegaws: there wasna muckle ye could learn auld Jeems aboot them; but the antiques, noo—they were different."

Merran accepted the kindly offer of help with real gratitude, being painfully conscious of her own inexperience; but Gregor patted her kindly on the shoulder and said, "Hoot, awa'! Gin ye've ony doots or misgivings, just come roon' to me, and I'll be only too willing to help ye, for your ain sake as weel as for the doctor's. Are ye living aboon the shop?"

"We're trying to," explained Julia, "but we haven't any beds."

"Yes," said Merran. "We wondered if you had any that weren't too expensive."

It transpired that Gregor had quite a few, and he conducted them to the back of his small warehouse, where he showed them what he had, then left them suddenly, as they were looking with some reluctance at the painted iron frames with brass knobs, which seemed to be the only choice within their means, to reappear dragging a mustard-coloured divan.

"I've just minded o' this," he said, a little breathless. "There's anither like it—twins, ye ken. The colour's no' everybuddy's choice, but when they're covered ower wi' the bedclaithes, wha's to ken? They're second-haund—that's it—they're second-haund, so I could let ye have them for less than new yins. Mind, I ken the hoose they come oot o' or I wouldna be showing them to ye. Umphm! it's no' Wullie Gregor would let the doctor's bairns buy second-haund deevans that he couldna vouch for."

"Oh, Merran, do have them!" urged Julia. "These iron frames would be utterly out of place with our furniture; but since we can't have four-posters, divans would be the next best. You see," she explained to the surprised Mr. Gregor, "we're furnishing with the stuff out of the shop because we haven't got anything else we can use."

"But," protested the little man, "yon's just leeving on your capital!"

"Only a very little of it," said Merran apologetically. "Just the things we absolutely need. It seemed to me it would be quicker in the long run; and I'll get you to price the things we've taken as well as what's down in the shop, Mr. Gregor, if you'd be so very kind. Then, if we are obliged to bring them down again and sell them, we'll know exactly what to ask. And if these divans are really cheaper than the other bedsteads, we shall be glad to take them. How much did you say?"

They left kindly Mr. Gregor's premises with light hearts and increased appetites, Julia calculating that if they lit the kitchen fire immediately after their return and hung the bedding round it as soon as the boxes arrived, they should be able to sleep under their own roof that night. But Merran prudently held out for longer airing.

"Besides," she added, "I'm afraid Mrs. Lamond might feel hurt if we were in such a hurry to leave them. And I want to talk over Mr. Bartle with Sandy, and get a legal point of view. There was something about that gentleman's attitude that made me feel a little uneasy; he was so very determined."

Julia tossed her mane of hair disdainfully.

"Pooh!" she said. "If it comes to that, we can be—and are—determined too. I shouldn't let Mr. Bartle disturb my night's rest."

CHAPTER VI

THE LENDRUMS SETTLE IN

AFTER a cheery lunch at Macrae's, where they managed to secure a table in the window of the restaurant above the big baker's shop, the girls went back with renewed energy to their task of making a home out of such materials as they could find, and worked so well that by tea-time Julia observed, "I think we've got the place nearly fit for William of Orange to live in. Don't you think we might bring him round to-morrow, Merran? The Lamond animals are very kind and forbearing, but Bill is definitely not a good mixer, you know, and he'd be happier in a spot he could call his own, however humble."

"He'll be happy enough indoors," agreed her sister, looking round with satisfaction on the cosy kitchen, where all the unromantic necessities had been shut away in the deep cupboards or banished to the scullery beyond. The Chippendale grandfather clock had been moved in and set going, and a copper warming-pan, retrieved from the back of the shop, had been polished by Julia and hung beside the old-fashioned range. "I'm not quite sure, however, that he'll be pleased to see that tiny flagged court instead of the big garden he owned at Slingsby."

"He'll adapt himself," Julia assured her, "and it will give him an interest in life to repel the neighbouring cats when they drop in. The great thing is to be the only pebble on his own beach, instead of being a visitor on other people's. And that reminds me, Merran—did Sandy give you the key of the deed-box where he put all the beads and pebbles? I'd love to see them."

"Not this afternoon," replied Merran firmly. "The box is on the bottom shelf of the left-hand press, but I daren't open it till we've quite finished all we have to do. Those beads hold a fatal fascination for me, and I shall simply waste time gloating over them. I don't mean to go near that box till everything is in order, and then I shall get it out and start on them at once—or at least directly Dave Nisbet reports on duty. That's another thing I mustn't forget to ask Sandy—if he knows what wage I should pay Dave."

"He won't know," foretold Julia. "Gregor could advise you better about that. Talk of angels—there's his van with our beds and cases pulling up at the workshop door. Have you got the key for *that*? Oh, I know: it's that big one hanging on the nail beside it."

The bustle began all over again, while the van-men tramped in and out, and up and down, carrying not only the stuff which they themselves had brought, but various articles of furniture which the girls had found too heavy to tackle unaided. When they had driven off, tipped and contented, the divans had to be set in place, blankets and bed-linen dragged out and hung up for airing, and Julia was only forcibly restrained from unpacking everything else straight away.

"I like to get things over and done with," she protested, but Merran replied:

"You'll be over and done with yourself if you keep on much longer—at any rate; I shall. We've done an immense lot to-day, and I think we should be able to move in to-morrow; but we're going back to the Lamonds' now for a good evening's rest—all the more so as I quite forgot to notify the electric people that we want our light turned on. Even you can't unpack and arrange in darkness, and we have no candles."

Julia cast a withering look at her.

"Come along, then," she said. "We must see them about it on our way home. Heaven knows how long it may take them to connect us up. They're sure to say their staff hasn't been demobbed."

After dinner that evening Sandy and his mother listened with interest to Merran's account of the day's doings, while Julia sat silently on the hearthrug, with her yellow Bill clasped in her arms and purring slumberously. Having already crossed swords with Bartle, Julia was quite prepared to draw again should occasion require it, but at the back of her mind was a sneaking kindness for this blustering self-made man. She felt that there was something of the spoilt child underneath his bullying and ostentation, and Julia had a mother's heart; she was sure that something could be done with Samuel Bartle if he were properly handled.

"No, of course he can't turn you out," said Sandy seriously. "The property's yours and the chap can't force you to sell, however much he may wish to do so. But, mind you, there are a hundred-and-one ways in which a man like that might make things very difficult for you in a small town such as Colmskirk; especially a man who isn't troubled with any fine feelings or sensitivity. He's out to get himself on to the Town Council—though nobody quite knows how he proposes to do it—and a bailie cuts a certain amount of ice."

"But why should he want to cut ice to my detriment?" demanded Merran. "I've done him no harm."

"Oh, yes, you have," broke in Julia. "From his point of view you have. He can't pull down and rebuild Gallowgate Square while you sit pretty in the corner obstructing all his schemes."

"I'm sure, my dear, it's a very good thing he can't!" exclaimed Mrs. Lamond, looking up from her knitting. "I only hope you'll go on obstructing him. What that man Bartle would do with Gallowgate Square if he had a free hand makes me shiver to contemplate."

"But you have to remember, Mother," urged Sandy, "that it's beastly awkward for him. Goodness knows I don't want to see the square pulled about! but Bartle bought it as a speculation, and he hasn't got much out of it so far."

"I presume he gets the rents from the cottages?"

Sandy threw back his head and laughed.

"You don't suppose he bought it for that! No, he's out for big business, and it must be annoying to find himself frustrated, first by old Jeems Roberton, and now by Merran. I expect he was hoping great things from her. Probably it never entered his head that a bit of a lassie would want to carry on the antique shop."

"Well, it's a pity," rejoined Merran resolutely, "but I'm afraid one of us must be disappointed, and I don't mean to be the one. Gregor has been a brick, Sandy. He has offered to check prices for me on my inventory. When do you want me to go over it with you?"

"That," replied Sandy, "will have to be done on the premises. If you're determined to move in to-morrow, I'll take you round, Bill, bag and baggage, and we can do it then, so that you may open as soon as you wish. A few of the summer steamer trips start next week, and they may bring you customers."

"I don't see how they can," said Julia argumentatively. "Those boats don't stay long enough at the pier for people to get off and explore the town. Colmskirk isn't like Rothesay or Whiting Bay."

"No, but don't you forget," retorted Sandy, "how many people come down here by train to catch these cruising steamers, and they nearly always arrive by the train before it, which gives them time to prowl round within easy dash of the pier. Those are the sort of folk who would buy Merran's beads, though possibly not the antiques."

Next morning, accordingly, the Misses Lendrum and Bill bade their kind hostess good-bye, with many invitations from her to return, soon and often, for any meal they might wish, and were driven by Sandy to their own quarters, where Julia joyfully resumed her unpacking and arranging, while the other two disappeared into the shop to compare its contents with the lawyers' list.

"Of course," Merran explained, "you'll find quantities of things missing, but we had to furnish the house somehow, and we simply couldn't afford to do it in any other way."

"The question is," remarked Sandy, casting his eye round the sitting-room, where she had taken him to show him their progress, "whether you can afford to do it this way either. Every article you've got up here represents a bit of your capital."

"That's what Gregor said," agreed Merran; "but he's going to price it just the same, and if we can't help selling it, why, I suppose we shall just have to; but meanwhile we may as well enjoy it. The best plan would be for me to take you through the rooms first, before we tackle the shop, so that you won't think there's a deficit on the inventory."

Sandy had scarcely finished his round and gone, when they heard a knock on the side-door opening into the workroom, and Julia went to open it. Outside stood a rosy-cheeked buxom woman, whose face was faintly familiar, with a large covered basket on her arm.

"Eh, it's Miss Julia!" she cried delightedly. "You'll no' mind me, Miss Julia, but Miss Merran will—"

"But I do mind you!" interrupted Julia, equally delighted. "It's Maggie, who used to be our cook when Daddy and Mummy were alive. Of course I remember you! Merran, come quickly! Here's

Maggie—though I can't think how on earth she knew we'd come back."

"Knew!" repeated Maggie with good-natured scorn as she followed her through into the kitchen. "It would be a funny-like thing if I didna know, and me married on Dave Nisbet! Why, it was me scrubbed down the place and got it ready for you. Eh, Miss Merran, but you've aged even mair than Miss Judy here. It's a grown-up leddy ye are noo."

"Well," said Merran, laughing, as she greeted their old friend, "if I'm not grown-up at twenty, when shall I be? But, Maggie, we'd no idea it was you who were Mrs. Nisbet, and left everything in such beautiful order for us. When did you get married?"

"No' verra lang after ye left Colmskirk, Miss Merran. It just seemed I couldna settle, and Dave appeared to need looking after, and he wanted me, so I thocht mebbe I'd better tak' him and be done wi't. He'll be roon' himsel' the morn's morn, to see you aboot the cutting and polishing, and whether you'd be willing to tak' him back at his auld job, seeing they say you're keeping on wi' the business—though I can't verra weel see hoo that can be," she finished, eyeing the two girls dubiously.

"But why not?" asked Merran gaily. "I've got to make my living, and I've always loved working with the stones. But of course I must have forgotten a lot that old Jeems taught me, and I shall need Dave's help badly, so I shall be only too glad to have him in the workroom again."

"That's a' richt then. He wanted to come roond the day, but I daured him to set foot across the sill till I'd fund out if you were settled. My certes, but you've made a bonnie place of this auld kitchen," and she gazed about her admiringly.

"Oh, we've not finished yet," Julia assured her. "We've got to make curtains and cushions out of what we can find among the things that have been stored. Put down that basket, Maggie, and come upstairs. We must show you what we've done so far."

Mrs. Nisbet followed them all over the small domain with suitable enthusiasm for their scheming and contriving.

"Though it's no' the way for the doctor's bairns to be living at a', at a'," she declared, when the tour was over and they had gone back to the kitchen. "And micht I ask, Miss Merran, wha's to see to the hoose when Miss Judy's at school, and you makin' geegaws wi' Dave, or minding the shop?"

"Why," responded Merran bravely, "there won't be so very much to do with only two of us, and one out all day. I shall get up early and do what I can before breakfast, and I can always prepare the meals in between whiles. It's wonderful what can be done with planning and method."

"Huh!" exclaimed Mrs. Nisbet sceptically, busying herself with her basket. "Weel, at least I'll be across Tuesdays, Thursdays and Saturdays to see to the rough work for you. We live just ower the square, and I can easy spare the time. Eh, what's that?"

For Merran, crimson-cheeked and stammering, was trying to interrupt.

"You're very, very kind, Maggie, and I only wish I could, but—you see, we can't afford any help—not yet, anyhow. We simply must do everything ourselves."

"Tits, bairn, dinna blether!" retorted their old retainer. "Ye can afford a' I'll be takin'—since I ken fine you'll no' let me come for naethin', which is what I'd prefer. I've no need to go oot helping, and I'd go nowhere else but to you, and a shilling a morning's a' I'll let you pay. So that's settled. And here's my haunsel' for your new hame. Ye aye liked Maggie's apple-pies and plum cakes when you were weans, so we'll see if you like them still. And yon's a wheen scones and oatcakes, till you've time to mak' them for yourselves. Noo, not anither word, for I've stayed ower lang as it is. The eggs are from my ain hens, and they're braw layers. I'll be back on Tuesday, and you'll be seeing Dave in the morning. Eh, but he'll be glad to ken you mean to keep him on at the cutting and polishing, for that's what his heart's set on."

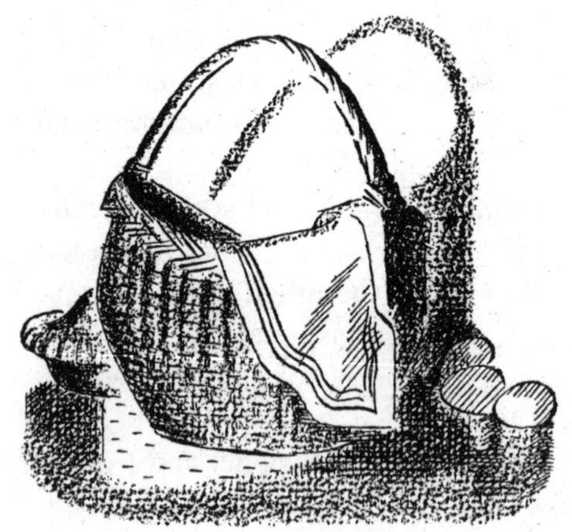

CHAPTER VII

A SIGN FOR THE SHOP

NEXT morning Dave arrived almost as soon as they had finished breakfasting on his wife's eggs. ("As a treat for our first breakfast," Merran warned her sister. "From now on it must be porridge or puffed wheat.") The treasure-chest, as Julia called it, was unlocked, and all the beads spilled out on the workroom table under the girls' admiring eyes. Merran had found and polished the old papier-maché tray, so she began at once to pile the finished articles on to it, arranging them with deft fingers, so that each trinket would show to the best advantage when she carried them through to the shop window.

"We must make a lot of new and different things, Dave," she cried enthusiastically. "Clasps and clips, and even hat-ornaments, if we used the tiniest scraps of stone and mounted them lightly enough."

Dave grunted discouragingly, for he was inclined to take a gloomy view of life.

"Lassies dinna wear hats these days," he reminded her, "just a pair o' trousers and a bit rag twisted roond their heids—that's no' the style o' dress that can be trimmed up wi' trinkets. I doot we'll no' be getting a big sale."

"Don't you worry, Dave," said Julia reassuringly. "That sort of utility dressing will go out directly they can get more material. And as for trinkets—there never was a period in the history of women when they didn't deck themselves out with all the jewellery they could afford, and a lot that they couldn't. The thing is to get the right touch about the stuff you make; you want to be *bizarre* without letting yourself get *outré*."

"Excuse me, Miss Julia, but we're not wanting anything of the sort. I've read aboot thae heathen bazaars oot in the East, and I'd be sorry if oor decent Christian wee shop was to copy the like o' them."

"That it shan't, Dave, while I have anything to do with it," Merran was quick to soothe him; and Julia added, nobly stifling her giggles, "I wasn't thinking of anything Eastern, Dave. What I should have said was 'quaint.' Sorry—my mistake." And she vanished into the shop, to spend a happy morning setting it in order; for Merran had decided to open on Monday, and had promised that Julia should help to sell, since all too soon the summer term would be starting at Westharbour Academy, and the joys of shop-keeping would have to yield to the toils of learning.

"Not that I shall mind beginning work again," she conceded later, as they lunched off bread and cheese and the remains of Maggie's apple-pie. "I've never been to school properly in Scotland, because I was too small when we lived here before for anything but that poky little place in Kerr Street. You were just beginning to outgrow it, I remember, and were to have gone to Westharbour."

"You mean Miss Dyson's? Yes. Mrs. Lamond says it is still going strong. We must go round and see them. But first of all I shall have to take you over to interview the Academy people. I'd better ring up and find out if they can see us to-morrow. It's rather short notice for them, since they reopen in a week, but I don't suppose there's the same difficulty with a big day-school. They should be able to squeeze in one more."

"Only a week—heavens! And there's so much to be done here that only I can do!"

"Such as—?"

Julia eyed her sister with a calculating look.

"Well, I don't quite see you, for one thing, out on the pavement on the top of a step-ladder, painting in the name of the shop, whereas I—"

"You'll probably see me in worse predicaments before we've finished," replied Merran calmly. "However, if you mean to infer that I don't know how to do it, you're quite right. Still, neither do you."

"No, but then," explained Julia earnestly, "that's just where you and I are different. I don't in the least mind tackling a job I know nothing about, while you only get dithery over it."

"All the same," retorted her sister unkindly, "I don't want the name-board spoilt through the inexperience of either of us. It would be better to leave it as it is till I can afford to have it done properly. After all, I'm quite glad that it should be 'J. Roberton' for a little longer."

"But it isn't better, because it won't be," declared Julia vigorously. "'J. Roberton' is barely legible, and you ought to have something that will attract people. I thought it would be an awfully good idea if I painted on 'The Serendipity Shop' in royal-blue picked out with scarlet. I'd rather have gold, of course, but that might be too expensive, and the scarlet would be very effective."

"It sounds perfectly appalling to me."

"That's because you don't see it in your mind's eye as I do. Moreover, you needn't be afraid I shall make a mess of it, as you suggested so ungratefully just now, because you know I have got a straight eye, and I can draw."

"I should imagine there's more to it than that."

"Now, look here, Merran, don't be such a wet blanket! We should get nowhere if I were as lacking in enterprise as you are. I propose to go to that little house-painter's near the bank and take him into my confidence. I shall ask him what kind of paint I need, and how much; and from there I shall lead him on to giving me tips as to how the thing should be done. When I've learnt enough I shall come back and use my natural intelligence. We've got a step-ladder, haven't we? If not, I must borrow Maggie's."

"I can see quite plainly that nothing will stop you," said Merran resignedly, though inwardly she was less perturbed than she appeared, for Julia, she knew from past experience, had a flair for getting away with her undertakings. "I only hope you won't try out too many of your long words on the painter, or he may be as perplexed as Dave was. But I don't believe a step-ladder will be necessary—not a long one, anyhow. Aren't those name-boards detachable?"

"That's an idea! Goodness, it will be child's play if I can get it down and lay it on the workroom floor. But I shall have to find out how to detach it—still, an ordinary ladder should do for that. And, Merran, there's just one thing more—it's really a brilliant notion, but you may not like it, of course."

"What on earth is it?" asked Merran in alarm.

"If you've finished lunch, come out into the shop and I'll show you. We can wash up afterwards while we discuss it, because you're sure to argue. But first, I'd better give Bill some bread and Oxo. He seems to be taking kindly enough to his new home, but that attitude of mind won't last if he isn't fed."

"I'll go round to Main Street presently and buy him some sprats," Merran promised. "I hadn't time this morning. Do you know, Judy, I haven't forgotten much. I was agreeably surprised to find myself quite at home with the tools. Between us we got through quite a lot of work."

"Luckily, you appear to have plenty of pebbles to work on at present," answered Julia. "Do you know where old Jeems got them?"

"No. I must ask Dave. Probably he had them on order from Skye, or somewhere up there. But what do you want me to look at in the shop, Julia? I'm always rather nervous when you're seized with a brilliant notion of any kind."

"I know—and that makes me diffident, though I may not show it. But this idea is really unique, and it will be the making of the business, if I can only get you to realize it."

She led the way into the shop and pushed forward a long, narrow panel which was leaning against the end of the counter. It was made of teak-wood, richly scrolled and painted in strong Oriental colours, and covered with Chinese characters. As Julia moved it so that the light from the small-paned windows fell on it, Merran cried out involuntarily.

"Why, I remember it quite well. That was one of Jeems's greatest joys, and nothing would ever induce him to sell it. It was brought to him from some port in China by one of the Boyd boys."

"Which Boyd boy? And what was he doing in China?"

"He was there in his ship, just before the war; he must have been a midshipman then. Don't you remember the Boyds who lived in that old house at the head of Glenbruie? They've been there for hundreds of years, and I expect they're there still, though I can't recall him very clearly. I don't think he was here often after I began coming, but he was very fond of old Jeems, and I think the antiques fascinated him very much as the beads drew me."

"He must have a good eye for useful antiques if he brought

this home. It's a marvellous piece of work, and probably he looted it from some old temple. I only hope there isn't some curse on it. You never know with these Eastern things."

Merran laughed. "Jeems didn't seem to think it was very old," she answered doubtfully. "I believe he valued it chiefly because Perry had brought it back for him, and I haven't the least idea what I should ask for it if anyone wants to buy the thing. It's frightful to be so inexperienced!"

"Don't you worry about the price," rejoined Julia cheerily, "because you won't need to sell it. That's where my inspiration comes in. I want you to let me hang it up outside for a signboard, just where everyone will catch sight of it as they come round from the Esplanade. It will advertise the shop better than anything else you could think of, because anyone who sees it will come along for a closer look; then they'll stare into the window, and the attractions there will finish them off."

Merran gazed down speculatively at the gay panel.

"It's certainly an original suggestion," she admitted, "but would it stand the weather sweeping up from the sea at all times of the year? Surely it would ruin the colours to be hung up outside."

"That wood," said Julia knowingly, "is teak. I wasn't taken twice a year by Uncle Basil to the South Kensington Museum for nothing. And teak will stand pretty nearly every weather there is. As for the colours, there is a kind of protective waterproof varnish that I've seen advertised. I'll get a pot of it when I go round to the painter's about the name-board, and then I can use it for both. The posters say it's clear and transparent, so it won't dim the colours down too much."

"But what about an iron bracket to hang it from? Or do you propose to fasten it to the end of an old broomstick and dangle it out of the sitting-room window?"

Julia elevated her nose scornfully.

"There's going to be nothing amateurish about this show. To tell you the truth, I haven't solved the question of the bracket yet, but something will occur to me—it always does. Often I think it's nothing short of providential."

"You certainly do have some inspirations from time to time," agreed Merran meekly. "Let's wash up now; it won't take us ten minutes. Then we can go out and do our shopping. That's going to be my difficulty in the future, when the shop is open and you are at school."

But Julia was prepared to cope with this also.

"It will take planning, of course," she remarked briskly, as she carried the tray of dishes through to the scullery, "but since it must be done, you'll find it can. Fortunately the shops have begun to send again, so I could leave notes at them on my way to the station."

"But," objected the conscientious Merran, "I ought to see the stuff I'm going to buy; it's bad housekeeping."

"What's more important," asserted Julia, "is that you can't be cooped up indoors all day long till closing time. I've got it, Merran! I told you I should. Not being a provision shop, you needn't open at break of day, as they do. You couldn't expect customers before ten-thirty—not for beads and junk—so don't open till then. We can breakfast at eight o'clock—we'll have to if I'm to get the eight forty-five—and then you can dash up and down Main Street, catching the pick of the early worms before the ordinary housewives arrive on the scene at all, and still be back behind your own counter in plenty of time."

"Julia," exclaimed Merran solemnly, drying the plates handed to her, "exasperating as you undoubtedly are at times, in your self-sufficiency, I simply couldn't imagine life without your brain. It's invaluable."

“Oh, I shouldn’t put it quite as strongly as that!” disclaimed Julia with belated modesty. “It’s only more practical than yours. But, then, it’s no good whatever for work like cutting beads.”

CHAPTER VIII

MAKING FRIENDS WITH THE ENEMY

One fresh, breezy day, a week later, Julia was balanced on the step-ladder propped against the front of the shop, while she tried to hang the name-board, newly painted and varnished, which she rightly regarded as a work of art. Each letter had been carefully spaced and measured to get it exactly straight, and the finished article would scarcely have disgraced a trained sign-painter. Julia regarded it with a certain amount of complacency, for she had not spared herself to get this result, and surely it was enough in itself to attract customers.

So far, not many of these had come into the Serendipity Shop since its opening on the previous Monday; but Merran, determined to look on the bright side, had maintained that this was just as well, since it had given her time to work without interruption in the background at increasing her stock of trinkets. Dave, too, stimulated by her enthusiasm, had been trying out some of his young mistress's new ideas, and allowed that they looked very attractive when arranged on the tray. But up till now only three customers had brought Merran through the string curtain at the back to answer the tinkling bell—Mrs. Lamond, who wanted an agate brooch to send to a sister in Canada and could, with difficulty, be dissuaded from paying far more than it was worth; the girl from the station bookstall, who bought a chain of bright-coloured beads to match her newest jumper; and some children asking hopefully for marbles. Julia had served—or rather, not served—these last, and their disappointed faces had left her sad.

"Couldn't you make some out of the stones on the beach?" she asked Merran. "I could bring you a bagful any day; and it wouldn't take you long to round them off, would it? You could put them in a basket in a corner of the window, and let the kids have them for two a penny. It would be better than having to refuse them."

"I might," said Merran, "in some of my many spare minutes; but I can't use good stones for them. I'll see what you bring me from the shingle."

But Julia, absorbed in her sign-painting, had not much time for going down to the shore, and now the end of the holidays was drawing very near. It was because of this time shortage that she had come out valiantly this afternoon, to hang the board single-handed. Merran had promised to help her when she had finished a clip on which she was working at the moment; but Julia disliked waiting; besides, a steamer was returning in an hour's time from one of the Arran cruises, and people coming off her might stroll into Gallowgate Square, and be tempted by the gorgeousness of the new board to look into the window below it.

Julia looped her bag of nails to the top of the ladder and descended a few rungs to reach the sign, which she had stood endways on the window-sill. It was heavy, but her arms were strong, and she hoped, with care and dexterity, to raise it until it could be slipped into a groove which ran along the top of the window for this very purpose. Once in there, it fitted neatly below the jutting sill of the sitting-room window above, and a few nails through the holes prepared for them were all that was needed to secure it in place.

"It's as easy as winking," declared Julia aloud, "if one only goes about it in the right way."

"It doesn't look it," commented a strange voice from the pavement below. "Why do you try to do it all by yourself?"

Julia started and dropped her hammer, which fell with a ringing crash on to the kerb, narrowly missing the speaker, a girl of her own age, who wore a hat with the colours of the Westharbour Academy on the back of her fluffy fair head.

"Heavens, I might have killed you! And then where would you have been? Why do I do it by myself? Because my sister's too busy to help me at the moment, and I can't wait."

"Why not?"

"Because the *Black Dwarf* will be in presently, and some of her passengers might catch sight of this and come in to buy. But I don't suppose you know much about shop-keeping. What are you laughing at? Do you mind handing me up that hammer?"

"I'll do more than that," offered the newcomer obligingly, as she obeyed. "I'll hand you up the board itself, and then you won't have to stoop and strain. This is a job for two."

"Well, I don't pretend I'm not grateful," Julia conceded, as the other girl raised the end of the plank towards her. "Once I get it into my arms—half-a-mo'!" and she stuffed the hammer into the pocket of her overall. "Safety first this time! Now I'm ready."

In a very few minutes the sign was up in its place, and after one or two nails had been firmly knocked in, Julia descended the ladder and stood beside her assistant to admire the effect.

"It does rather stand out, doesn't it? My sister didn't altogether agree about the colours I was using, but I think I was right all the same."

"You don't mean to say you painted that yourself? Gosh, you're clever!"

"No, I'm not," replied Julia modestly, "but I like doing things, and doing them differently. Thanks awfully for your help."

"Did you think of that name?" asked the girl, jerking her head upwards in its direction. “Because that’s different, if you like! What does it mean?”

“Serendipity? Oh, a little of everything—like liquorice allsorts. It comes out of some Eastern fable. No—I didn’t think of it. My father christened it that when old Jeems Roberton had it. By-the-by, I see you’re at Westharbour Academy, and I’m starting there on Monday, so I’m glad to get to know someone beforehand. What’s your name?”

A queer quizzical smile came over the other girl’s face, which was pink and pretty, with a becoming sprinkling of freckles. It was beginning to dawn hazily on Julia that she had seen her somewhere before.

“You mayn’t be as glad as all that when you hear what it is—I’m Lisbeth Bartle.”

“Lisbeth *what*? Not—not—”

She nodded, her grey eyes twinkling a trifle apprehensively.

“Yes. My father is Samuel Bartle of Bartle’s Stores. A very remarkable man,” she added with proud defiance. “Not many girls have a father to touch him.”

“I’m quite sure they haven’t,” assented Julia with hasty courtesy and some mental reservation. “That’s where I’ve seen you before, of course—you were with him at the station the evening we arrived.”

“Yes,” said Lisbeth, still on the defensive. “And next day he came to see you about buying the shop, but your sister won’t sell it any more than old Jeems would. It’s a frightful disappointment to him.”

“I’m sorry about that,” said Julia sympathetically. “I mean I’m sorry he’s disappointed. I could see he wasn’t used to it, and he took it hardly. And, of course, it didn’t make him like us at all.”

Lisbeth turned and looked down towards the sea. There was a

west wind blowing up the little street, and the high voices of children were blown along it on shrill gusts of laughter from the shore, where they were playing among the fishing-boats.

"No," she admitted, "it didn't. But, then, Daddy is terribly set on his own way—especially if he can't get it. Why shouldn't your sister stick to her own shop if she wants to? Certainly she has made the window look most alluring—and I love her beads."

Julia grinned at her suddenly.

"That's rather big-minded of you," she said, "so I don't mind telling you I liked *him*. There's something about him—and I could see he really does want to give Colmskirk a leg up, even though I don't agree with his ideas of doing so. It's a pity we can't see eye to eye, but I hope that won't make it awkward for us."

"Oh, no," said Lisbeth promptly, accepting without surprise the assumption that she and Julia were to be friends. The girls had liked each other at sight, and saw no reason to pretend otherwise; one of the qualities they shared was a straightforward lack of affectation that was to spare them many misunderstandings in the future. "Daddy never interferes with me in any way—at least, not in that sort of way—but I think I should warn you that he isn't the kind of person to sit down under a defeat, and if he can get possession of your sister's shop, he will."

Julia stood on the pavement, her hands in the pockets of her gay chintz overall, the breeze tossing her dark curls, and wrinkled her tip-tilted nose consideringly.

"Do you know," she said, "I don't see how he can. Merran asked Sandy Lamond about it, and it's so very legally hers. It wouldn't be possible to biff her out."

"Oh, not that way, of course," assented Lisbeth, "but there might be other means. I don't exactly see myself how it could be done—I only know that Daddy is most fearfully determined. He's not a scrap stingy, either—he might offer her such a big price that she couldn't resist it, and get round her that way."

"He wouldn't!" retorted Julia with conviction. "Merran's queer about money in some ways. I mean—there are things she finds more important. As long as we can jog along in reasonable comfort and keep out of debt, she'd rather be successful than rich. And she's dead set on making a success of the Serendipity Shop. It wouldn't be any use to try to bribe her."

"Oh, well," said Lisbeth philosophically, giving up the argument, "they must fight it out their own way. Your name-board looks awfully nice, anyhow, though it's a pity it doesn't show downwards towards the Esplanade. Strangers are apt to go strolling past without wandering into Gallowgate Square, and this wouldn't catch their eye unless they did."

"No, but," responded Julia mysteriously, "I've got something else that will. Wait a second!" and she dived into the shop, to reappear with the Chinese panel held triumphantly before her. "There," she exclaimed, "what do you think of that? The varnish is quite dry now, and I'm only waiting for the man at the paint-shop to bring me over an old iron bar he promised me with a hook at the end of it. It was lying on a heap of rubbish in his yard, and when I asked if I might buy it he was quite insulted—said he'd thrown it away for scrap, and he'd not only give it to me, but would come and fix it up this evening. Isn't he a pet? When that's up, Lisbeth, it ought to collect a crowd!"

"You couldn't have anything more kenspeckle!" agreed Lisbeth, gazing at it with awe. "It's really quite unique. Have you any idea what it means?"

"Not the foggiest," answered Julia cheerfully. "But then, neither has anybody else. It's the look of the thing that matters, and it certainly is good-looking."

Three indignant blasts sounded from somewhere out on the bay, and Lisbeth cried, "That must be the *Black Dwarf* hooting. I expect the ferry-boat from Inchmore is keeping her out of the pier, but she'll be in directly, and her trippers will be swarming all over the town. I hope some of them will be coming up this way. See you at school on Monday morning. By-the-by, I don't know your name. You see," with laughing eyes, "I've only heard you called the younger Lendrum girl."

"I'm Julia," she replied, as she prepared to carry in the panel. "Next time you must come in, if you think your father wouldn't mind, and meet Merran and William of Orange, my marmalade cat."

CHAPTER IX

MERRAN GOES OUT TO LUNCH

Two passengers from the boat did find out the Serendipity Shop that afternoon, buying, not beads, but a wag-at-the-wa' clock with a painted face, which Merran had some difficulty in tying up securely before they bore it off to the train. That purchase apparently set the ball rolling. By the beginning of the week, when Julia had been swallowed up in Westharbour Academy, her sign was creaking merrily in the breeze, and customers were coming in at the rate of one or two each day. A few came for antiques, and a few, not finding what they sought, withdrew without buying anything; but it was chiefly the hand-made ornaments that attracted them, and Merran began to work in the evenings, after hours, in order to keep up her stock. Dave Nisbet could always be relied on for the rougher work—the actual cutting, polishing and shaping of the stones in their cruder forms—but it required Merran's defter and more imaginative fingers to evolve the completed gem; and the lame craftsman never knew what flight of fancy his tools might be called upon to follow, though he was always the first to admire the result. Fortunately he had had some training in metal-work, which he was able to pass on to her, and this soon provided suitable settings for their pebbles. Merran speculated in a small second-hand furnace, which she had seen advertised in some trade journal, and when this had been put up in the workroom, they were able to melt their metals with more ease.

It was a strenuous life, and left very little time for anything more than the absolutely necessary housekeeping, since Julia was now too fully occupied with her school work to be of much use when she was at home. But many people in Colmskirk still remembered their old doctor with affection, and were eager to seek out his daughters and make much of them. They were intrigued by the story of Merran's legacy, and impressed by her plucky determination to make a living out of it. The girls could have had many invitations to supper in the evenings, after the shop was closed, if they could have found time to accept them; and on Sundays they were hailed, coming out of church, by old acquaintances who would fain have carried them back to share their midday meal. The hospitality of Colmskirk had learnt to surmount even post-war austerity, and "pot-luck" was something they were always ready to proffer. Merran tried her best to respond when she could spare an evening, or on early-closing days, and Julia, if she could fit in her preparation, was always eager to come too.

"We must keep up with Colmskirk people," explained Merran, "because if we're going to make our living in the town it's only right to pull our weight in such ways as we can, though they mayn't be many, I'm afraid."

"Oh, I know," answered Julia cheerfully. "Even though we haven't much time to play around, we can always show ourselves friendly, and take an interest in what interests them. I find that's really the best way to go about people, and it's easy here, where everyone's so kind—not starched and artificial, as they used to be in Slingsby."

"They weren't," protested Merran, "not all of them. But I know what you mean—they were more conventional. How do you get on with the girls at school?"

"Quite all right. They don't seem to mind me even if I am

new—though I try not to be any newer than I can help. I'm frightfully self-effacing—very backward in coming forward, in fact."

"It doesn't sound much like you," replied Merran, laughing, but Julia favoured her with a solemn wink.

"I know my place, and I can assure you it works. I like most of them immensely, and I don't think I'm altogether unpopular. The one I like best, though, is Lisbeth Bartle. There's something very sound about that girl."

"It's queer that you and she should have clicked in the circumstances. So far, I've only seen her in church, but I should like to know her, since she is your particular friend."

"Well, I think she's going to be," amended Julia cautiously, "but I don't hold with rushing one's relationships, even at school. Safety first. Anyhow, you'll probably get to know her quite soon, because I mean to ask her to tea in about another fortnight."

"Oh!" said Merran, rather startled. "Will her father let her come?"

Julia grinned as she gathered her books together and prepared to go upstairs to the sitting-room, where she usually did her evening's work.

"Between you and me," she replied, "I fancy Lisbeth does pretty well as she pleases; but she does it very tactfully—she wouldn't come if she thought it would hurt his feelings; she'll just manage things so that it doesn't. She's an only child, you know, and her mother died when she was born, so she has had sixteen years in which to practise managing."

It was on the following day that Mrs. Binnie called. Mrs. Binnie was "the Provost's lady," and a person of importance in the burgh. Her husband was a retired Glasgow merchant who had his roots in Colmskirk, and had built himself a very comfortable villa just above the Bruie Burn on the north side of the town. Merran had pleasant recollections of opulent children's parties at Fernbank in the days before Mr. Binnie became Provost, but she had not expected them to recall her, and was agreeably surprised when the shop-bell tinkled just as she was preparing her solitary lunch, and she went through to find Mrs. Binnie inspecting the bead-trays.

"My dear, you don't remember me in the least, I expect, but I was very fond of your parents, and directly I heard about all this," with a comprehensive sweep of her hand, "I came along to give you my blessing. I should have been here weeks ago, but had to go off to England at an hour's notice to nurse a sick relation. Bad for my engagements in the town, but one's own flesh and blood comes first, and anyhow it gave Mrs. Stiles a chance—and did she enjoy it! She's my deputy, you know, on the Town Council—you don't know, of course, but you soon will. Now, don't let's waste any more time, but get on your coat and come along. I've got the car outside and I'm taking you back to lunch with me."

"But—but—the shop!" stammered the startled Merran. "Thank you very much, Mrs. Binnie, but—"

"Nothing of the sort!" interrupted the lady breezily. "Lock it up and come. Bless me, you've got to have lunch somewhere, and it may just as well be at Fernbank. Who do you suppose is going to buy beads at this hour of the day? There won't be a steamer at the pier till three o'clock, and all the natives are busy at home, eating such food as the times allow. Don't keep me waiting, there's a good girl! I'll run you back again in plenty of time for your next customers."

So Merran, having put down Bill's dinner-plate and fetched her coat, followed Mrs. Binnie out obediently and took her seat in the car. It gave her a delightful feeling of adventure to lock up like this and come out in the very middle of the day. Hitherto her excursions, except on Sundays, had always been in the early morning or after closing hours. It was a luxury, too, to find herself eating a well-cooked meal without any effort on her part, and to respond to Mrs. Binnie's kindly inquiries.

"I hadn't time to examine your work properly just now, but what I saw struck me as being charming and very tastefully shown. I mean to advertise you a bit among my friends up in town, for I have an idea that you may very well become the fashion when people know about you. It's so delightful in these austerity days to find anything distinctive in the way of presents, and your designs look as though they were original."

"They are," said Merran, "as far as I can make them so. I'm tremendously keen on the work itself, quite apart from the profit."

"That's why it has got a personal touch about it. My dear, you ought to do well, and I hope you will; but I suppose you know you inherited more than the shop from old Jeems? He has bequeathed you an enemy as well, and a pretty formidable one, too!"

"Who?" exclaimed Merran in alarm. "Oh, you mean Mr. Bartle? But he can't do me any harm. Sandy Lamond says my title-deeds are perfectly water-tight, and no one can force me to sell if I don't want to."

Mrs. Binnie looked grave as she helped herself to a biscuit.

"Perhaps not; but I shouldn't be too sure that Bartle is harmless. He is a very determined man, who has risen from small beginnings chiefly by his dogged persistence in sticking to his own way till he gets it."

Merran lifted her small chin defiantly.

"Well, I haven't got beyond my small beginnings yet, but I can take a leaf out of his book and be equally determined in sticking to my own way."

Mrs. Binnie regarded her meditatively.

"Have some of that cream-cheese with your biscuits," she said. "I admire your spirit, and—as I said before—I'll do all I can to help you, but I do want you to understand what you're up against. It's so much better not to under-estimate the enemy, and Bartle is a very wealthy man, which gives him the initial advantage."

"I don't quite see how, in this case," maintained Merran obstinately.

"Don't you? Then I'll give you one example—for Bartle has mounted his first gun this very week. He has started a counter in his store for hand-made jewellery and such-like, and has ordered a big consignment from some place in Skye where they specialize in the making of it. And I fancy he'll try to undersell you at first, for he can afford to do so. That's Sam Bartle's opening move. If Miss Naboth won't let him buy her vineyard, then he'll go all out to sour her grapes."

The colour rose in Merran's face and her blue eyes flashed indignantly, but her voice was quite calm as she retorted, "He's a beast, of course, but it just means I shall have to work a lot harder to raise the quality of my goods. He may sell hand-worked jewellery made of Scottish stones, but if he orders it like that it's bound to be what everyone else is selling up and down the country. You were kind enough to call mine distinctive, Mrs. Binnie."

"Tits, lassie! I called it that because it is. Nobody with judgment would look twice at Sam Bartle's after seeing yours. But you have to bear in mind that it isn't every day-tripper off the steamers who has sufficient judgment to see the difference—nor even every summer visitor at the Hydro. What they will consider will be the difference in the price."

"But I can't lower mine," objected Merran.

"Exactly! It would be a great mistake if you did; the things you put out aren't meant to be two a penny. But that, you see, is what Bartle is counting on. And, mind, his stock is by no means cheap and nasty; he's too clever for that."

Merran nodded thoughtfully as she rose from the table and followed her hostess into the flower-filled drawing-room.

"I begin to see a little of what I'm facing up to," she said. "Thank you very much, Mrs. Binnie, for explaining it to me; but I'm not going to be frozen out, all the same, and I'm not going to sell my Serendipity Shop. Why, apart from everything else, do you know what he means to do if he can add it to his other purchases in Gallowgate Square?"

Mrs. Binnie pulled up a chair for her guest and rang for the coffee.

"Yes," she said, "I know all about it. So does most of Colmskirk. He is going to take down the old white-washed cottages and put up a great modern store, all windows and chromium plating, which will surround the whole square in four sections, and glitter in the sun so that it will be seen miles out at sea, like a huge daylight beacon. Oh, Sam Bartle is going to put Colmskirk on the map all right!"

Merran grinned impishly as she accepted the cigarette her hostess offered her.

"Well, he can't commit these atrocities as long as I sit tight, and I'm prepared to martyr myself in the cause of the burgh. But you've made me realize that it's going to be a stiff fight, Mrs. Binnie, so perhaps I'd better be going back and getting on with it now. Thank you very much for bringing me here, and for my delightful time—"

Mrs. Binnie knocked the ash off her cigarette.

"Sit still," she commanded. "I'll do more than that—I'll run you back again; but not for another ten minutes. I've got a committee at the Burgh Chambers, and I'll drop you on my way to it. You must come on Sunday next time, when you'll see my husband. You were always a great favourite of his—or was it Julia? Where is she, by the way? You must bring her too."

"She'd love it. She goes to the Westharbour Academy, and doesn't get back till five o'clock. It may amuse you to hear that her greatest friend there is Lisbeth Bartle."

Mrs. Binnie laughed heartily.

"Splendid! Lisbeth is a nice child, and no one can understand it. By rights she should be an insufferable little hussy, for she's an only child and the apple of her father's eye. There's nothing he wouldn't do for Lisbeth. You see, her mother died at her birth, and Sam Bartle was very much in love with his wife; she was a lady, and she ran away from home to marry him in the old romantic style. I always think that little history explains a good deal of Bartle. All he really lives for now is Lisbeth—and his hope of getting on the Town Council. He's a queer fish, and I think he wouldn't stick at much to attain his ambitions, but he's not bad at heart; anyway, I prefer him to Brolly Tait, the other candidate for that bailieship. In short, you may regard Sam as an enemy to be respected, in various senses of the word."

CHAPTER X

THE UPWARD TREND

WHEN the shop was shut that evening, and Julia had returned in time for their high tea at half-past five, she listened with keen interest to Merran's account of her luncheon at Fernbank.

"So that's what Mr. Bartle is up to, is it?" was her comment at the end. "Still, Mrs. Binnie is right, Merran. The things you make are quite individual, so you've got something there which he can't touch. Even if he does undersell you, that won't affect the customers who have sense enough to prefer the best and go straight for it."

"You're very flattering," responded Merran, smiling. "All the same, I wish my dignity would allow me to go and look at the goods on Mr. Bartle's trinket counter."

"I shouldn't worry," said Julia comfortably. "You wouldn't find them half so inspiring as the illustrations in that book I got you from Westharbour library last week—the one on Celtic jewellery."

"I wasn't expecting inspiration," said Merran, "but I should like to gratify my curiosity. You're right about the book, though. I've got lots of valuable ideas from its pictures, and I'm trying to work them out, with Dave's help. If one tries, however clumsily, to copy that sort of thing, one can learn a good deal; besides, there's some hope of success when one knows they were all made by hand originally, with the use of very primitive tools."

"And that," said Julia conclusively, "is a line which Bartle could never take up, even if he wished to, because it requires an artist."

Accordingly, Merran bent herself more than ever to the task of finding and working out distinctive designs for her ornaments, and to her great delight the Serendipity Shop started to prosper amain. Soon she was no longer dependent for patronage on stray passengers wandering between pier and station, whose eyes might be caught, as they strolled, by Julia's strange swinging sign. First came people from the Hydropathic above the Broomieknowes, and then cars from other parts of the county began to pull up in Gallowgate Square; some even came all the way from town, attracted by what they had heard from Mrs. Binnie and her friends. Those were the people who bought up her dearer and more ambitious efforts, and were her best advertisements, for they talked about her and showed their purchases wherever they went.

"Yes, I found it in such a quaint little place down in Colmskirk, tucked away round the corner from the Esplanade. You might easily miss it but for an extraordinary Chinese board that hangs out from the front. It's kept by such a nice girl—oh! quite young—a doctor's daughter and *most* artistic. She designs all these things herself, and makes most of them, too, with the help of a lame workman. Rose Binnie told me about her. You should run down, my dear, and see what you can pick up."

The Provost's lady herself was delighted with Merran's growing success, and visited her shop to tell her so, on a Saturday morning, when bound for one of the innumerable local committees on which she sat by reason of her husband's office. Julia was behind the counter, and received her with warmth, for, like most people in Colmskirk, the Binnies were great friends of hers.

"Shall I call Merran," she asked, "or will I do? I can get her in a minute. She's only slipping our week-end joint into the oven.

It's almost infinitesimal, though Daker cut me off as big a bit as he dared."

"I see you haven't lost your love of long words," observed Mrs. Binnie, amused. "I've never forgotten you, at six years old, assuring my husband that the price of something—your new shoes, I believe—had been 'perfectly pre-postiverous.' No, don't disturb Merran. I only wanted to tell her I'd heard from Mrs. Scott, who bought that pink crystal pendant when she was down lunching with me last week, and that it has been greatly admired. I shouldn't be surprised if it brought her in some orders, for it was very uncommon."

Julia coloured with pleasure and pride.

"I'm so glad people like her work," she said, "for I do think it's beautiful. She feels she owes a great deal to your kindness, Mrs. Binnie."

"Oh, nonsense, my dear! When young people show enterprise it's up to us elderly folk to lend a helping hand. How are you getting on at the Academy? Like it?"

"Very much, thank you. I'm taking up shorthand and typing next term, so that I can go in for secretarial training. I want to grow up into being a super-secretary, if I can get that sort of job."

"I don't know what a super-secretary is exactly," said Mrs. Binnie, "but you'd better come along with Merran to tea to-morrow and talk to my husband. He might be able to give you some tips."

"I'd love to, thank you," replied Julia regretfully, "but I've promised to take my tea up Glenbruie to-morrow afternoon with Lisbeth Bartle. She knows a good place for picnicking up there, by that little lochan beyond Faraway."

"Some other Sunday afternoon then," said Mrs. Binnie. "I'm glad you have made friends with that child, Lisbeth. She doesn't have much of a time, for all her father's wealth. He isn't popular about here, and that reacts on her, which is a shame, for she's a nice girl if only people wouldn't visit her father's sins on her."

"I think that's perfectly futile!" exclaimed Julia hotly. "And you know, Mrs. Binnie, he isn't such a bad sort if he wasn't always dashing up the wrong turning and upsetting people. He means well, even if he is trying to push us out of Gallowgate Square and raze it to the ground—that's just one of his wrong turnings."

Mrs. Binnie moved towards the door, her face still wearing that look of faint amusement.

"Well, it's very open-minded of you to regard it like that, for it's small thanks to Sam Bartle that the Serendipity is flourishing. But I'm glad about you and Lisbeth because there's so much you can give her. Good-bye—and don't forget my message to your sister about that pink pendant."

Julia delivered it as they ate their midday dinner in the sunny kitchen, which had had its weekly scrubbing from Maggie earlier in the day. Merran had unearthed a pair of red-checked curtains from the boxes lately stored at Gregor's, and these now hung on either side of the broad stone sill where stood the famous geraniums in full flower; a gingham cloth to match was spread on the table, and the whole effect, though plain, was home-like.

Julia looked round her with approval.

"This may not be sumptuous," she remarked, "but it's pleasant, and the warming-pan gives it a tone. I don't wonder William of Orange seems entirely satisfied; it would be awkward for us if he wasn't, but I've never regretted bringing him north. What do you suppose Mrs. Binnie meant, Merran, by saying there was such a lot I could give Lisbeth?"

"Possessions aren't everything," replied her sister. "I expect your friendship means a good deal to Lisbeth, because I think Mrs. Binnie is quite right in saying that she suffers from her father's unpopularity. He rubs the townsfolk the wrong way, and it's difficult for them to show kindness to Lisbeth when their feelings towards him are far from kind. Why, I'd love to have her to tea here if it wasn't for this absurd feud he insists upon."

Julia helped herself thoughtfully to potatoes.

"After all," she said, "it's a silent feud. We haven't come across him or spoken a word to him since you refused to sell him the shop. He has a perfect right to keep hand-made jewellery if he wants to. Even though we know it's done to spoil your sales, we needn't recognize it as such. And it is only at second-hand that we hear he's going about abusing you—so we needn't recognize that either."

"I don't intend to," returned Merran promptly. "It would be most undignified to take any notice. But what are you getting at?"

"Only that, if we don't admit we've got a feud with him, whatever he may suppose, I can't see what's to hinder me from asking Lisbeth to tea. I always intended to when I'd known her a little longer. I told you so."

A worried line appeared on Merran's smooth brow.

"I know—and I felt that it might be awkward, much as I should like to have her. You see, Judy, I'd hate him to think we were trying to suck up to him through his daughter."

Julia eyed her severely.

"I can't see how you can sit in judgment on me for using vulgar expressions after using one like that yourself—but that's by the way. I don't think your argument applies. *We* don't want anything out of Mr. Bartle; if anybody's going to do any sucking-up, to borrow your low phrase, it should be him. I know Lisbeth would like to be asked here—and anyhow, we can't go on meeting up Glenbruie, or on the boat across to Inchmore, whenever we want to see each other out of school. Even now the weather is likely to hold us up. Can't we set an example to Colmskirk and be decent to Lisbeth in spite of her father?"

"All right," yielded Merran suddenly, "if you put it that way. After all, it is hard on the kid. Invite her for next Saturday. I shall have to be in the shop, of course, till six o'clock, but you can take her up to the sitting-room and entertain her in your own way."

"Oh, that won't be difficult," Julia assured her. "Thanks awfully, Merran. I've been feeling I wanted to do something for her, and that will be a beginning. It's a pity, for old Lisbeth's sake, that her father can't find some way of benefiting Colmskirk without setting everyone by the ears. He should have taken my hint about the hospital. He wouldn't have had to complain of ingratitude then."

Merran laughed as she rose to fetch the pudding.

"He has got a very different idea at present. Mrs. Stiles came in this morning to look at those brass-studded bellows, and she was fizzing up like a soda-water siphon because someone she'd met in Macrae's had just told her old Bartle is going to buy Meadows, and convert it into a fun-fair."

Julia gasped.

"Oh, no, Merran, he can't! That lovely house and garden! It would be iniquitous!"

"There's nothing to stop him, as far as I know. But you can imagine the wrath of Mrs. Stiles, living as she does next door to Meadows."

"She should buy it herself, then. They can very well afford it. Did she take the bellows this time?"

"Yes, but she tried to make me reduce them—said she could get them for half the price up in town if she had time to go and look for them. Julia, if you'd fetch me some common or garden chuckie-stones from the beach this afternoon, I believe I could find a few minutes to cut some marbles for the children, as you asked me to do a while ago. They come and look in at the windows, and I always wish I had something within their little means."

"I'll bring you a bagful," promised Julia readily. "As a matter of fact, I've just had an inspiration. It came to me this morning when I was behind the counter, and I meant to put it before you at once, but Mrs. Binnie drove it out of my mind."

"What is it?" asked Merran apprehensively.

"Only that I thought we might start a hand-made toy department to be open on Saturdays only. I could get some patterns and make them in the evenings when I'd finished my prep. I'm fairly quick-fingered at that sort of thing, you know, and I'd simply love selling them at the end of the week."

"Very well—but if you once begin you'll have to keep it up," Merran warned her, "or else the children will be disappointed. And anyhow I can't see how you can find time to make more than five or six a week. They'll sell out in ten minutes."

"Perhaps—but the kids who get them will be pleased, and the others can come back the following week," replied Julia, undaunted. "And being made out of scraps by me, we can keep the prices down. We don't want to make money out of babes."

CHAPTER XI

A PICNIC AT GLENBRUIE

JULIA sang softly to herself next afternoon as she changed from her best frock of cherry-coloured tussore, into something plainer and more serviceable for scrambling about among rocks and trees—a brown linen with yellow cuffs and collar, and round her neck she fastened a short string of cornelians which Merran had given her the week before. She was looking forward to this picnic. Coming out of church that morning, Lisbeth had squeezed up to her, whispering, "Top of Gallowgate Lane at two-thirty. I've got a huge surprise for you!" and had vanished again into the emerging congregation without giving her friend time to ask questions.

Julia popped her head round the sitting-room door to bid her sister good-bye, then ran lightly downstairs and out through the workroom, picking up her packet of sandwiches as she passed the kitchen table. She had concocted the fillings of these with great care and originality, for Lisbeth was sure to bring a box of Macrae's more elaborate cakes, and Julia wished to live up to them in the matter of her own provisions; so she had ransacked the store cupboard, and was fairly well pleased with the result. The brown-bread sandwiches contained shredded sardines folded in lettuce-leaves, and the white bread was spread with cheese and tomato ketchup; to these she had added some tea-rolls stuffed with chutney and chopped walnuts. The drinks were to be Lisbeth's responsibility, which, Julia felt, was a pity, since she herself had evolved in her mind a marvellous "cocktail" recipe composed of lemon-squash and ginger-ale with a strong dash of apple-juice.

"Next time," she thought, as she hurried across the square, "I shall insist on doing that part of it; I may think of something even better. What a mercy it's fine! Nothing can be so damping as a picnic in dread of rain every minute."

Gallowgate Lane was a long, narrow street running straight through to the back of the town, and Julia, when she reached the end of it, found Lisbeth already waiting at the tryst, sitting with studied calm at the wheel of an open car, the very latest of a famous firm's "baby" models.

"My goodness!" exclaimed Julia, coming to an abrupt stand as she stared, goggle-eyed, at this apparition. "Surely this isn't the surprise? Why, how on earth did you get hold of it?"

"Isn't she a beauty?" cried Lisbeth gleefully. "Get in, quick, before we collect an admiring crowd of urchins. I knew you'd be knocked all of a heap. Daddy gave her to me for my next birthday. He has let me have her in advance so that I shan't lose all the decent weather. Think what fun we can have in her during the holidays!"

Julia got in, depositing her packet of sandwiches on the top of a picnic-basket at the back.

"But it isn't your birthday—you're too young," she protested. "No one can have a licence before they're seventeen."

Lisbeth winked deliberately while she let in the clutch with an expert movement—seventeen or not, she had long ago learned to drive on her father's car—and they ran smoothly out on to the country road skirting the back of Colmskirk.

"I've persuaded Daddy to let me take a risk," she said. "I simply could not wait till the end of September for Dulcibel—that's her name—so, against his better judgment, he gave way and allowed me to have her. The local police aren't likely to fuss, and if we go farther afield I'm banking on the fact that I look quite seventeen; it's not as though I had one of those baby faces."

Julia swerved half round and examined her critically.

"Perhaps not," she conceded, "but you don't look so frightfully sophisticated, nevertheless. Still, let's hope you'll get away with it, for your driving is all that the most exacting policeman could desire. Where are we going to, in the meantime?"

"Up to the far end of Glenbruie, as we arranged. We can park Dulcibel on the edge of the woods there and explore. I daren't leave her too long, of course; you never know who may be about on a Sunday afternoon, though it's usually pretty quiet in those wilds."

"Too far from the pier and Esplanade to be popular," agreed Julia. "I say, Leebie, she's a ripping little car! I've never seen a baby car before which opened right out, and it's so much nicer than a saloon with a sunshine roof."

"I know," said Lisbeth. "I love to feel the air all round me, unless it's pouring. And this hood has a patent contrivance for raising it in two shakes of a lamb's tail, before you've time to get soaked struggling with it. She's the last word in everything."

And she proceeded to put the new possession through all its tricks for Julia's benefit, as they skimmed inland up the long valley of the Bruie Burn.

"There's only one thing I ask," she said earnestly, as they turned into a little-used track that bent off on the left towards the wooded glen. "Don't talk about her at school. If Gracie Tait and that lot discover I've got a car of my own to do as I like with, they'll come all over friendly, and I can bear them better when they're not!"

Julia chuckled. "Taters has found out whom she has to thank

for her new nickname. It's spreading like wildfire through the school, and you can't expect anyone to like being called 'Tattie-bogle.' It's clever, certainly, but hardly kind."

Lisbeth looked uncomfortable.

"Oh, do you think so? I didn't mean it that way. I shouldn't mind if anyone called me 'Tattie-bogle.'"

Julia glanced at the dainty blue-clad figure beside her.

"I don't suppose so—you can afford not to mind. But Taters is deficient in humour, to begin with, and anyhow, I shouldn't think she can help knowing she's got the face and colouring of a pure-bred weasel."

"But I gave her the name because she's always so untidy," objected Lisbeth. "You can't deny she's an awful mess to have in the form, and that's something she can help. I wasn't thinking about her ugliness."

"But I bet *she* was," Julia persisted, "and she doesn't love you any the better. One can't afford to be personal, except about raving beauties; the other kind are sure to take it the wrong way."

Lisbeth's sunny face was clouded as she backed the car in under a thicket of wild rhododendrons and shut off her engine.

"Well, I'm sorry," she said. "I don't really like hurting people's feelings—though I think we've a right to object if they come to school all bits and pieces, with holes in their stockings, and let our form down. It mightn't matter so much, perhaps, in IVa, but I do think the Upper Sixth should sew on their buttons and brush their hair."

"Yes," assented Julia, "and we can do more about it than the staff; but you require to adapt your methods to the people you're dealing with, and ridicule doesn't pay when applied to the Gracie Taits of this life."

"I hate to think I've really hurt her feelings," reiterated Lisbeth.

"I must think what I can do to make it up to her. Meantime, Julia, let's get out and explore. Dulcibel will be safe here, if anywhere, and we must find some place nearer to the lochan where we can sit and eat all this food."

They wandered off downwards through the trees and bushes till they reached the Bruie Burn tumbling about its boulders, and found a comfortable seat above a tiny fall, among the roots of an old gnarled oak, where they squashed themselves in together and unwrapped the provisions.

"I hope you'll like the sandwiches," said Julia, a trifle anxiously. "I tried to invent something unusual, but the ideas I worked out are a bit new, so they may prove to be acquired tastes, and there won't be time for you to acquire them in one afternoon. Leebie, do you think you could come to tea with us next Saturday? Merran told me to ask you."

Lisbeth coloured with pleasure.

"I'd love to," she answered simply, "and I'd love to meet your sister. I look at her in church and think what an interesting face she has. It's pretty, but more than pretty. You're jolly lucky to have her, you know."

"I do know," answered Julia soberly. "Try one of the rolls."

It was very seldom that Lisbeth hinted, even so indirectly, at her own loneliness, but Julia knew she was lonely in that big luxurious home of hers above the Broomieknowes; and it was not likely to be any better when she grew up and left school next year, unless some way could be found to break the barriers of her father's unpopularity. That, Julia felt, was the most unlikely contingency of all, as things were at present. There were plenty of people in Colmskirk who would object very strongly to Meadows being converted into a fun-fair, apart from Sam Bartle's other well-meant indiscretions.

"I think, if you don't mind, Julia," said Lisbeth politely, "I'd rather not finish this roll. The—the flavour's very nice, but it's a little too hot for me. I think it must be one of the tastes I've still to acquire."

Julia's wandering thoughts were abruptly recalled.

"Oh, sorry!" she exclaimed contritely. "I thought the chutney was a little insipid when we had it at supper last night, so I added a sprinkling of ginger to the filling, and maybe I've overdone it a bit. Have one of these sandwiches instead. They must be cool enough, because they've got lettuce in them."

She took the remains of the discarded roll from her friend, and, standing up, flung it with force and precision right over the little fall into a deep, dark pool below, where it dropped with a soft splash—and immediately an irate masculine voice called up from the screen of bushes on the farther bank, "Hi! Look out! You're disturbing the fish! That spoilt a bite for me—and you're trespassing, anyhow!"

Both girls stared in astonishment as a dark, ruffled head rose through the greenery below them, and they heard the skirl of a line being wound in. Then a young man stepped out of the rhododendrons, fishing-tackle in hand, and glared up at the disturbers of his peace.

Julia was the first to recover herself.

"We're not trespassing," she retorted indignantly. "I'm sorry about your fish, and I shouldn't have done it if I'd known you were there, but we are entirely within our rights."

The fisherman continued to glare. He clearly felt that it was bad enough to have lost his bite without having an argument thrust upon him.

"Pardon me, but you're not—you're within mine. This part of the glen is private property."

"Yes," said Julia, "it belongs to Drumbruie House, but old Mr. Boyd told my father we might come into it whenever we liked. Probably you don't know who I am, but my name is Julia Lendrum."

"And mine," responded the fisherman, "is Peregrine Boyd."

Lisbeth, as an interested onlooker, felt that he had achieved the last word, and made a move to gather up the half-eaten picnic, when, to her astonishment, things took a different trend.

"Dear me!" exclaimed Julia, all her arrogance melting like snow in the sun. "Then you must be the midshipman who brought the painted panel back from China for old Jeems Roberton. My sister, Merran, thinks she can remember you at children's parties years ago, but I was too small then. Are you home on leave just now? Do come up here and have some of our picnic. There's too much for only two."

Perry Boyd gazed up at her for a moment, then burst out laughing. It was impossible to mistake Julia's frank friendliness for anything but what it was. She had effectually destroyed his sport for one afternoon, but she was offering a different form of entertainment, and one that might be more amusing at the moment. A picnic in the wood with a couple of schoolgirls was a new experience for Perry, and he decided to sample it.

"Thanks awfully!" he called back. "I was just beginning to get hungry, but couldn't be bothered to go home. Sure you can spare me some?"

"Rather!" responded Julia, while Lisbeth began to get out the food again.

In a few seconds he had joined them, and was introduced to Lisbeth, who plied him with sandwiches in shy silence, while Julia, who never knew the meaning of shyness, advised him kindly to avoid the rolls unless he had a special fancy for curry.

"You probably have," she said, "having served in the East, but anyhow you'd be better with something else. Safety first! I'm sorry I messed up your fishing, but I'm very glad to meet you all the same, because I want to know the history of the Chinese panel."

"The fishing doesn't really matter," he assured her. "It wasn't a good day for sport anyway—too much sun coming through the branches. As to the panel—I'm afraid I've forgotten it. I usually brought something back for old Jeems, because I always had an affection for him and his shop. Who has it now, do you know?"

"My sister," replied Julia promptly.

"Your sister?" he echoed in astonishment.

"Yes. Jeems left it to her, and as she wanted a job, she wouldn't sell—she decided to carry it on," with a hurried glance at Lisbeth. "She makes the beads, you know, and she's got all sorts of new ideas for them. But I'm sorry you don't remember the panel. I've always felt it had some story behind it."

CHAPTER XII

PERRY BOYD AND THE CHINESE PANEL

Lieutenant Peregrine Boyd, R.N., came round the corner from the Esplanade and strolled up towards Gallowgate Square till he arrived opposite the Serendipity Shop, where he halted and stared across at the corner window, looking both ways under its queer swinging sign. The sign itself he eyed first with incredulity, then with great and growing amusement.

"So that's what she was talking about," he exclaimed aloud. "Lord! I'd forgotten all about the thing! And to think they've hung it up—the innocents—to advertise their wares! Well, well!"

The curtains at the back of the window parted, and a girl leaned in, to place a basket containing some small wares in the right-hand corner; he watched as she rearranged one or two of the articles, and though he could see little but the parting in her rippling gold-brown hair, something about her held his attention, so that, as she drew back again behind the blue net curtains, he crossed the street and pushed open the door of the shop.

Merran turned with a start at the sound of the bell, and looked dubiously at this tall young man in his shabby tweeds, who seemed to take up more room than his spare figure justified. He had keen eyes, whose straight lids slanted downwards at the corners; his mouth, which was large and also straight, cocked up at the ends;

and this combination of features produced a quizzical effect that was vaguely familiar to her.

"Good afternoon," she said politely. "Can I show you anything?"

"Why, yes," he answered, with an engaging smile. "Pretty nearly everything, in fact—though, alas! I can't buy much of it. You see, I used to have the run of this place when I was a kid, in old Jeems Roberton's time, and I've been seized with a terrible urge to poke about in it again, if you will allow me."

"Now I know who you are," cried Merran triumphantly. "You must be Perry Boyd, and my young sister met you up the glen last Sunday. But you've changed a good deal, you know, since I danced with you at Mrs. Binnie's Hallow-e'en parties."

"There's been a war," he answered soberly. "Come to that, you've changed a good deal yourself since you were wee Merran Lendrum, running round the town in a scarlet coat and tammy. You did me a dirty turn, if you like, supplanting me in old Roberton's affections after I went to sea. I might have been his heir if it hadn't been for you, and then I should have been asking you to-day what I could show *you*, instead of the other way about."

"Oh, he always kept a warm corner in his heart for you," declared Merran, "but I expect he thought it was enough for you to inherit Glenbruie without having this as well."

"Lord, yes!" he said with another lapse into gravity. "He only died last year, didn't he, so he must have known that Hugh went at Alamein, and Billy was shot down over Germany—and that there was no one left but me for Glenbruie."

"I'm sorry," said Merran softly. "They were so much older—I never knew them, though my father did. Are you all alone up there now?"

He nodded. "When I'm there," he answered briefly. "Mostly

Perry

I'm at sea, and then I let it. Just now I'm waiting for a ship. I say, you've tidied the old shop up a lot. I like it. Can see round things a great deal better."

"I'm afraid there's not as much in it as there used to be," she said apologetically. "I haven't sold much in the ten weeks we've been here—nothing very big, at least—but then I haven't bought any more stuff either. To tell you the truth, I'm rather afraid of buying antiques. I know so little; I might get badly stung."

He seated himself sideways on the edge of the counter and looked across at her with considerable amusement.

"But how are you going to replenish your stock if you funk it? How do you propose to keep the business going?"

"I'm concentrating more on the beads," she confessed. "Let me show you what I've been doing lately, with Dave's help—you haven't forgotten Dave Nisbet?"

"Rather not! But he was always working in the background on his stones and things; and it was the antiques that appealed to me. Look here, Merran, I could help you to do a spot of buying while I'm here. I'm supposed to have a natural flair for knowing the real article when I see it, so I'm not easily had."

The girl coloured hotly and bent her head.

"It's frightfully good of you, but—well, I haven't got any spare cash to buy with at the moment. I'll have to work things up a bit first. But thank you very much, all the same. I know you have a gift for buying. There are several things here that you brought back to Jeems from abroad, and he never would sell them if he could help it. Look round and you may recognize some. There was that inlaid tea-caddy with the mother-of-pearl fishes, and the carved brass incense-burner—oh! and the Chinese panel that my sister, Julia, has made into a sign. Did you notice it as you came in?"

He grinned broadly. "Did I not! First thing I saw when I

rounded the corner. And if you'll take my advice, you'll haul it down and replace it with something more respectable, even if less attractive. After all, there's a good deal of coming and going in the world these days, and somebody might conceivably blow into Colmskirk who knows Chinese."

Merran's blue eyes widened apprehensively.

"Perry, what does it mean?"

"Various things," he replied evasively, "none of which I'd care to repeat to you. And it isn't even a genuine antique, so it needn't break your heart to remove it. It's nothing more nor less than a prank I played on old Jeems, and he knew it, and relished the joke—just a kind of mascot I picked up in a Chinese market at a port where the ship chanced to put in. Didn't pay much for it either, but I knew it would amuse the old chap."

"Roughly, what does it mean?" insisted Merran, "for it evidently does mean something, and I may as well know the worst. You needn't, of course, go into the lurid details."

"It begins all right," he told her reassuringly. "Starts off with something like 'Blessed be all who enter here to buy.'"

"And—?"

"Well, I'm afraid it goes on, 'But such as do not spend, may they be cursed with something—something—something,' and it proceeds to go into particulars. I think that's all you need know about it, Merran, but, believe me, it's a sign no lady should have above her shop door, however artistic and bright of hue."

Merran sighed. "I think it will probably break Julia's heart if it has to come down. She has taken such a lot of trouble about it. And, really, you know, Perry, it isn't at all probable that any Chinese would come this way."

"Perhaps not. But a missionary home on furlough might pop up at any moment, and what would he think of you?"

"Just that I couldn't read Chinese," replied Merran innocently, "which would be perfectly true."

"All right. But you've been warned. Now let's see the beads if I may. I expect your productions are more exciting than those old Jeems put up. You've got the long fingers of a craftsman, and I bet you can use them."

"I try to," said Merran, laughing, "but that's for you to judge. Come and look!"

The old papier-maché tray no longer sufficed for her pebble trinkets, and she had moved a small glass-fronted cabinet into one side of the window where the afternoon light shone full on it; and here, on its faded velvet shelves, were arranged the things on which she had been working during the last few weeks—brooches and clasps made of pale amethyst or tawny cairngorm, set in thin rims of silver or pewter; a metal bangle thickly studded with tiny chips of different coloured stones; drop pendants and ear-rings of topaz or clear sparkling crystal; beads, too, in long strings or short, the hues of the polished pebbles beautifully matched or contrasted.

"Heavens!" he exclaimed. "You must have worked to make all that since you came here—besides what, I presume, you've sold. It's a marvellous show."

"Dave is a very quick worker—quick and dexterous," she explained; "besides, I didn't start right from scratch. Jeems left a whole box of stones, shaped and polished and only waiting to be made up, though I'm getting to the end of them now, alas! Some of those we had to re-cut a little to get the shapes I wanted. Jeems hadn't bothered much about anything but beads, mostly round."

"You must be simply bursting with ideas," he declared admiringly. "I like that string hanging up on the left. It reminds me of a necklace we used to have, which we called 'the Luck of Drumbruie.' It belonged to my great-great-grandmother. The story was that her lover bought it from a gipsy-wife and gave it to Jenty for her betrothal gift, and that the gipsy foretold it would bring them luck. There's a portrait of Jenty in the drawing-room at home, wearing her beads. One of Raeburn's best efforts, I should say—not that I know much about pictures. But the girl was a beauty all right, and they say she had a marvellous voice."

"But what became of the necklace?" asked Merran. "Haven't you got it now?"

Perry's face clouded. "No," he said shortly; "it was lost—the summer before war started—and it's true enough our luck went with it. Well, I musn't take up any more of your valuable time. You should be making more of those wonderful gems instead of listening to my idle chatter. But I hope you'll let me look in again some day soon?"

"Yes, rather!" she answered readily, "and perhaps I may have something else to show you. I'm glad you like my things."

She told Julia the whole story when that young lady burst in an hour later, ravenous for tea, but intensely interested, as usual, in all that had been happening during her absence.

"I like Perry Boyd," she said decidedly. "He was very decent to us last Sunday, after he'd recovered from the loss of his fish. Because, I suppose, we were trespassing, since the permission Daddy had from old Drumbruie must have lapsed long ago. I expect he enjoyed sharing our picnic, though. It must be pretty lonely for him up there, with both parents dead, and his brothers killed in the war. I hope you were nice to him, Merran?"

"Of course I was!" retorted her sister indignantly. "Why shouldn't I be?"

"Oh, well, you've been rather stand-offish to Sandy Lamond lately, when he has looked in, and I thought perhaps you might be adopting a professional manner for young men who come to the shop."

"What rubbish you talk, Julia! Anyhow, Sandy Lamond is in possession of both parents, and has lost no one in the war that I know of."

"I see," said Julia meditatively. "Yes, I should think that might make a difference if you wanted to make one. But there's another thing—you really mustn't pay any attention to that nonsense about the sign. It's the making of the shop, and since we don't know what it means we're not in any way responsible. To the pure all things are pure—even Chinese swears."

"That's more or less what I thought," agreed Merran.

"I admit I was a trifle nervous about it," pursued Julia, "when I thought he might have pinched it from some temple and brought a curse on us by doing so. But if it has no religious significance, and only curses customers who don't buy anything, why, I can't see that we need worry. After all, that's their look-out."

CHAPTER XIII

A RED-SAILED YACHT

It so happened—probably by arrangement—that the weekly half-holiday at Westharbour Academy coincided with early-closing day at the various places in its vicinity; so one fine Wednesday afternoon the Lendrum girls locked up the Serendipity Shop, and set out for the pier, having planned to take the three o'clock boat to Rothesay.

"From there," said Merran, "we may find a steamer which is going through the Kyles, and get some tea at Tighnabruiach; then we'll be home in fine time for supper. This is our first sail since we came back to Colmskirk, and I feel we're entitled to one."

Julia agreed. She had found life ashore so intensely interesting since their return that she had not hankered after many hours afloat; but as the *Duchess* steamed out into the Firth and set her course for the long, green island ahead, she decided that there could be no better way to spend a half-holiday; and besides, it was undoubtedly good for Merran to get completely away from her beads and brooches for a few hours. She mentioned this, adding kindly that her sister would find herself better able to work after the little break.

"Thanks," responded Merran drily. "But my output is going to be slowed up soon when I run through my stock of stones, which is dwindling rapidly now. The worst of it is that I can't find out where old Jeems used to order them, so I can't send for more."

"Doesn't Dave know?"

"Apparently not. He just says vaguely that 'Jeems aye had stanes,' but he doesn't seem to have the faintest idea where they came from."

Julia, leaning on the rail, gazed with puckered brows at the receding coast of Ayrshire.

"That's awkward," she said, "but not insurmountable. We shall have to think out something different. After all, it must have been pretty expensive to have cases of stones sent down here from Skye, or wherever it was they came from—quite apart from what had to be paid to the sender. Stones are not light, as I realized when I brought you in that basketful for the kids' marbles last week. By the way, they sold like hot cakes on Saturday, and I was surprised to see how pretty they looked. You made a good job of them."

"You chose good pebbles for them. In fact, I actually kept back one or two for my own purposes. There was a yellow topaz, and a really fine bit of agate, though I don't suppose you recognized them as such when you picked them up. You'll see what they're like when I've finished with them—much too good for marbles."

Julia looked interested. "That's given me an inspiration," she announced, "—at least, I think so. Anyhow, it's an idea. Why send away for material that you can pick up on your own shingle? Are not the stones of Colmskirk and Langsands better than all the pebbles of Skye or Mull?"

"That remains to be seen," replied Merran doubtfully, "but it is, as you say, an idea. Certainly you did very well, and you didn't even know what to look for. I think I must take a basket out on to the beach to-morrow after closing time and see what I can find."

"I'll come with you," said Julia obligingly, "if we don't get too much prep. I may as well learn what to look for. And it would be a great draw if I were to paint you a neat poster to put in the window—'Buy Colmskirk gems. Only local stones used.' The summer visitors would snap them up like anything to take home as mementoes—those that were souvenir-minded, at any rate."

They changed into a smaller boat at Rothesay, and conversation languished as they entered the Kyles and sat on the forward deck, inhaling long breaths of fragrance from the bog-myrtle that grew on the green slopes closing in upon the Narrows. White yachts skimmed by them so near that it seemed they might easily put out their hands and touch them; one with red sails specially intrigued Julia as she leaned over to watch it.

"I love that one," she exclaimed. "I've seen her once or twice in Colmskirk Bay, and now I'm near enough to make out her name if she'd only keep still for half a moment. She's the—the *Fia—Fiammetta*, and she looks like a flame, too. Oh, Merran, do you see the rhododendrons among the trees along Loch Ridden? Aren't they glorious?"

Their boat left the curtseying yachts behind and steamed into Tighnabruiach, where she lay off the pier for a short time so that those who wished to do so might go ashore. The Lendrums hurried off to the little hotel where their father had often taken them as children, and Merran, at Julia's instigation, ordered a high tea, because, as her younger sister sagely reminded her, if they had a substantial meal there they wouldn't need to bother with much when they got home.

"I hope we shall have time to eat it, however," observed Merran rather uneasily. "We mustn't lose the boat. There isn't another connection with Colmskirk this evening."

"That's all right. She waits here for an hour," said Julia positively. "We can easily eat more than this in an hour," and proceeded to demonstrate her statement.

It was amusing to sit in their corner, devouring home-made

scones and honey, and watching the people drift in and out of the tea-room, while an invisible wireless set discoursed soft music in the background. Between its own resident visitors and those who came on the boats, the little place was full of a pleasant busy-ness, and the girls found plenty to interest them.

"It will soon be time to go, Judy," said Merran reluctantly, "if you have eaten nearly all you can eat. I heard a steamer's whistle five minutes ago, but it must have been that Craigendoran boat that came in just ahead of us. Ours won't leave for another quarter of an hour—why, look who's just come in! Over there—in the navy pullover and slacks."

Julia looked.

"Gracious, it's Perry Boyd!" she cried. "He must have come in on a yacht. Oh, he's seen us. He's coming this way. There's room for him at our table."

"All the room there is," replied Merran firmly, "because we daren't stay any longer. Good afternoon, Perry. What a pity you didn't come in sooner. We're just off to catch our boat."

"Then you'll have to swim," stated the newcomer calmly, as he seated himself beside her with cheerful nonchalance, "—at least, if it's the Rothesay steamer you're after, because I met her heading back for the Kyles as I came in on my yacht just now."

"Oh, but that's ours!" cried Merran, springing up in dismay. "I mean—that's the one we came by, and the only one that will get us back in time to catch the *Duchess* on her return trip. There must be some mistake. She always waits here for an hour."

Perry grinned unfeelingly.

"Not she! The mistake is yours. She never waits longer than forty minutes. But you needn't look so disturbed, my dear girl. Give me time to appease the inner man, and I'll run you over in no time in *Fiammetta* with a good following wind."

"Oh, *Fiammetta*!—is she yours?" asked Julia, clapping her

hands. "We passed her in the Kyles, and I loved her at sight; she's got the most heavenly lines. Merran, isn't it providential we missed the boat?"

"Not at all," retorted Merran crossly. "It's rank carelessness, and entirely your fault. It was you who insisted she lay off for an hour. Why should Perry have to load up with us when he's out for a pleasure sail?"

"We'll add to his pleasure," declared Julia confidently. "At least, we'll try to, when you've recovered your temper."

"And as to loading up," added Perry mildly, "you're neither of you very heavy, and we're not going to race any other craft as far as I know. Don't say you've finished tea just as I'm about to begin! Well, anyhow, couldn't you mark time with an ice or two, just to keep me company? Here, waitress, please bring a couple of large strawberry ices—and a pot of tea with the usual etceteras. Now, Merran, sit back and relax—you've nothing to worry about. This breeze won't drop before sunset."

Merran soon recovered from her momentary irritation, and settled down to enjoy the rest of the afternoon as much as Julia. There was no question of that young lady's enjoyment, and it was plain that she and Perry were already fast friends. He inquired after Lisbeth.

"I saw her this afternoon," he said, "as I was getting *Fiammetta* out. She whizzed past on the shore road in that dinky little car of hers, with a sandy-haired, sandy-faced damsel sitting beside her. They were heading for Seaward Point."

Julia looked disturbed.

"That must have been Taters—Gracie Tait, I mean. She's in our form at school, and Lisbeth loathes her. That's why she's taking her out in her car."

Perry swallowed his last cup of tea, and offered his cigarette case to Merran.

"I can't see that it's a sufficient reason myself," he said politely, "but doubtless you do."

"No, I don't," answered Julia with vigour, "but Lisbeth does. She believes she inadvertently hurt Taters' feelings the other day, and that she ought to make it up to her in consequence. I think it's a pity myself. It was a mistake to hurt Taters' feelings in the first instance, because she's the type to bear malice; but having done so, it would be much better to let it stand. Taters is a bit of an owl, and she doesn't understand gestures."

"She looks it," rejoined Perry, regarding Julia's vivid face with amusement through his cigarette smoke. "Like an owl, I mean. Just the same complexion—but her eyes are too near together."

"You seem to have made quite a study of her in a moment of time," commented Merran, laughing, "if the car really whizzed."

"I'm good at getting lightning impressions," he explained, "and I didn't take to that girl."

"No," replied Julia thoughtfully, "she's a venomous owl. That may not be good natural history but it describes her. And what's more, she won't forgive or forget just because Lisbeth has given her a treat; she'll still have it in for her if she gets a chance. Not that old Leebie did it with that end in view. She was genuinely repentant."

"What I admire in Julia," remarked Perry to the elder sister, "is her command of the English language. I never came across a girl of her age who knew so many long words, and could use 'em in just the proper places. But I bet she can't spell 'em all."

"Well, I can then," retorted Julia serenely. "It's all part of my training to be a super-secretary. I've got an end in view, and I'm working towards it. Don't you think we ought to vacate this table if you've finished? There are some people over there looking at it hungrily—and I'm dying to get on board *Fiammetta*."

"Julia!" rebuked Merran, scandalized; but Perry only laughed.

"You're perfectly right," he admitted. "We've sat here much too long and if the sunset calm overtakes us you may get more of *Fiammetta* than you really care for. Just a moment till I pay the bill."

The sail back to Colmskirk in the late afternoon sunshine was all that Julia's enthusiasm had pictured it, and when they made their way up the shingle, after bidding their host a grateful farewell, Merran said, with a sigh of satisfaction, "I don't know when I've enjoyed myself more. Oh, Judy, aren't you glad we came up here instead of living an ordinary life with the cousins in Slingsby? I wouldn't give up my dear Serendipity Shop for anything."

"I should be more than sorry if you did," agreed Julia. "Hullo! there's the postie. I'll run and ask him if he has anything for us. I can't endure waiting while he goes all round the square."

She returned a little breathless as Merran was putting her key into the door, and presented her sister with a typed business envelope.

"It's local," she said, "and it looks like a bill; but you aren't expecting any, are you? I thought we were paying as we go."

"So we are," Merran answered as she stepped inside and flicked on the light. "Do see to Bill's supper, Julia, there's a dear. He'll be fearfully huffy anyhow about our being out all afternoon, and we daren't keep him waiting."

She tore open her letter and read it as she followed Julia into the kitchen.

"Good gracious," she cried, "it's from Bartle! Listen to this—he's returning to the charge. 'Dear Miss Lendrum, I shall be glad if you can make it convenient to see me on business to-morrow morning at 11.30. I have a new proposition to make to you regarding the premises you now occupy. Assuring you of my best attention at all times.'—Julia,"—she laid the letter down on the table and stared across it with exasperated eyes—"he's at it again! That man won't take no for an answer!"

"He'll have to learn, then," said Julia briskly, "though I can't help admiring his pertinacity. And that letter is very badly worded; he uses 'make' twice in as many lines; and that isn't the correct formula for ending a communication of this description. What he needs is a secretary—and he needs one badly!"

"Perhaps you'd like to apply for the job?" suggested Merran. "Well, I shall have to cope with him again to-morrow morning, and this time you won't be here to support me. I almost think you ought to take a day off from school!"

CHAPTER XIV

MR. BARTLE MOVES AGAIN

MERRAN awaited her visitor next morning with the same exasperated amusement that had come over her when reading his letter. She had hoped, because of the time that had elapsed since his last visit, that he had accepted his defeat and bent his energies elsewhere—especially after she had heard about the purchase of Meadows—but Mrs. Binnie had warned her that she was mistaken.

"I've never yet known Sam Bartle to abandon any project on which his heart was set," she asserted, "and this is more than a project, because it involves the whole side of a square which he has bought, and he'll want some return for his money. They know all about him on the Town Council! He's always bombarding them with offers and suggestions that none of them want. What it will be like when he actually gets on the Council next autumn I can't imagine. He means to stand as a bailie then, and the rest are all shivering in their shoes."

"Anyhow, he shan't get the better of me," thought Merran obstinately, as she carried in her morning's marketing and put it down on the kitchen table before going through to open up the shop. She could hear Dave busy already in the workroom, and meant to join him there until the bell summoned her back to the counter. A great deal of her chipping and polishing was done thus, between the comings and goings of customers, and she was anxious to-day to handle the yellow topaz which Julia had brought in among her collection of common pebbles, and which Dave had been cutting for her the day before.

"It's a fine bit, yon," he observed, passing it over to her when she came in, "and no' sae wee either. It didna cut to waste, as I was feart it would. Whaur did Miss Julia find it?"

"I don't know. Down on the shore below the Broomieknowes, I think. It was just a piece of luck, of course, because she doesn't know yet what to look for."

"Umphm!" said Dave, bending near-sightedly over his bench. "But gin somebuddy went wha did ken what she was after—gin ye was to gang yoursel', Miss Merran—there's no sayin' what ye michtna find. I've aye thocht yon was a guid stretch o' the shore for pickin' up chuckies. I've found some there mysel' that would be hard to beat."

"I think I'll go along and try my own luck in the evenings," Merran replied. "We're needing more stones badly, and it would be a tremendous saving if I could get them as easily as that. I wonder if—oh, there's the bell! I don't suppose I shall be very long."

Out in the shop she found Mr. Bartle awaiting her, square and purposeful, staring at the cabinet in the window that held her trinkets.

"You've got some good stuff there," he opened the conversation unexpectedly, jerking his head in their direction. "Don't know where I've seen anything much better. Make it all yourself, eh?"

"Most of it," replied Merran modestly. "Dave Nisbet does all the rough work and most of the settings. I'm not very good at metal-work yet, though he's teaching me."

"Humph! Made to your own designs, isn't it? Heard about it from my daughter. She's very friendly with your young sister."

"Yes, very," assented Merran, wondering when he meant to come to business. She had not long to wait. Sam Bartle was trying a new and more genial line of approach, but he had no intention of letting it deflect him from the main issue. He felt that he had somehow blundered at their previous encounter, and he did not wish to make the same mistake this time. He felt glad that Lisbeth's friend, the managing young madam, was safely out of the way, and for that reason he had chosen the morning for his appointment. Mr. Bartle had an uneasy suspicion that Julia was a match for him.

"Now, see here, Miss Lendrum," he began, in what he conceived to be a persuasive tone, "I've come along this forenoon to make you a new suggestion, and one that I hope you may be disposed to regard more favourably. Time's getting on, and I'm no nearer to my bit of reconstruction in Gallowgate Square. Too late to do anything for this season, of course, but the sooner I get started the sooner everything'll be ship-shape for next year. It'll take a lot of time to do all I want, and I can't even begin till I've got possession of this corner. It's the keystone of my whole scheme, so to speak."

Merran's blue eyes began to flash dangerously.

"But I thought we had gone into all this before, Mr. Bartle, and I told you then I haven't the least intention of selling my shop. I can't help what you do to the part of the square which you've bought already, however much I may dislike your ideas, but I can and will keep my own property intact."

"That's exactly what you said last time, but I was hoping you might have learnt more sense by now. An intelligent girl like you ought to want the best for her home town, and I'm prepared to give the best to Colmskirk. I'm not a chap who grudges anything in reason—"

"Probably not," interrupted Merran with spirit, "but you want to give the town what you consider to be best—not what it wants for itself."

He glared back at her indignantly.

"How can you possibly judge, not being a man of business abilities? However, I haven't come here to argue about that. I've got a proposal to make, and this is what it is—if you're prepared to accept a generous price for your property here—and I'm ready to make your lawyers a thumping good offer—then I'm prepared to set you up in my store and pay you a salary to design and run a jewellery counter on the lines along which you've been working here, *and* a percentage on the profits. Then, when the new Gallowgate store is opened, I'll move you back into it with a department of your own—and let me tell you, young lady, as a business man, that's not an offer to be sneezed at!"

Merran had listened to this dazzling proposal with growing amazement. There was no doubt in her mind that Sam Bartle honestly meant to carry out every word of it, and for one dizzy moment such a scheme for getting rich quick shook her unexpectedly. Then a picture rose swiftly before her of the quaint old square demolished, and in its place some glittering monstrosity of a modern store flaunting its ostentation to the public gaze, with herself working in it as an employee of Bartle's, forced by her dependent position to conform to his whims and fancies, no longer free to follow her own ideas and inclinations in the work she loved.

"I am very sorry to disappoint you, Mr. Bartle," she said firmly, "but I am quite content with my own circumstances, and quite determined to carry on as I am doing at present. I take a certain pride in owning this scrap of the town, and I prefer to be my own mistress. Thank you very much all the same for your kind suggestion, which, I know, is very generous. It's just that—well, it doesn't appeal to me."

Sam Bartle's face had grown darker and darker as he listened to her, and now he brought his fist down on the counter with a resounding thump.

"Then I'd like to know what I'm to do with my property here—the rest of the cottages and shops that I've bought already in this confounded square? I can do nothing with them—nothing at all—while you block my plans by sitting tight in this ramshackle old place, and I won't have it, I tell you! I won't have it! That all my grand schemes should be foiled by a chit of a girl who doesn't know which side her bread is buttered—the thing's unthinkable, and I won't have it!"

Merran had been growing steadily cooler as her visitor's temperature rose, and now she answered calmly, "But I'm afraid you must have it, for there isn't anything more to be said. I'm sorry to hold you up so badly, but I've a perfect right to my own property, and it's not a bit of use for you to bluster and bully me—so good morning, Mr. Bartle!"

She stood fast behind her counter while he stumbled towards the door, growling under his breath as he went. Then, with his hand on the latch, he flung a final defiance at her over his shoulder.

"I'm not finished yet, madam, and you needn't think so! I'll find some means still of making you regret your obstinacy in this affair, or my name is not Samuel Bartle!"

And he stamped out, leaving Merran to go back, angry but victorious, to her work on the yellow topaz.

"He may storm and rage as he likes," she said to Julia that evening, when telling the story, "but there's nothing he can do to harm me—nor Gallowgate Square either—as long as I hold on. Apart from everything else, I should feel that I was letting poor old Jeems down if I sold his legacy, knowing how he felt about Bartle's notions. The one thing that does worry me is whether it may lead to strained relations between you and Lisbeth."

The Serendipity Shop

The Serendipity Shop

But Julia only laughed as she drew her satchel towards her and prepared to start her home-work.

"No fear of that," she answered cheerfully. "Old Bartle doesn't mix his public and his private lives, and I come into the latter category as Leebie's friend; he doesn't consider me as your sister at all—indeed, I believe he's quite surprised that I won't go to his house, since Lisbeth comes here—but that's different."

"How?" asked Merran curiously.

Julia reddened and looked a little embarrassed.

"Oh, well, you haven't done her father any harm, but he's definitely out to injure you, if by doing so he can get his own way. So naturally I can't take hospitality from him. Do you know that he means to run for the Town Council in November?"

"Rather! The Binnies have told me all about that, and the fights they are looking forward to if he gets in, to prevent him from 'benefiting' the town."

"All the same," stated Julia, taking out her geometry, "I'd rather have him, if he'd behave himself, than the man who means to stand against him—Henry Tait, our Gracie's father."

"What's wrong with him?"

"I've told you—he's Gracie's father! But as if that wasn't enough, he's exactly like her to look at—takes after her in every feature."

"Who or what is he, anyhow?"

"Don't know, but I should think he's been a money-lender of shady antecedents. Anyway, he has retired now and lives in one of those staring new houses on the Langsands road. Look here, Merran, if you'll wait till I get these two propositions done, I'll come down on the shore with you and help to hunt for pebbles."

"Good!" returned Merran. "With or without you I shall have to go and do something about it this evening. I had an order from town by the afternoon post, and I must get the wherewithal to carry it out."

She left Julia to her preparation, and carried out the tea-things to wash them up in the scullery. Presently, when the geometry problems had been solved and they were free to go out, she had more to reveal about this new order, for it was not an ordinary one. It came from the big Glasgow firm of Godbin and Clark, and hinted that it might be the forerunner of many others if her work proved to be all they had been led to expect. Customers had spoken to them about Miss Lendrum's productions, and one lady had shown them a pink crystal pendant, bought at Colmskirk, which had struck them as being attractive and unusual. They would be glad if Miss Lendrum would quote them the trade price for another similar article, also for a long bead chain, two necklets and a clasp. This would give them an opportunity to judge of her style, and also to test its appeal to their customers.

Merran sang happily to herself as she rinsed the tea-cups. A connection of this sort would be a tremendous help to her in the winter months, when the steamer cruises ceased and visitors no longer thronged into the Hydro and lesser hotels. The letter had instantly inspired some new designs which she was eager to carry out as soon as possible, but to do so she must get more stones from somewhere, and she voiced a silent prayer that she might find what she needed presently on the shore below the Broomieknowes.

CHAPTER XV

TOM TIDDLER'S GROUND

MERRAN could not help feeling, after two or three evening strolls on the shore below the Broomieknowes, that her prayer had been abundantly answered. Elsewhere on the shingly beach that stretched from one end of Colmskirk to the other the harvest was not so rich; but for some reason only understood, perhaps, by geologists, there seemed to be a wealth of pebbles suitable for her purposes on the strip just below the rough stretch of grass and broom-bushes that separated the older and larger houses of the little town from the sea. The stones were not all semi-precious, though she found a good percentage of these also, but her practised eye soon taught her to seek those of certain colours and appearance, which would repay her workmanship and be useful for her requirements. And Julia, always quick to learn, soon became nearly as much of an adept as herself in picking out what was wanted. The pebble-bin in the workroom was full again, and polishing went on apace. The order from Godbin and Clark was finished and despatched, and Merran settled down to work hard on stock for her own shelves.

Julia's special "Children's Corner" on Saturday mornings was also proving a success. She had talked about it at school, and some of her friends, catching fire from her own enthusiasm, had begged her to let them join in making toys for it. She had been ready enough, for it was hard, in her limited spare time, to keep up the supply, as her small customers became every week more numerous; but Merran, when consulted, had made one firm condition.

"They can all help," she said, "and you can fill half the window if you wish on Saturdays; but all the profits must go to charity, and I should suggest the Cripple Children's Holiday Home at Langsands. It's quite impossible, of course, that their takings should go into our till."

Julia was very much relieved.

"That seemed to me an awful snag," she admitted frankly, "and yet I hated to refuse them. But the Cripples' Home will put it all on a proper footing, and even Lisbeth can join in. She makes wonderful rag elephants, but naturally I couldn't let her until you thought of this. Now it will be the same kind of thing as any bazaar, and the girls who work for it can take it in turns to come and help me sell. That's what they're really dying to do, and it's more than one person can cope with, anyhow, when the rush begins."

So everybody was pleased, including the customers, though Merran privately wondered how Lisbeth managed to square her parent in the matter, and was scarcely surprised to find that she was not among the Saturday sellers, though rag elephants of various shapes and sizes flourished their trunks in the window every week along with other strange beasts never seen on land or sea; and Perry Boyd, having looked in accidentally one week-end, christened it "The Dipsomaniac's Dream." However, they served a generation of children starved of toys by the war, and therefore less critical than Lieutenant Boyd.

The legitimate earnings of the Serendipity Shop were mounting with satisfactory steadiness, and Merran was beginning to feel that even Uncle Basil would soon be forced to admit she had been justified in her venture. True, the antique side of the business could hardly be termed flourishing, but that did not disturb her overmuch. Then one day came another letter from Godbin and Clark, requesting her, if she could make it convenient, to come up and call upon them on a certain date.

"I wonder what they want," she exclaimed, passing the letter across the breakfast-table to Julia.

"Go up and find out. But if *they* try to beguile you into running a department for Scottish jewellery in Sauchiehall Street, be just as firm with them as you were with Sam Bartle. I couldn't bear to be wrenched away from Colmskirk again, however dazzling their allurements. What day do they want you? The 29th? Luckily the holidays will have started by then, so I can mind the shop."

"I'm afraid the holidays won't be much fun for you," said Merran, sighing a little; but Julia had no self-pity.

"Leave me to make my own amusements," she replied loftily. "Lisbeth and I are planning some good times with Dulcibel; we're going to explore the county. Besides, I've got another project on hand. I mean to take up citizenship."

"Oh!" said Merran faintly. "How?"

"By making a complete study of the town I live in—historically, socially and—er—commercially. Sam Bartle isn't the only person who takes an interest in Colmskirk. By the time I've finished I shall know a number of things—including the reason why the gallows-mound is right outside our bathroom window."

"If it actually is the gallows-mound," amended Merran.

"Certainly it is. A thing like that couldn't be an accident—but it's a queer place to have one. I wonder where they hang people nowadays?"

Merran thoroughly enjoyed her day in town, and had a most satisfactory interview with the managing director of the big Glasgow shop. It appeared that—though they had no immediate desire to transplant her to Sauchiehall Street—the firm was very well pleased with the work she had done for them, and wished to place a much larger order with her. Further, they wanted to make sure that they would have the monopoly of her things as far as Glasgow was concerned, and for this assurance they were prepared to pay very handsomely.

"The truth is, Miss Lendrum, that we are able to use all you can supply us with, so you should have no temptation to work for anyone else. Candidly, we are anxious to prevent that, for your stuff has a distinctive quality which is already interesting customers, and we prefer to be your sole agents. That we may be assured of this we are even willing to pay you a small retaining fee."

Altogether, it was in a very jubilant state of mind that Merran made her way back to St. Enoch's in time for the evening train, and she rejoiced inwardly that she had not listened to Mr. Bartle's proposal and pledged herself to the new store which it was impossible for him to build—at least in Gallowgate Square—so long as she maintained her hold on the corner site. Her refusal had left her independent and in a position to serve a firm of far greater prestige than even the great Bartle's Stores. She could afford, too, to buy more and better metal for her settings since the actual stones were, apparently, to cost her nothing but the trouble of picking them up. It might even be possible next year, if all went on well, to send Julia to college. Merran was convinced that Julia, with a University education behind her, would go far.

The Colmskirk train was actually starting to move out of the station when the door of Merran's compartment was wrenched violently open, and Sandy Lamond fell into it over the feet of a startled old lady, who was nursing a large pilgrim basket on her knee. The basket was knocked flying, and while Merran helped to retrieve it, the owner lectured him severely on carelessness and lack of consideration for the public.

"It's just as easy," she told him, "to start too soon for a train as too late. Personally, I always make a point of allowing ten minutes longer than is really necessary. You might have killed yourself, quite apart from breaking everything in my basket."

"I say, I'm most awfully sorry!" exclaimed Sandy penitently. "I do hope I haven't done any serious damage. Is there any way of finding out, short of opening it here and now?"

"That won't be necessary," replied the lady, still severely, "because it happens that I've nothing breakable in it—but that's no thanks to you, so I hope it will be a lesson to you, young man. Thank you, my dear," to Merran. "No, I don't think it would be any safer in the rack, because you never know with racks. Besides, I'm getting out at Lochwinnoch, so it would hardly be worth while."

Sandy, crushed and repentant, settled himself in the corner farthest from his victim and opposite Merran, whom he greeted in a subdued manner which she at first put down to the recent contretemps; but after one or two unsuccessful attempts to start a conversation, she concluded that he had something on his mind, and that it was kindest to leave him in peace to his evening paper, of which he offered her half. It was not until they had jointly helped the old lady out at Lochwinnoch, and were left with the carriage to themselves, that Sandy made any effort to expand.

"I say, Merran," he began, "this is an unfortunate business."

"Oh, I shouldn't worry," she answered consolingly. "You didn't do any damage, you know, and when she'd recovered from her first shock I don't think the old dear really minded very much. She parted from us on quite friendly terms."

"I wasn't talking about that," he assured her. "It's this Bartle affair and your stones. What? Hasn't he said anything to you about it himself? Oh lord, then he's left it all to me!"

"Left what?" asked Merran in astonishment. "He came to see me about three weeks ago with a fresh plan for buying me out on the most advantageous terms. But I wouldn't accept them, so he flung off in high dudgeon, and I've heard nothing since. Is there some fresh development? And how do you come to be mixed up in it? As my lawyer?"

"No," he responded, slumping back in his corner with a groan, "as his. But of course I told him I'd have nothing to do with it, so he withdrew, breathing fire and slaughter, and I understood he meant to take it to some chap in town. Evidently he hasn't or you would have heard by now; so I suppose he's banking on my warning you."

"It would be a great help," Merran pointed out gently, "if you could give me some inkling as to what it's all about. At present I'm completely in the dark."

"Well, naturally, I thought he'd cautioned you first, before coming to our office, but apparently he hasn't. It's the most utter rot, of course, but there's no getting away from the fact that you seem to have been picking gold and silver off Tom Tiddler's ground—at least, he declares you have. Unluckily, that part of the foreshore does belong to him; in fact, he recently bought the whole of the Broomieknowes from the Monument to where Robin Water runs into the sea."

"Look here, Sandy Lamond," said Merran firmly, "either you or I must be quite mad, and it's more likely to be you, for I know I was sane enough when I got into this train. Try to stop burbling about Tom Tiddler's ground and Robin Water, and tell me quite simply and quietly what fresh grievance Sam Bartle has got against me, and why he took it to you."

"Because he wanted me to send you an injunction warning you not to lift pebbles from his part of the foreshore. You *have* been gathering them there, I take it?"

"Certainly I have. I didn't know anything about his claims to that particular part of the beach, naturally—I supposed it was all public property."

"Well, it isn't—none of it. The bay belongs to the town as far as the mouth of the Bruie Burn, and the stretches beyond that are owned by the people whose gardens run down to them. The Broomieknowes and the shingle there used to belong to old Keyes, the baccy magnate, who died last spring. But his executors have sold it now to Bartle, and that's where you have tripped up."

Merran sat in dumbfounded silence for a few minutes while the train rattled its way along between the sand-dunes and the sea, with Arran raising its blue-black peaks across the shining Firth, and the sunset splendour spreading itself over the sky behind.

"It would never have entered my head," she exclaimed at last, "to imagine that any of the stones on any part of the shore were private property. What does he propose to do—prosecute me?"

"Heaven only knows! I haven't had time yet to read up the law on the subject. I just told him to go to the devil, and left it at that!"

"Did you really?"

"Well, in professional language. I told him that, as your solicitor, I could hardly be expected to act against you, and that if it came to choosing between you—if he meant to push it that far—then I should obviously choose you."

"That was extremely decent of you, Sandy," said Merran, much touched, "but I can't let you do such a thing. I'm never likely to be a profitable client to you, while Sam Bartle might bring no end of grist to your mill—especially if he takes to suing everybody who picks up chuckies off his shore."

"You're the senior client," retorted Sandy gruffly. "Oh, well, you know what I mean. We've always had charge of your family's affairs, and I trust we always shall. And as for old Sam Bartle and his foreshore, I doubt whether he'd bother to lift a finger in protest if anyone else were to remove large boulders in a cart. I warned you before he's got it in for you, and it's not likely he'll sit quietly by and watch you collecting off his very ground the means to keep the Serendipity Shop in prosperity. Sam is a man of determination, and he's determined to shift you out of Gallowgate Square. Fair means having failed, he's now out to do it otherwise."

Merran's chin was raised at a firm angle.

"He isn't going to, then!" she said.

CHAPTER XVI

JULIA HAS A VISITOR

NOTHING more was heard at the Serendipity Shop of any injunction from Mr. Bartle. Apparently he had not, as Sandy expected, taken his business to another solicitor, but had changed his mind about challenging Merran regarding her gleanings from his shingle.

"I should think so too!" snorted Mrs. Binnie indignantly, when the story was confided to her one Sunday afternoon at Fernbank. "The man's no fool or he wouldn't be where he is to-day. He knows that if he did anything of the sort the whole town would hear of it, and that would mean good-bye to any faint chance of his ever becoming a bailie. Your father, my dears, was Colmskirk's 'beloved physician,' and the townsfolk wouldn't stand for such treatment of his daughter. Small wonder he took a second thought."

"I believe," said Julia reflectively, "he really dropped the idea because he felt rather ashamed of it after Sandy had finished with him. I've been studying Mr. Bartle's psychology lately, as well as I can at a respectable distance, and I fancy he's a creature of impulse. Once he takes the bit between his teeth nothing can stop him, but if you can manage to pull him up before he gets too far—well, he may think again. I don't believe he's always as sure of himself as he likes to make out."

The Provost roared with delighted laughter.

"You're a wise little lady, Julia!" he cried. "We'll have you on the Town Council yet, and be glad of you—that is, if you don't marry into the diplomatic service first. Any more sidelights on the character of the great Sam?"

Julia threw him a swift smile.

"Why, yes! He really is devoted to Colmskirk in his own funny way, and one reason why he isn't going on with this trumped-up attack on Merran is because Lamond and Beith turned it down, and they are the local lawyers. He doesn't want to deal with any strange firm up in Glasgow. He'd rather let it go."

"Especially," added Mrs. Binnie drily, "as the man couldn't have been serious. I never heard of anything so absurd in my life! A few chuckies on the beach—what use are they to him? No, no! he only wanted to annoy Merran—that's all. Piece of petty persecution."

"Oh, I think it was more than that," rejoined Julia shrewdly. "He knew Sandy would warn her privately, even if he refused to injunct her; and he was pretty certain Merran would never touch so much as a broken crab-shell off his shore again. That's what Bartle is out for—to injure her bead business so that she'll have to climb down and let him get her shop in the end."

"That he never will!" declared Merran heatedly. "But I wish all the best stones in Colmskirk didn't lie on his foreshore, for my store is running low again."

"That mustn't hold you up," said the Provost kindly. "You know you are welcome to take all you want from the shores round the bay; that belongs to the town."

"Thanks very much, Mr. Binnie," replied Merran gratefully, and forbore to tell him that she and Julia had already combed the bay with some thoroughness but very little profit. Sam Bartle's latest manœuvre had hit her harder than she cared to confess, because it had cut her off from certain pebbles of a curious pale-green colour which her customers specially admired. Indeed, Godbin and Clark had ordered a pendant and ear-rings of those very stones, and she did not know at the moment how to carry out the commission.

“Don’t worry about it,” said Julia philosophically, as they walked back from the Binnies’ through the Sunday afternoon crowd on the Esplanade. “If you can’t find the right shade, you can’t; and sensible people must realize that it’s impossible to bank on what you’re going to pick up from the sea-shore. We’ll try a new stretch to-morrow evening, and probably collect an entirely fresh range of colours.”

“I’m just wondering,” said Merran, “if you would look after the shop for me to-morrow afternoon? Then I might take the boat over to Inchmore and investigate the beach there, immediately opposite the Broomieknowes. It’s just possible it might hold the same kind of stones.”

“No harm in trying anyhow,” assented Julia briskly. “Yes, of course I’ll see to the shop—I always enjoy that job.”

But the following afternoon it rained, and Perry Boyd came to tea—to the great discomfiture of William of Orange; never a man’s cat at any time, he had lately developed an active dislike to his own sex, and fled before all of them except Dave Nisbet, whom he tolerated as being, practically, a member of the household; besides, Maggie, who adored Bill, was in the habit of sending over succulent scraps by her husband, who, in consequence, got the credit. All this Julia explained to Perry, who was fond of animals and rather hurt when Bill behaved as though he were a burglar or cut-throat.

“He can’t help it, poor darling! It’s nerves,” she said. “He has never been the same cat since his long journey up from London; but we hope, with sea-air and good strengthening food, to overcome it in time. Meanwhile, he prefers to sit in my bedroom if there's a man about downstairs. Perry, do you mind telling me the story about your singing great-grandmother and her lucky beads? Merran heard it, but I wasn't there, and I'd like to hear some more."

"Certainly, if you're interested," said Perry obligingly. "Perhaps you'd bring Merran to tea with me on Wednesday, and then I could show you great-grandmother Jenty's portrait, and her harp and song-book. The Raeburn, at any rate, is worth seeing. The beads, alas! I can't show you."

"What happened to them?" asked Julia in her forthright manner. "I know you lost them, but how?"

"I didn't lose them," responded Perry, passing his cup to Merran. "No Boyd would have been so careless of their luck. It was a girl to whom Hugh got engaged just before the war. She came to stay at Drumbruie, and one day she persuaded my mother to let her wear the necklace for an afternoon; but she forgot to take it off before starting out for an evening sail, and it dropped off her as she was stepping out on to the rocks at Inchmore. She searched and Hugh searched, and next day we took *Fiammetta* across and spent hours hunting, but the luck was gone; we guessed the tide had carried it out. We never saw it again. But you can see it in the portrait; old Raeburn made a marvellous job of the light reflected back from the crystals. You'll come, won't you?" he appealed to Merran. "I'll fetch you in my little old run-about. It just holds three when two of them are slim."

The girls accepted with pleasure. Their friendship with Perry was making rapid strides in spite of the fact that Merran, at least, had very little time to cultivate it. Now and again he took them out in the yacht after closing time, and himself came frequently to the shop on various pretexts—or no pretext at all beyond the vague one that he had formed the habit in boyhood, during old

Roberton's time, so could not be expected to break it now.

"Besides," he usually added, "they can't in reason keep me without a ship much longer, and when I'm gone overseas you'll like to remember you were kind to a lonely bloke on half-pay."

"Oh, we'll be as kind as you like," Julia promised readily, "especially when it means going out in *Fiammetta* by moonlight," that being the height of her ambition at the moment, but one on which her sister frowned sternly.

"No," she told her with decision. "There are certain limits which I mean to observe, even at the risk of being called stuffy and old-fashioned. I know chaperons have gone out, and so have a lot of other things that must have been pretty useful in their time; but I shall only go sailing by moonlight if Perry can persuade Mrs. Binnie, or someone like her, to come with us."

"I know," Julia nodded. "To lend an air of respectability to the proceedings. Well, Mrs. Binnie is such a sport, I believe she'd come if Perry asked her, and like it, too."

The weather cleared next day, and Merran took the first afternoon boat for Inchmore, leaving Julia in charge, much to that young lady's satisfaction; but she did not get her usual meed of entertainment from serving the varied assortment of customers, as very few came in before tea, and, though trade was a little brisker afterwards, she did not find the people as interesting as she had hoped. Just before it was time to shut up, however, the bell tinkled for the last time, and the door opened just enough to admit a foxy-faced schoolgirl with straight sandy hair combed back from her face and confined in a bright green net. She slipped in with a furtive air which would have given a stranger the impression that there was something secretive about her movements, and that she had possibly no business there at all; but Julia was no stranger to Gracie Tait, and knew well that she was the type of girl who was sly by instinct rather than for any reason.

"Hullo, Taters!" she hailed her briskly. "What can I do for you?"

"Oh, I haven't come to buy anything, Julia," replied her schoolfellow deprecatingly. "Just to bring you a toy for your Saturday morning sale and to have a little chat. We don't seem to have seen much of each other these holidays."

Julia forbore to reply that she knew of no particular reason why they should. Instead she opened the bulgy parcel which Gracie handed to her across the counter, and revealed a somewhat clumsily knitted penguin of plump proportions.

"Thank you very much," she said courteously. "I'll put him out on Saturday, and I expect he'll be speedily snapped up. Sit down, Taters, if you want to chat. Are you having nice hols.?"

"So-so!" replied Miss Tait discontentedly. "I saw you bathing the other morning with Lisbeth Bartle. Colmskirk's a rotten place for bathing—not enough sand."

"Oh, well, one has to make the best of what one can get and wear plimsolls," replied Julia philosophically. "There's more than enough at Langsands, but then it quakes. I'd rather have our good solid shingle even if it is a bit painful."

Gracie eyed her sharply out of her small, close-set eyes.

"I rather wonder," she remarked, "that Lisbeth doesn't drive down in that posh car of hers to where the bathing's better—beyond Westharbour or Peterston. But perhaps she thinks discretion is the better part of valour."

"In what way?" demanded Julia, falling into the trap. "It's quite a good road along there, and Lisbeth drives well."

Gracie looked if possible more secretive and mysterious than she had done before.

"It isn't that," she said, "but—haven't you heard? The police have found out that she's not seventeen yet, and there's going to be trouble about it."

Julia looked startled, for this was a contingency she had partly foreseen.

"No," she said, "I hadn't heard; but I haven't seen Lisbeth for a day or two. However, I'm not surprised. I've always told her it was a risky game."

"I suppose she'll wriggle out of it somehow," said Gracie, with the suspicion of a sneer; "but it won't help her father when he comes to stand against mine for the vacant place on the Town Council. If the case gets into the papers everyone will know he has been conniving at her breaking the law."

"I don't suppose it will get into the papers," retorted Julia shortly. "I must ask her about it to-morrow."

Taters looked genuinely alarmed.

"Oh, no, you mustn't! You mustn't say anything to her about it, Julia. I only told you in confidence and because you're such a friend of hers that I thought you'd be sure to know all about it already. Lisbeth would be furious with me if she fancied I was discussing her affairs."

"Yes," assented Julia gravely, "she certainly would. Oh, well, I expect she'll tell me the whole story herself whenever she sees me."

"She may not. She mightn't want to talk about it even to you, because of her father and the Town Council. Promise me you'll say nothing about it, Julia, not to your sister or anybody. After all, I trusted you."

"Oh, very well," conceded Julia reluctantly. "But I didn't ask you to, and I hate having secrets."

"It isn't that," protested Gracie, "but you can see how awkward it might be for me, when my father is opposing hers. And I haven't mentioned it to anyone else."

"But who told you?"

Gracie Tait's face closed down again, like a plaster mask splashed with mustard freckles.

"That," she replied loftily, "I am not at liberty to reveal. If you want to shut the shop now, perhaps I'd better go."

CHAPTER XVII

MR. BARTLE'S PROSPECTS

MERRAN came back in time for supper, well pleased on the whole with the result of her afternoon on Inchmore. True, she had seen none of the pale-green pebbles she had gone out to seek, but she had brought back a number of different coloured stones that were quite attractive, including some dull yellow pieces which, she assured Julia, were quite good crystals.

"It's wonderful how you can tell. I should never have given them a second glance," confessed Julia. "They look supremely uninteresting to me."

"Ah, but I dipped them in a rock-pool and they glittered. Wait till Dave gets hold of them to-morrow and you won't know them! Still, I'm not any nearer to getting that set done for Godbin and Clark. It's maddening to know I could so easily pick up what I want below the Broomieknowes."

"I suppose," said Julia tentatively, "you wouldn't let me go over there with your little serge bag just at daybreak? I've got a strong conviction that Mr. Bartle is not an early riser."

"Of course I shouldn't let you! I wouldn't touch anything from that strip of beach now, not with a ten-foot barge-pole! I shall just have to write and ask if a darker green will do—or they might fancy my new yellow crystals."

Julia, who was scrambling eggs for the evening meal, paused suddenly, the pan suspended above the gas-ring.

"I nearly forgot!" she exclaimed. "Could you do anything with stones that have been already worked? Because Mrs. Stiles brought back that string of blended beads she bought last week to change them for cornelians. She said they weren't the right shade for her daughter's frock—and some of them were pale green."

"That's saved me!" cried Merran. "I'll take that string to pieces to-morrow and see what I can do. Look out, Judy, those eggs will burn."

"They won't," retorted Julia, "but they're thickening, and I'm ready for the toast if you've made it."

"Did you have any other customers?" queried her sister, buttering the hot crisp slices with rapid fingers.

"Nobody special. Taters came in and havered for half an hour, but you couldn't call her a customer."

"I dislike that girl," observed Merran. "She's sly. What did she come for?"

"Goodness only knows!" replied Julia evasively, spooning her scramble on to the toast. "Oh—she brought a knitted penguin for my Children's Corner. I don't like her any better than you do. After all, you're not at school with her. Just a moment, Bill, my precious, and you shall have the scrapings."

Inwardly Julia had been a good deal perturbed by Gracie's gossip, and she would have liked to discuss it with Merran—especially as she could see no sensible reason for refraining. But having given her word, however grudgingly, to Taters, she felt obliged to keep it—at least, until such time as the same news should reach her from some other source. At first she had felt more uncomfortable than usual when out in the car with Lisbeth, and showed a tendency to shy at policemen which caused her friend some amusement.

"Your conscience is far more tender than mine," declared

Lisbeth airily. "I don't really bother, because I can't see a great deal of difference between sixteen and three-quarters and seventeen. It doesn't look as though the police noticed it much either. I haven't been asked for my licence."

"What would happen if you were?"

"Oh, there might be some unpleasantness, but I expect I should get off with a warning. But I'm not inviting one, because then I *should* have to lay up Dulcibel for the next six weeks, or Daddy would probably be fined, and that wouldn't do him any good."

Julia pondered. It was quite evident that Lisbeth knew nothing—at present, anyhow—of the danger which, according to Taters, hung over her so imminently; possibly the gossip had been exaggerated.

"You mean because of the Town Council election?" she asked.

"Yes. It comes along in November, so it might be cutting it rather close if he landed in the police-courts before that." Then she added more seriously, "You know, Julia, Daddy is desperately keen on getting in, and it's not just because he'd like the importance of being a bailie. He's full of schemes for the good of Colmskirk, but so far the Council has turned down most of them. If he was one of the Council himself he thinks he might get on better."

"Not unless he could count on a majority," said Julia involuntarily.

"Oh, well, he thinks he might work up a following if he once got in." Lisbeth glanced round at her friend with a twinkle in her violet eyes. "I know you don't altogether agree with some of his propositions—I don't, myself—but he does mean most awfully well, and it's hard to be thwarted at every turn."

"As a matter of fact," said Julia soberly, "I can't help feeling sorry for him, just because of that. He's so public spirited, and yet it seems to me he's always shinning up the wrong tree."

"What?" exclaimed Lisbeth, startled.

Julia gave her a considering glance.

"I don't care to discuss your father with you," she explained delicately, "but I feel I ought to, as things are, because if anything is to be done it will have to be done soon. There isn't a great deal of time between now and November—not if he's to reverse his present policy and get himself on a different footing."

"I can't see Daddy changing his footing or reversing anything," declared Lisbeth; and running the car up a side turning under some overhanging nut-trees, she switched off her engine. "Now, let's talk," she said. "Knowing you, I'm not afraid you'll say anything about Daddy which I would mind listening to; but I'm rather troubled myself about his chances for the Council, so if you know anything about that, we'd better thrash it out together."

"Well," said Julia warily, "there's his scheme for Meadows, to begin with. It's getting the town by the ears—or at least all the more articulate of them—because they don't fancy the idea of a fun-fair right on the Esplanade, in the most residential part of it, and they're all saying so in a very loud voice, especially Mrs. Stiles."

Lisbeth nodded. "They think it would be vulgar," she said coolly, "and I'm inclined to agree with them. But when I said so to Daddy, he was rather hurt; he said it would bring crowds to the place."

"But the wrong sort," protested Julia. "He could do better things for Colmskirk than fill it with trippers. Crowds aren't everything, and that's what most of the townsfolk feel. They don't want it converted into a Scottish Blackpool."

"And so they'll vote against Daddy. I see what you mean, Julia, but what I don't see is how to avoid it. When I try to discuss it with him, he just says it isn't to be expected that a schoolgirl would understand municipal affairs."

"The modern schoolgirl," replied Julia loftily, "is full of common sense—except, of course, those who are incurably fluffy, and you find them in every generation. But that's not the point. We want to get Mr. Bartle on the Council—"

She paused abruptly as she met Lisbeth's quizzical smile.

"Do you?" asked the latter pointedly. "After his crusade against your sister? That's very decent of you, old thing!"

Julia reddened hotly.

"Don't think for one moment I admire him for that," she retorted with vigour. "If I thought there was anything personal about it I'd be simply furious! But I know there isn't. Business men—especially big-business men like your father—can be quite ruthless officially, and yet as mild as milk in private. It's called having a dual personality."

Lisbeth shifted slightly in her seat and ran her slim brown hand round the steering-wheel.

"I shouldn't describe Daddy as being mild at any time," she said doubtfully, "fond as I am of him. But if you mean that he would be perfectly friendly to Merran if her shop was anywhere except on the corner of Gallowgate Square, then you're quite right. He never likes to feel he has made a bad investment, and that's what the square stands for to him, unless she'll consent to sell."

"Well, she won't," answered Julia decidedly, and sat in silence, wrinkling her brows in thought for a few minutes before bursting out suddenly, "I wish we could think of something else for him to do with that side of the square. I don't like to feel we've made it into a bad bargain for him."

"You might think of a dozen things," Lisbeth assured her wisely, "but to get him to do any of them would be quite another pair of shoes. Oh, well, I suppose we'd better be moving home now, but I'm glad we've had this talk, and that you really want

Daddy to get in when the election comes along."

"I think I'd wish him luck in any case," Julia stated, "but when the alternative is Taters' father, I'm all for yours!"

Lisbeth looked amused as she started up the car again and ran it backwards into the road.

"You don't like Mr. Tait?"

"Certainly not! His eyes are too close together—like his daughter's—so I fear he may be like her in other ways as well."

"You know, I think Taters is rather keen on you," remarked Lisbeth carelessly. "Sometimes I even fancy she's a bit jealous of me, and that she would gladly put a spoke in my wheel where you're concerned if she could. Luckily, however, I don't believe she can."

Julia joined in her laugh.

"Rather not!" she agreed emphatically. "It would take more than the Tattie-bogle to achieve that!"

Lisbeth dropped her at the corner of Gallowgate Lane, and she hurried home to find Merran shutting up for the evening with a somewhat depressed air.

"Had a good run?" she asked. "Where did you go? By the way, you've missed Perry. He came in to say good-bye. His appointment arrived last night, and he's off to-morrow to join his ship at Portsmouth."

"What?" Julia wheeled round in the kitchen doorway. "But isn't this rather sudden?"

"I suppose it is—in the end—but he knew he was marking time and that the appointment might come at any moment. He told me to give you his love and many regrets that the moonlight sail is off. I was afraid you would be disappointed."

"Oh, well," replied Julia, with her usual philosophical acceptance of all disappointments, "it's no use grousing about what can't be helped—but I'd just brought Mrs. Binnie to the

Julia

scratch, and I believe she'll be as sorry as anybody; Mrs. Binnie is a bit of a sport, you know. What ship has he got?"

"The *Calliope*—a new rather super destroyer, he says, and just commissioned. He hopes they'll be coming up to Lamlash before long for their speed trials, and if so he may get a few hours' leave to come over and look us up."

"We shall miss him," said Julia soberly; "but, with school beginning next week, I shall probably miss him less than you will. Did you remember Bill's fish this morning, Merran? Because he's saying it's about time he had it. I wish my watch kept as perfect time as William's!"

Though Julia's active brain was buzzing happily about its own affairs, she could not help noticing, as the evening wore on, that Merran was unusually listless and distrait, and quietly drew her own conclusions. She doubted whether Merran had diagnosed her own complaint, but to Julia it was very evident; indeed, she had had her suspicions for some time, and felt it was most unfortunate that the Royal Navy should have awakened so suddenly to its need for Perry's services.

"Another month—even another week," she thought regretfully, "might have been enough to get things started. Now it's left hanging in the air, and goodness knows what may happen before he comes back again! I don't believe Merran knows her own mind yet, though I'm quite sure Perry does. And then there's Sandy Lamond. Oh dear, it's all very complicated! but I feel myself Perry is the most suitable, and it would be a frightful disappointment to him if Sandy nipped in when his back was turned and caught her on the rebound. I must keep my eye on things as far as possible and discourage Sandy if I get a chance; and yet—I don't know! It's never wise to interfere in the game. Perhaps the best plan would be to keep Merran's mind occupied as much as possible with outside affairs, but it's a heavy responsibility for an inexperienced person like myself."

Accordingly, after a moment or two, she said aloud, "You know, Merran, I think we should take more interest in the welfare of the town. At least, I can't very well during term-time, but I feel you ought to belong to something municipal and do things about it."

Merran looked up with some natural surprise from a stone on which she was working, for Julia had followed her into the workroom after supper and ensconced herself in a corner with a book.

"I'm fairly busy myself," she expostulated mildly. "With all these orders on hand, I don't get a great many spare hours for going to town meetings. And then there are the stones to hunt for as well, and that takes time—especially now that I have to search so far afield."

"Still, I think you ought to," persisted Julia. "After all, as a tradeswoman of Colmskirk you've got certain obligations and responsibilities about which I feel you should see Mrs. Binnie. I mean to offer to do a spot of typing for her when the Burgh elections come round—in the evenings, I mean, after I've finished my prep."

Merran, however, looked singularly unimpressed by this display of public spirit; her mind appeared at the moment to be on other things.

"I may see about it sometime," she answered vaguely. "After all, isn't it enough to have Mr. Bartle taking an interest in the welfare of the town, without anybody else butting in as well?"

CHAPTER XVIII

AN IMPASSE

The last of the summer visitors departed from Colmskirk; the pleasure steamers vanished off the steel-grey Firth, and the white-winged yachts went away to hibernate in various nooks and corners of the coast; the coloured leaves swirled down off the trees in the gardens, but clung a little longer in their splendour of crimson and gold to the woods up Robin Water and Glenbruie; and the little town settled in to the privacy of its own winter life, undisturbed by invasions from the outer world.

Fewer customers came now to the Serendipity Shop, though Perry's sign still creaked and flaunted its Chinese profanity above the door, and the children still flocked in on Saturday mornings to spend their pennies at Julia's corner. But though Merran sold less across the counter, she was increasingly busy with orders from outside, and constant practice was giving her an added dexterity in her craft. She was not earning a fortune, but she was able to assure the relations at Slingsby, in answer to anxious letters of inquiry, that she was able to make her venture pay and was perfectly happy about it. Now and again other letters reached her on headed notepaper from H.M.S. *Calliope*—very friendly and amusing, and such as she could share quite openly with Julia—which caused that young lady some secret disappointment.

The Westharbour Academy had reopened for the winter term, and Julia had hurled herself headlong into all the work and play on its Senior programme. Her personality made her a natural leader among the other girls, and though she did not seek leadership for herself, she thoroughly enjoyed her popularity, and was ready to take part in all the school's activities. Though Lisbeth was unquestionably her chief friend, she had many lesser strings to her bow, and was very happy in the midst of it all, for she knew herself to be a favourite with the staff as well as with the girls, and as she confessed to Merran, "I like everybody to like me. There's something so pleasant and satisfactory about it."

And then suddenly, like a bolt from the blue, came something that shook all this satisfaction into ruin, and life in a moment looked very bleak for Julia.

It was a fortnight after the commencement of term that she was summoned away, one Friday morning, in the middle of an algebra class, by a message from the headmistress, and wondered very much, as she hurried down the long stone passages to the office, what Miss Craig could possibly want with her at such an unseemly hour; but since her conscience was clear, she went lightheartedly enough to her doom, and it was not until she actually found herself in the presence that any foreboding fell upon her.

Not many women surviving into modern days can be correctly described as august: it is an adjective more applicable to the Victorians; but it certainly applied to Miss Craig of Westharbour Academy at such times as she was annoyed. There was a cold glitter in her fine eyes, and her handsome nose looked more high-bridged than ever.

"Sit down, Julia," she commanded icily, pointing to a chair in front of her desk. "I sent for you to ask if you can give me any explanation of a letter which I have received this morning from Mr. Bartle of Colmskirk, whose daughter, I have always been led to believe, is a particular friend of yours. It is a most disagreeable letter for any headmistress to read about any pupil in her school, but it is, of course, my duty to sift Mr. Bartle's complaint to the bottom. I cannot allow any stigma to rest on the Academy."

"No, Miss Craig, of course not," agreed Julia in respectful astonishment, "but I don't quite understand. Why has Mr. Bartle written to complain of me?"

"He hasn't," admitted the Head, "but I am sorry to say it has come back upon you. However," relaxing a little as she saw the girl's genuine bewilderment, "you may quite well be able to clear yourself of anything except a little indiscreet gossiping. That is bad enough, but I should be sorry to think anything worse of you, Julia."

Julia's dark curly head went up proudly.

"I hope you won't even have to think that, Miss Craig," she answered. "I don't usually gossip, and never about Mr. Bartle."

"I think," said Miss Craig, "the best plan is to show you his letter," and she passed across a large typed sheet, which Julia took and read in growing amazement.

"Dear Madam," (it ran)

"I have been very much disturbed during the last few weeks by a rumour which has reached me from different quarters, to the effect that you intend to expel my daughter from your school because she has been seen driving a car without a licence, being under age. As you have not communicated with me direct I can only conclude that this is a piece of malicious gossip, and I will ask you kindly to find out who is putting this story about, as I have already traced it to four girls who attend your Academy and are in my daughter's classes. Unless I receive a full and immediate apology from the author of the libel I shall be reluctantly compelled to withdraw my daughter from the school."

Here followed a list of four names, among them being Gracie Tait's, but as Julia was not mentioned, she found it harder than ever to guess why she had been summoned; so she handed the letter back in silence.

"Did you know," asked the Head, watching her keenly, "that Lisbeth Bartle was driving without a licence?"

"I knew she was under age," answered Julia cautiously, "—in the holidays; she's all right now."

"And did you think that was a proper thing to do?"

"It was Lisbeth's business, not mine," she replied still more guardedly, adding with a burst, "But anyhow, Miss Craig, the school isn't responsible for what we do in the holidays."

Miss Craig tapped gently on her desk with the end of her pencil.

"No," she said at last, "but you are responsible to the school for your behaviour at any time, because on that depends its reputation, as I am always trying to impress on you girls. However much I may disapprove of what Lisbeth has been doing, it is, of course, an absolute falsehood that I had any intention of expelling her—so much a falsehood that I am inclined to agree with her father in thinking that it was intended maliciously. And that is why I cannot comprehend, Julia, how you come to be connected with it—you who are Lisbeth's friend!"

If the Head had purposely tried to get under Julia's guard by this last remark, she had every reason to be satisfied with the result of her little stratagem. There was no mistaking the complete sincerity of the girl's innocence as she retorted hotly,

"But I'm not concerned with it, Miss Craig! I *am* Lisbeth's friend; and even if I were her greatest enemy I wouldn't do a dirty trick like that! I can't understand why you should suspect me, because I'm quite sure Lisbeth doesn't—nor even Mr. Bartle."

"I did not say I suspected you, Julia," the Head responded quietly, "but I sent for you because I require an explanation which possibly you can give. Before doing so I saw the four girls who are named in this letter, and all of them frankly admitted having heard the tale and discussed it among themselves—which, I suppose, knowing schoolgirls, is natural enough, however undesirable. Maisie, Joan and Betty each told me in turn that she had heard it from Grace Tait, so finally I had Grace in and questioned her as to where she had got her information. She said she had been told by Julia Lendrum, and thought it must be true because Julia and Lisbeth were always together."

Julia's face as she listened was a study in various emotions, all of which the Head was quick to note as they passed. But when she had finished speaking, the girl only said slowly, as though wishing to be quite sure of her facts, "Then Gracie Tait said it was I who told her this?"

"She did—at once and without any hesitation. Is it the truth, Julia?"

Julia flung back her head and met the Head's scrutiny with clear brown eyes. "No, Miss Craig," she replied emphatically, "it is not," but said no more.

The Head tried another tack.

"Did you and Grace discuss the matter at all?"

Julia's eyes dropped now, and she answered unwillingly, "Yes, we did—one afternoon when Grace came to see me."

"Was anyone else there at the time?"

"No. My sister was out. We were alone in the shop."

"H'm!" Miss Craig leaned back in her chair and began to play again with her pencil. "Will you repeat the conversation to me as nearly as you can remember it?"

Julia's bright colour faded a little.

"I'm afraid I can't, Miss Craig," she said bluntly.

"Do you mean you don't remember?"

"No—I remember it all quite well, but I don't want to tell you what was said."

The Head made an impatient little movement with her shoulders.

"But I am afraid I must insist upon your doing so. I have had perfectly straightforward answers from the other four, and I require the same from you. No, don't reply till you hear what I have got to say. Not only did Grace assure me that she had got this story—this absolutely false story—from you, but each of the other three (and I saw them separately) told me that Grace, when repeating it to them, added that there could be no mistake because she had heard it from Julia Lendrum. Now do you see why you must be perfectly open with me? It's the only way in which you can clear yourself."

"Oh, I see that all right," replied Julia bitterly. "But all the same I can't say any more than I have done. I'm very sorry, Miss Craig—I don't wish or mean to be impertinent, but I can't repeat that conversation, however much you insist!"

The Head's exasperation was rising. She had wasted a good deal of valuable time over this affair, and her investigations up till then had been plain sailing. Now it was evident that she was up against an impasse, and that Julia, for some reason known only to herself, had no intention of being candid. She had denied the authorship of the tale glibly enough, but she would make no attempt to prove her innocence, and for the first time Miss Craig began to doubt it. On the girl's own showing she and Grace had been alone, so there could be no question of some third person whom she was trying to shield, unless—

Curbing her mounting impatience, the Head tried again. "You

admit you and Grace discussed this story about Lisbeth—"

"I didn't, Miss Craig! I only meant we talked about Lisbeth—and her car."

"Don't quibble, Julia! It's the same thing, naturally. I am only questioning you and these other girls so that I may find out the real inventor of this lie. I do not blame you so much for repeating it—though I may have something to say to you all later, on the subject of idle chatter—but I am absolutely determined to discover the girl who first started it. That, I feel, we owe to Mr. Bartle, since it was through other Academy girls the rumour was spread. And I may tell you he is equally determined to get a full apology from whoever was responsible—you can see that yourself in his letter. No matter how you passed the gossip on to Grace—what I now ask you to tell me is who repeated it to you in the first instance?"

"Nobody, Miss Craig."

"Nobody? My dear Julia, how can you be so absurd? You have just said that you both discussed Lisbeth and this matter of her driving, and yet—"

"It's not absurd, Miss Craig—it's absolutely true! I never heard a word about Lisbeth being expelled. I should certainly have thought that was ridiculous, but I knew nothing about it till I read Mr. Bartle's letter just now. If Grace says I told her that, she's simply—making a mistake!"

The Head pressed the bulb of an electric bell which lay on her desk, and when her secretary appeared from the next room, she said: "Will you kindly find Grace Tait, Miss Field, and send her to me at once? I imagine she is in the gymnasium, so please ask Miss Walton to excuse her."

Miss Field went obediently, while Miss Craig scrutinized in chilly silence some notes lying on her desk, and Julia stared unhappily out of the window. From where she sat she could see the Belfast steamer rolling a little as she made her way down Clyde, and the sea-gulls sweeping and dipping about her, hoping to be fed. For the first time in her life Julia's self-confidence had been shaken, and she had no idea what to do next. At the end of five minutes Taters arrived, breathless and faintly green under her orange freckles. Avoiding any glance in Julia's direction, she fixed her shifty gaze on the Head and said meekly, "Miss Field says you want me, Miss Craig?"

The headmistress looked across at her with a distaste that she was careful to hide; but it came into her mind that, of the two suspects before her, Julia was decidedly the more attractive.

"Miss Field is right. I sent for you, Grace, because I want you to repeat what you have already told me this morning about your conversation with Julia and what it was she told you. I am quite resolved that this matter shall be cleared up before you leave the Academy to-day, if it takes me all forenoon to do so."

CHAPTER XIX

JULIA UP AGAINST IT

GRACIE TAIT'S close-set eyes moved from the headmistress to Julia and back again, and finally her gaze wavered down to the carpet to remain fixed there; but her answer when it came was quite cool and self-possessed.

"I went to see Julia, Miss Craig, to take her a toy I had made for her weekly Cripples' Sale, and we got talking about the bathing round Colmskirk, and how hard it was to find any sand. Then I said I wondered she and Lisbeth didn't go farther along the coast to bathe since it wouldn't take long in Lisbeth's car. Isn't that right, Julia?"

"Perfectly," replied Julia stonily.

"Go on, Grace," ordered the Head.

"Then Julia said she wasn't too keen on going far afield with Lisbeth because she was under age, and there was going to be trouble about it before long, as it had got round to the Academy that she was driving without a licence, and that meant she'd be expelled, since you wouldn't risk having one of your pupils mixed up with a court case."

"Thank you," said the Head. "That will do. No, I did not say you might go. Well, Julia? You have heard what Grace has told me. What have you got to say about it?"

"That it's an absolute lie," burst forth Julia furiously, "and all the worse for being partly twisted up with the truth. But unluckily I'm the only person who knows that."

"Very well, then," said Miss Craig calmly. "I am now waiting to hear your version of the story. You say it is true up to a point, so perhaps you will tell me where the truth ends and the falsehood begins?"

Julia remained silent for a few minutes, staring straight at Gracie, who, after one swift look at her classmate, riveted her eyes again to the carpet.

"No," Julia said at last, slowly and unwillingly, "I can't do that—though I'd simply love to!—and Gracie knows very well why I can't. But, anyhow, it doesn't much matter, does it, as it's merely my word against hers?"

"It matters this much," retorted the Head, whose patience was wearing very thin, "that Mr. Bartle must have a full apology from the originator of this tale. I have traced it back to you two girls—one of you heard it from the other, who obviously either invented it for some motive I can't pretend to fathom, or got it herself from some third person still unknown. Now, I must have the name of that third person, or else the apology must come from one of you; for I shall have to assume that this invention came from one of you likewise."

"Not from me, Miss Craig," protested Grace quickly. "I know I was very wrong and foolish in repeating it to the others, but it was Julia who told me, so I thought it must be true. Don't you remember, Julia? I was so surprised to hear it."

Again she lifted her eyes for a moment, and again they fluttered away from the other girl's cold, accusing stare.

"Oh, yes, I remember," answered Julia bitterly, "but not, I'm afraid, the same things as you—though I do remember some that you've left out!"

The Head glanced sharply from one girl to the other.

"This is a deadlock," she exclaimed, "and I am getting no

farther. You will both go back to your classes now, and at dinner-time you will come to me again, when I hope you will both have reached a proper frame of mind and decided to speak the truth. For it is abundantly clear to me that one of you is lying; and a girl who lies to me persistently and in cold blood cannot remain at Westharbour Academy. I have no use for that type of person, and neither has the school."

Somehow or other the two girls found themselves outside in the passage, where their ways separated; for Julia knew that the algebra class must long ago have merged into French History, and a glance at the clock told Gracie Tait that she was overdue at a music lesson. Nevertheless, she lingered to mutter, "I'm really grateful to you, Julia, for keeping your promise to me. Of course I had no idea it would lead you into such a mess, but you must see for yourself—I mean, Father would be in a most awful rage if I had to go and apologize to Mr. Bartle of all people, and now of all times. It wouldn't matter in the least, though, if you were to do so, and then everything would quiet down again all right and be forgotten—"

She broke off, slightly, alarmed by the concentrated scorn and wrath in Julia's brown eyes.

"Would it?" she said. "You've got considerable nerve, Taters, haven't you? I may be expelled for lying, as the Head hinted just now, but at any rate I don't mean to deserve it simply to save your skin. Get out!"

And Taters got.

The Head's determination to clear the matter up before either girl left the school that afternoon came to nothing, for her second interview with them took her no farther than the first, and left her even more bewildered. At one moment she was convinced of Julia's innocence, and at the next her conviction was shaken by the unswerving fashion in which Gracie Tait stuck to her story.

She was an austerely just woman, and the fact that her own preference had always been for Julia made her harder to the girl than she actually felt. Besides, she was unwilling to recognize that such evidence as there was seemed entirely against the pupil whom she preferred. And still Mr. Bartle was no nearer to receiving his apology.

Of course the entire Sixth Form and most of the Upper School as well knew all about it by dinner-time. The three girls whose names had been mentioned with Gracie's in the letter told everything they knew without reserve, as well as a good deal which they surmised; other people, who knew nothing at all, added their surmises, and so the snowball grew. Taters, when questioned, proved eagerly communicative, while Julia, on the other hand, refused to discuss it.

"I should think there's been enough gossip already," she said darkly. "You can guess what you like, but I can't help you—beyond affirming what you probably know already, that Taters is a most accomplished young liar. I can't see any good and sufficient reason for hiding that from you."

"Shut up, Julia!" one of the prefects rebuked her. "She hates you quite enough already without adding fuel to the flame."

"I'm glad and proud to be hated by her," retorted Julia quickly, and went her way with haughty indifference; but inwardly she wished with her whole heart that Lisbeth had not been away from school for the past three days with a bad cold. Not that this was a matter she could have discussed with Lisbeth in complete candour, tied as she was by that unfortunate promise to Gracie Tait; in fact, Julia began to realize with increasing desolation, her promise prevented her from being completely candid with anyone; not even to Merran could she give a full explanation. And, that being so, she decided to keep her troubles altogether to herself. What need to bother Merran when neither she nor anyone else could be of any help? Time enough for her to know about it when she learned that her sister had been expelled for lying. At least that was one thing Merran would never believe.

"Though, if the Head expels one of us, she must in common decency expel both," Julia argued with herself, "and I don't think somehow she's likely to do that. For it's just a case of one person's word against another's."

Since the trouble had flared up on a Friday, it had perforce to be given the week-end in which to simmer, and the Head privately hoped that this might prove to be a good thing; she at any rate was quite helpless to do any more. So she wrote a letter to Mr. Bartle, regretting the whole thing exceedingly, but adding that she had already taken steps, and hoped to be able soon to give him more and fuller information.

Julia carried out her Saturday morning duties with a kind of dull conscientiousness very unlike her usual bubbling enthusiasm, and had not much appetite for her midday dinner, though it had been cooked by Maggie with a special eye to Miss Julia's tastes. Merran, looking at her anxiously, hoped she was not sickening for Lisbeth's cold, and suggested a good long walk for the afternoon.

"Why not go up Cock Robin Hill?" she said. "I know it's not much fun alone, and I wish I could come too, but the air up there is so marvellous that it's bound to blow away every germ."

"I haven't got any germs," maintained Julia. "If I'd caught any of Lisbeth's they would have shown their cloven hooves three days ago. But I'd like to climb Cock Robin all the same. I haven't been up it since we came back, and it's such a clear day, the view will be wonderful."

Bareheaded, in a thick brown coat, and with an ash-stick in her hand, she walked rapidly through the week-end bustle of Main Street, and coming out on the Langsands road beyond the station yard, turned left after a few yards into the wild and shaggy public park which climbed upwards through trees and rocks and faded heather towards the steep, bare hillside. Julia, however, did not follow the well-marked path along which little groups of townsfolk were taking their Saturday walk; instead she struck into a low thicket of whins and tawny bracken that covered the shoulder of the hill, and presently found herself among the rocks and myrtle bushes of a deserted region. Here, wedged between two large boulders, with the short thymy slope making a back for her perch, she sat and gazed. Below her, in its screen of rowans, crouched a solitary white cottage, a shepherd's home, from which the ground fell steeply down into the distant huddle of the town with its grey roofs and red spires; beyond all spread the wide expanse of Firth like a stretch of beaten pewter, with the blue Highland mountains fading into the distance.

Julia stayed quietly there, letting the wonder and the beauty of it soak into her troubled young spirit, while swift clouds trailed their shadows over hills and woods and sea, and a sudden shower swept across her cranny, gone as quickly as it came, blown like a silver veil out and away to the far purple islands in the west.

"I'm hidden on the cleft of a rock," she exclaimed exultantly; and that thought started a whole train of others. "Why, of course, there's still something left for me to do about this mess at school. I'm surprised I didn't think of it sooner. It seems somehow rather mean, only to try it now when I'm at my wits' end; but it has only just struck me that I can pray to be helped out of it. Anyhow, I'll start at once, and then wait and see what happens. It's wonderful how things do work out when you least expect it—like Merran getting the Serendipity Shop. Perhaps I've been too much in the habit of depending on my own common sense up till now, but apparently that doesn't solve everything. Or else—unpleasant thought!—there may be limits to my stock of sense.

At least, it's letting me down rather badly now.—Hullo! who's this?"

Someone was plunging downwards through the dying bracken, calling and whistling to a dog as he came. The next minute he rounded the corner that hid him and strode into sight, a red cocker spaniel at his heels.

"Sandy Lamond!" cried Julia. "The very person! But it's the first time I've ever heard of an angel of deliverance wearing plus-fours and a pipe in his mouth!"

Sandy pulled up short and stared at her in mild amazement, as well he might.

"What on earth are you blethering about?" he demanded, removing the pipe, since he had no cap to raise. "You never struck me as being the kind of person to require the services of a delivering angel, suitably garbed or otherwise."

"Well, I do now," Julia assured him earnestly. "Nobody is as self-sufficient as they think they are, and I've just taken a nasty jolt. But I have very good reasons for believing you've been sent along this way by Providence just now to help me out; for I don't mind confessing I was pretty near my wits' end when you came round that corner!"

A second look at her convinced him of her sincerity. There was a strained look in her eyes, and her lips were trembling a little, though she tried to steady them as she spoke. Sandy dropped down on a flat boulder among the bracken at her feet, and nursed his knees with both arms.

"Let's have it, then," he said laconically, adding, "though personally I think Providence might have made a better choice."

Julia leaned forward eagerly. Already some of her dejection was beginning to fall away from her.

"Oh, no," she protested, "because—don't you see?—being a lawyer makes you much the same as a doctor or a parson, only much more useful to me. I don't know the doctor or the minister very well yet, so it's far better it should be you."

"Well, I'm glad you're satisfied," rejoined Sandy modestly, "though I can't say I've ever regarded myself hitherto as being a suitable substitute for either."

"Perhaps not," said Julia, "but the point is this—one can tell you things in strict confidence that one couldn't honourably repeat to anyone else—not even one's own sister. It's like speaking under the seal of the confessional, and that's exactly what I'm dying to do at the present moment. I'm far too full of perplexity to keep it all to myself. In fact, if you hadn't happened to be you just now I should probably have burst!"

"Oh!" said Sandy. "Yes—quite! Oh, of course! Hang it all, Julia, what the dickens have you been up to?"

CHAPTER XX

LEGAL ADVICE

JULIA sank back once more against the bank of turf behind her.

"It isn't what I've been up to," she answered ruefully. "It's what other people have dragged me into. Honestly, Sandy, I've gone over and over it all in my mind, and I can't see that I did anything specially foolish—except, perhaps, when I promised that little beast, Taters, not to repeat to a soul what she told me. Mercifully, however, a lawyer isn't a soul in the ordinary sense of the word. If I'd thought of you sooner I should have been saved a lot of worry."

"What made you think of me now?"

"Why, you came crashing down through the fern just when I'd—anyhow, never mind about that! You're here, and I'm consulting you professionally. Sandy, what would you do supposing somebody came and told you a bit of scandal that you didn't particularly want to hear, seeing it was about your best friend—and made you promise not to repeat it—and then went and repeated it all round the town herself, and said she'd got it from you."

"Gosh!" exclaimed her lawyer frankly, "you've got me there! I'd—I expect I should—no, I shouldn't, either! I'd tell her to get to blazes out of it, and then go round spreading the truth—though I admit it's difficult for the truth ever to overtake a lie with a good start. Still, if by Taters you mean that furtive-looking kid who belongs to Brolly Tait, the retired umbrella merchant, in the house with the windows over towards Langsands—that's whom you mean, isn't it?"

"Well, their house has got rather more windows than it needs," agreed Julia, "but I didn't know her father made umbrellas; I thought he looked more like a money-lender. But that's Taters all right—I mean, it's her father."

"Then," finished Sandy with decision, "I should think your word would go as far as hers any day with most people. Why not try?"

"Because, I told you, I promised."

"Maybe you did, but she can hardly expect the promise to bind you when she goes round telling lies and getting you into trouble."

"But *I* expect it to," replied Julia stoutly. "You can't just wriggle out of a promise because it has become inconvenient—at least, that may be legal, but it's not at all moral. Besides, if I were to sneak she'd get expelled—if they believed me."

"And she jolly well deserves to!"

"Well, her deserts aren't my affair."

"I should think, under the circumstances, they were—very much so!"

Julia shook her head obstinately, and bent to caress the dog, who had come back, much mystified, to see what had become of his master.

"You must find some other way to get me out of it," she insisted. "That's why I'm consulting you. I shouldn't need to if I were to go to the Head and make a clean breast of it. That would be simple enough—though even then she mightn't take my word for it."

Sandy considered this with the legal side of his brain, and agreed that there might be something in it.

"She might want to," he said, "but she couldn't, in justice, believe one of you against the other without some sort of evidence, and apparently there isn't any. Pity Merran happened to be out that afternoon. It strikes me, my child, there's only one way out of this—Miss Tait must be made to confess."

Julia looked sceptical. "Then it's up to you to say how," she informed him. "Personally, I should think that, short of thumbscrews, it can't be done."

"I don't know," reasoned Sandy thoughtfully. "Being the guilty party, she's probably a bit jumpy by now, and a little pressure on the right spot—oh, no, I'm not advocating thumbscrews, unless, perhaps, the mental variety—but it strikes me that your friend, Taters, would be the better for a wholesome fright—something to scare her back to the paths of rectitude."

"She's no friend of mine," said Julia disgustedly, "and she's quite scared enough as it is of what the Head and Mr. Bartle between them might do to her if they knew the truth."

"Just what I said—jumpy! What's wanted is a greater fear to cast out the less; but it requires thinking about. We've got till Monday, I take it, before the matter comes up again? Leave it to me, Julia. I'll work out some scheme before to-morrow night, and then I'll ring you up."

"It will have to be when Merran has gone to evening service, then. I'm not going to have her bothered about this before it's absolutely necessary."

Sandy chuckled. "At this rate we'll have to arrange a clandestine meeting on the shore or somewhere in order to discuss the case. Most awkward! Ever since you proposed to me at the age of six—"

"I didn't!" contradicted Julia indignantly, with flaming cheeks.

"But you did, I assure you! At one of the Binnies' Christmas parties. I was just home from my first term at Fettes, and apparently found favour in your sight, but it was acutely embarrassing."

"It must have been!" Julia began to laugh, as he had intended, and when he rose from his rock, she too slipped out of her cranny, and they walked down the hill together, pausing half-way for one more look at the widespread view before the trees screened it.

"The town is spreading," remarked Sandy, regarding it with a critical eye. "I dislike that bungaloid growth which is rapidly eating up the fields at the back of it. Builders have no imagination—no feeling for a place's personality."

"And Colmskirk has such lots of it," added Julia. "It should be preserved at all costs; but the Burgh Council don't appear to bother. They have no imagination, if you like."

"Luckily, some parts of it can't be messed up," said Sandy, "however much they might like to try their hand at it. This park, for instance, was only bequeathed to the town on condition that they left it more or less to Nature. And as long as Merran holds on, Bartle can't meddle badly with Gallowgate Square. The old kirkyard, too, behind Main Street—that's immune."

"Which reminds me," exclaimed Julia, "you can probably tell me the meaning of that big conical mound outside our bathroom window. I never thought of asking you before, but nobody else seems to know, though Merran has an idea it may be the old gallows-mound; she has a vague fancy that Colmskirk once had such a thing."

"It certainly had," confirmed Sandy, "but I had no idea it was quite so close to your premises. I suppose it must be, though. Look, we can just see it from here," and he pointed down with his stick. "Yonder's the square, and that green spot behind it must be the mound."

"If Sam Bartle got his way and our shop," mused Julia, gazing below her with narrowed eyes, "he would have to level the gallows-mound as well before he could carry out his nefarious designs. I wonder if that has ever occurred to him?"

"Shouldn't think so," replied Sandy as they went on their way again. "Probably doesn't even know of its existence. Anyhow, he couldn't touch that."

"Why not? I don't suppose he has much respect for any ancient monument that gets in his way."

"Perhaps not; but it so happens that 'monument' is the word for the big heap at your back door. Before the earliest burghers of Colmskirk started using it to hang people on it had another significance. That, my child, though few know it and fewer care, is the original cairn where they piled the Norwegian dead after the big battle on the shore in the days of King Alexander. Very convenient, as you see, just outside the kirkyard wall. I don't expect they were ready, so soon after the fray, to offer the invaders the hospitality of their kirkyard, but they planted them on the verge of it, and there they have been ever since. Even Sam Bartle could hardly do away with that to make room for a business proposition."

"No," assented Julia rather doubtfully, "I should think he might stick at that. Anyhow, I'm very glad to know the full story of our earthwork. I feel I've spent a most profitable afternoon with you, Sandy, and if you can only think out some method of circumventing Taters, I shall be more grateful still."

They parted at the head of Main Street, and Julia made her way homewards to find Merran watching for her at the shop door.

"Oh, there you are!" she exclaimed with obvious relief. "That shifty-looking schoolfellow of yours is waiting upstairs in the sitting-room to see you, and won't go away till she does. I sent her there because I couldn't be bothered with her hanging round me in the shop."

"Who? Taters?" asked Julia in amazement. "What on earth does she want here? It shows considerable nerve on her part to come at all."

"Why? Have you been quarrelling at school?"

"I don't demean myself to quarrel with grass-snakes," replied Julia with dignity, and Merran laughed.

"She certainly looks green enough, and I don't think somehow she's very happy in her mind. Go and see what she wants, and get rid of her as soon as possible. I want my tea."

Julia went quietly upstairs and into the sitting-room, having first washed her hands and run a comb through her wind-tossed curls to give herself a little extra self-possession. Taters was standing by the window, looking down into the square, but she swung round with nervous abruptness as the door opened behind her. Julia closed it again and stood with her back against it.

"Well?" she asked curtly.

"Oh, Julia," exclaimed the other girl, blinking in a scared fashion, "I came because I thought we ought to reach some sort of understanding before Monday. It's—well—it's extremely awkward at school."

"Yes, isn't it?" Julia agreed. "But what do you propose to do about it? It's up to you, isn't it? We needn't exactly pretend anything else now that we are not in the Academy buildings."

"I don't know what you mean," said Taters in an injured tone.

"Oh, yes, I think you do. I told you we needn't pretend, but just as a matter of curiosity I should like to know what's at the bottom of all this. What have I ever done to you that you should concoct such a network of lies and land me in such a predicament?"

"Nothing," replied Taters sulkily, "and I wasn't trying to get you into trouble. I never thought it would come to this, or that it would ever reach the Head's ears, seeing it happened in the hols.

Believe it or not, Julia Lendrum, but I have always rather liked you; I have even wanted to be friends with you, only you never look at anyone but Lisbeth Bartle."

"You have taken a queer way of showing your preference."

"I keep on saying I never meant to do you any harm—only to start a coolness between you and Lisbeth, so that I might get a look-in myself. That's why I said I'd heard the rumour from you—because I thought it would make Lisbeth mad with you."

Julia laughed contemptuously.

"You're rather an ass, aren't you? Did it never strike you that Lisbeth's first move would have been to come straight to me and ask me if I'd heard all this? Then we should have got to the bottom of it together. But unfortunately this 'flu of hers has kept her isolated, and meanwhile the tale got to her father's ears, and now the fat's in the fire and sizzling!"

"Anyhow, you can't sneak—you promised not to!"

Julia looked at her thoughtfully.

"I wonder if you'd be as scrupulous if things were the other way round. You seem to rely rather a lot on my promise—which is flattering, though inconvenient. You're right, however—I can't sneak. It's all very difficult, and I've been feeling the need of a little outside advice—so this afternoon I've been consulting my lawyer."

"Your *what*?" Taters turned a paler shade of green, against which her orange freckles stood out with a sickly distinctness.

"My lawyer," repeated Julia. "He seemed to think my promise didn't hold under the circumstances; but I said it did. So he's thinking the matter over now to see if he can find a way out. I expect he will; he's a very clever lawyer."

CHAPTER XXI

TATERS WRIGGLES OUT

In the end it was Julia who telephoned Sandy, choosing that evening to do it, when Merran had gone round to consult Gregor about the price of an old Chippendale chair which she had been asked to buy.

"I don't want to give less than the fair price," she explained to Julia, "and I haven't the foggiest idea what that may be—or even if the chair is a genuine Chippendale piece. I shall bring old Gregor back with me to look at it if he can spare the time. It's most inconvenient to be so inexperienced about antiques when I have to sell them. If I even had a natural flair like Perry Boyd it wouldn't be so bad; but I only know what I like and what I don't."

"You should arrange," said the sage Julia, "to buy only when Perry Boyd is at home on leave and can help."

"Well, he's not at home now," Merran pointed out impatiently, "and the man who brought in that chair to-day won't wait till he is. What about coming with me?"

"No, thanks," returned Julia. "I've got business of my own to see to."

Merran took this to mean lessons, and remarked sympathetically that it was a shame she should have prep to do on a Saturday. "But of course that Tait girl wasted what was left of the afternoon after you came in from your walk. I hope she won't make a practice of blowing in on you at week-ends."

"Not much danger of that," Julia assured her, with a peculiar grin which her sister was too busy at the moment to notice, and Merran had hardly crossed the square before she was at the telephone in haste to get Sandy.

"Hullo!" came his astonished voice at the other end. "That you, Julia? Has anything further happened to your case? Or have you merely had a brain-wave before I could?"

"Not I," she answered; "but I've had a visit from—from the other party. You warned me, you know, not to mention names on the 'phone. You were quite right, Sandy, about her being jumpy. I mean—that's why she came—but she was jumpier still when she left. I mentioned that I had been consulting my lawyer."

A deep chuckle came over the wire.

"That gave her the jitters, did it? Thought we might take the matter to court? But what will be the net result of this? Is she going to make a clean breast of it?"

"I doubt if she would make a clean breast of anything, however scared she might be—she'd still hedge and prevaricate. But I do believe she's going to do something about it, though I can't think what. Anyhow, I've promised to ask you to hold your hand till after Monday, so she evidently means to take steps of some sort then—do something to satisfy the Head, at least, if not Mr. Bartle."

"I take it the lady will be able to cope with him," Sandy rejoined, "given any data on which to do so. Well, Julia, I congratulate you. It looks as though you might not require my professional services after all."

"Oh, but I've had them already," declared Julia fervently. "If I hadn't been able to say that you were advising me, we should still be where we were. You provided the greater fear which seems to be casting out the less, as you guessed it would. I'm tremendously obliged to you, Sandy. I feel like a different being to-night, and it's all thanks to you."

"Tut, tut!" said Sandy. "I wish all cases were as easily settled out of court. Let me hear how you get on—and remember, if you should ever be in need of legal advice again, I'm your man. It's a pleasure to act for you."

Taters was missing from her classes on Monday morning, and Julia went through her work with outward serenity, while inwardly she was on needles and pins from hour to hour, wondering what was going to happen and when she might expect another summons to face the Head.

The message came for her towards the end of the afternoon, during the last lesson, when she had almost ceased to expect it, and she reached the Head's office to find Taters there, no longer wearing school uniform, but cool and self-possessed in a very grown-up costume and small tilted hat, with a subtle air of suppressed triumph about her.

"Come in, Julia," said the Head grimly. "I have brought you here because I consider you are entitled to an explanation from Grace Tait, as the very least she can do before she leaves us, to compensate for the unpleasantness she has caused you. Grace's father requires her to help him with the clerical work in connection with the Town Council elections next month, so, as she was leaving school in any case at Christmas, he has decided to withdraw her now; and personally I think it is a very good arrangement. Perhaps, Grace, you will yourself tell Julia why you chose to accuse her of something she had not done, and so allowed suspicion to rest on her unfairly. I find the whole thing beyond any explanation of mine."

"Oh, I hope Julia will understand, Miss Craig," murmured Gracie deprecatingly, and the Head retorted with a snap:

"Well, if she does, it's more than I do!"

Gracie turned suavely to her erstwhile schoolfellow.

"I'm afraid, Julia," she said, "I really do owe you an

explanation, since I have been using you to shield someone else, and so was obliged to give Miss Craig a wrong impression of you for a day or two—but of course I always meant to clear it up in the end, when I'd got permission to do so from—from the person concerned."

"Oh!" said Julia drily. "And did you?"

Taters blinked her light lashes rapidly.

"Yes—but only on condition that her name isn't mentioned. So I'm afraid it won't be possible for Miss Craig to get the apology Mr. Bartle has been demanding. I could only get leave to clear you, Julia, because I explained how very awkward it was to leave you bearing the blame for what someone else had said; but of course she wouldn't hear of apologizing to Mr. Bartle or Lisbeth; she said she didn't see why she should."

"That's as it may be," said the Head curtly. "I shall at least be able to tell Mr. Bartle—*now*—that the author of the falsehood is not in Westharbour Academy, and there my responsibility ceases. I shall not even inquire, Julia, why you refused to be open with me in the first instance. I presume you had your own reasons, and I suspect them of being very mistaken. The affair is not cleared up, but it is now beyond my jurisdiction."

Her tone added that she was extremely thankful it should be so, and Taters took her leave with an uneasy impression that the Head had been quite undeceived by her tale, which, she was forced to admit to herself, was not after all a very convincing one.

"But it was the best I could do at such short notice," she thought as she hurried off to the station, anxious to get a train that would start for Colmskirk before the school was released and the girls poured on to the platform. Miss Grace Tait had answered enough questions for one day; "And anyhow, all's well that ends well, since Pa has let me leave in the middle of the term. He didn't want to, but he saw well enough there was nothing else to be done when I told him what a fix I was in. If he hopes to get on the Town Council next month he can't afford a scandal with the Bartles and Julia Lendrum's lawyer, whoever he may be. He was furious when he heard what a mess I'd made of things. I shall have to mind my P's and Q's at home for a bit after this, I'm afraid, but it's worth it on the whole. I'm sick of that old Academy and everybody in it!"

And Miss Craig, left alone in her study to write her final findings to Mr. Bartle, was heartily relieved to know that a bad influence had gone out of the school without need for drastic action on her part.

"I couldn't prove my convictions," she thought, "but I had them nevertheless. Now, I wonder what scared that little liar into such a sudden flight? Because I'm quite sure she meant on Friday to brazen it out."

Julia could have told her, but Julia told no one. The happenings of the week-end were a secret she shared with none but Sandy Lamond, though, when Lisbeth returned to school later in the week, recovered from her influenza, her friend said laconically, "We've lost our little Taters—left to learn electioneering—and Westharbour Academy is a pleasanter place in consequence."

"Yes, I should think so!" agreed Lisbeth with enthusiasm. "Did you hear that story she was spreading around—about my being expelled for furious driving or something?"

"For driving without a licence," corrected Julia. "Yes, the rumour reached me. In fact, she tried to father it on me, but found it wouldn't answer."

"I thought it was merely funny," laughed Lisbeth, "but Daddy was inclined to take it up and make a fuss. However, I had a temperature at the time, and couldn't be bothered with it, and when I got better I found the thing had apparently petered out. Daddy couldn't get any farther with it, and anyhow I *had* been running round without a licence, so I expect he wisely decided it was better to let the matter drop."

"I'm quite sure it was," Julia assented. "He doesn't want the wrong sort of publicity just now. When you come to think of it, there's a humorous side to this bailie-making. Both the candidates go walking about on eggs lest anything should happen to swing the balance of the voting against them. Between your car and Taters' penchant for scandal, your respective parents are putting in a pretty poor time."

Lisbeth laughed carelessly.

"Oh, my licence is all square and shipshape now," she declared, "and what Taters does we need no longer bother about, since we don't need to meet her every day at school. I should think her father might find her talents most useful now that he's going to employ her in this campaign. She'll find out all Daddy's secret schemes and use them against him."

"Has he got any?" asked Julia with curiosity. "I mean—the town knows all about Meadows and what he wants to do to Gallowgate Square if he can only bring it off. Mr. Tait can't make much capital out of plans that are public enough already, though you may be sure he'll do his best."

Lisbeth shook her fair head doubtfully.

"I never really know what Daddy is up to," she confessed. "We don't see eye to eye over his ideas for Colmskirk, so he never tells me any of them now if he thinks I'm going to argue against them. But I've got an uneasy feeling that once he gets in—if he does—he means to splash about a bit."

Julia puckered her brows in a worried fashion.

"I wish you could stop him, Leebie! It won't do either himself or Colmskirk any good."

"I know, my dear, and I wish I could, but—there's the bell! Meet me after games, and we'll go home together on the early train. I want to discuss heaps of things."

Lisbeth's discussions—the accumulation of a fortnight without any—made Julia rather late in reaching home that afternoon, but she found her sister still later with the preparations for tea. Merran was standing by a half-laid table with an open letter in her hand and a look of distress on her face, while William of Orange mewed unheeded about her feet—an outrage, for William of Orange expected his tea at least half an hour before anyone else.

"What's up?" asked Julia, throwing her satchel down on the armchair. "Nothing gone wrong with the last order you sent up to town, I hope? Oh, I see!" as she caught sight of the familiar heading on the notepaper. "But Perry's all right, isn't he?"

"I don't see why you should be so sure of that!" retorted Merran, most unwontedly irritated. "He's just as liable to go wrong as others or anything else. Anyhow, he has this time! and I'm very much worried about him."

Julia gave her a penetrating stare before stooping down to satisfy the requirements of the neglected Bill.

"I'm sorry," she said sympathetically. "What's up? Has he had 'flu, like everybody else? It's some weeks, isn't it, since you heard from him last?"

"Not 'flu—measles. That's why I didn't get a letter. He didn't know whether I'd had it or not. But that's not the worst of it, Judy. Poor lad, his eyes are affected. Measles does that sometimes, you know."

"But not seriously," protested Julia, still feeling that her sister's distress was a little out of proportion. "I've never heard of anyone losing their sight from measles. Hang it all, Merran, he's not going blind!"

"I didn't say he was," replied Merran with dignity. "I said his sight was permanently injured—well, that's what I meant, anyhow. He has seen the very best oculist in London, and was told he'd always have to wear glasses. I don't believe, Julia, you've the least idea what that means to a naval officer—especially a gunnery man. Poor old Perry will have to leave the Service—give up his career and come home to farm Glenbruie—if he knows how, which I don't suppose he does. This letter is to tell me that he has sent in his papers and expects to be back before the end of the month. It's a real tragedy to any man as keen on the Navy as Perry has been from his cradle, and I can't help feeling desperately sorry!"

CHAPTER XXII

"B.B.B.B."

THE Royal and Ancient Burgh of St. Columba's Kirk (to give it the proper title set forth on its charter) was full of a pleasant and exciting stir. In two weeks' time the stir might be less pleasant but much more exciting, for then the battle would be joined in good earnest, and the struggle, towards which they were now moving happily, would determine events in the municipal life of Colmskirk for three years to come—that being the span of a bailie's office.

Hitherto the town had taken these triennial crises very placidly. Officials had fallen due to retire at the end of their time, had stood almost automatically for re-election, and had been as automatically re-elected. Mr. Binnie, for example, had been Provost for nine years, and seemed all set for another nine, and his fellow-townsmen were very well pleased about it. In any case, his position was not in question this autumn, because he and the other bailies had another year of office before them. The impending election was something extra—something outside the usual smooth-running conduct of affairs—and was being caused by the resignation of a certain Mr. Thompson, who had gone to live in the south of England.

Feeling with regard to the two candidates was mounting week by week. Henry Tait, the umbrella manufacturer, was considered harmless inasmuch as he had done nothing so far either to please or upset his fellow-burghers; he had the reputation of being a good business man, and was believed to be a Liberal as far as he had any politics at all; in fact, his was a negative personality, but he was regarded as being safe. Sam Bartle, on the other hand, was far from safe, because he left people with the uncomfortable feeling that it was impossible to say what he might be up to next. True, he gave generously to every good cause, but Colmskirk had learnt to shy away nervously from the various good causes he was eager to start on his own. It was known that he wanted to pull down and rebuild the Burgh Chambers to a strange but striking design. He had already demolished a fine old house at the back of the town and had erected a block of workmen's flats on the site. His scheme for Meadows was only too well known and very little liked, and, but for Dr. Lendrum's daughter, he would soon be playing old Harry with Gallowgate Square.

Altogether, it was felt that Sam Bartle was far too fond of knocking things down, and there was general apprehension as to what he might put up in their place. Merran, who was becoming well liked in the town for her own sake as well as her father's, came in for a good deal of commendation for her firm stand regarding her shop and its site; but Bartle had already bought Meadows, and moreover he now owned the Broomieknowes, though what he could possibly do with that strip of common ground and shingle was beyond his neighbours' imagination. There was a rumour that he meant to graze a flock of goats on it and supply the school-children with free milk; but as they already received that from accredited cows the story was not given much credence. Up to a fortnight before the election day the attitude of Colmskirk was very much, "If we vote for Tait, nothing will happen. If we vote for Bartle, anything may. Better to be on the safe side and keep under Tait's umbrellas."

And then there arose a new feature in the campaign—one that

bewildered all voters equally, for none could fathom its meaning. On all places throughout the town where bills might be stuck, and in many where they might not, there appeared the simple yet mystifying sign, in large letters of coloured paper—"B.B.B.B." Nothing less and nothing more, and with no indication of their meaning and nothing to show who had put them there. For a whole day Colmskirk argued, debated and conjectured, but without arriving at any solution; and next morning four large Bs were painted boldly in red across the plate-glass windows of Bartle's Stores.

"It's some election stunt—it must be!" declared Julia, pausing on her way to the Westharbour train that she might study the glaring legend from different angles. "It isn't on any of the other shop windows."

"But what does it mean?" demanded Violet Stiles, who had been the first among the group of Academy girls to discover it as they were hurrying towards the station. "And is it Mr. Bartle who is putting it up, or the other side? There are groups of four Bs chalked at intervals along the garden wall of Meadows where it joins the Esplanade. It was the first thing I saw when I came out of our gate just now. And of course, Meadows belongs to Mr. Bartle now—worse luck!"

"Nevertheless, it's not he who is putting up all those signs," said Lisbeth coolly, joining them from the side street up which she had come. "I can tell you that much, though I know no more than you what it means. It must be the Tait party who are doing it—and it's beastly cheek to disfigure other people's windows!"

"But it must stand for something," persisted Violet, "or where's the sense in splashing it about at all?"

"There isn't much," retorted Julia. "A slogan that can't be interpreted doesn't help anybody's cause. Come on, girls, or we'll lose that train."

By the time they got back from school, however, the whole town knew that the four Bs must be the work of Mr. Tait and his minions, for they had been expeditiously removed from Bartle's windows and also from the walls of Meadows, only to reappear on Mr. Bartle's own garden wall during the dinner-hour when the place was deserted and nobody about. And by next day there was a crop of calico pennons fluttering from poles dotted up and down the Broomieknowes, each displaying four Bs in varied and gaudy colours, and people racked their brains to guess what they could possibly stand for.

"Nothing very flattering, anyhow," observed Lisbeth, "since we know now who puts them there. I suppose an explanation will follow in the fullness of time—when the Taits think it's most likely to bring them in votes."

"What I don't like," said Julia vigorously, "is that your father is doing nothing to snatch a few for himself. Oh, I know he's addressing meetings, but what's the good of that?"

"It's supposed to be the usual thing to do, isn't it?" demurred Lisbeth. "The customary way of putting your views across to the voters."

"I dare say it is," replied Julia impatiently, "but you know, and I know, that the voters don't like Mr. Bartle's views, and if he's to be made a bailie, the less he says about them the better. I wish you could convince him of that, Leebie, though I don't suppose he'll listen to you. It's only natural, after all."

"But what do you want him to do?" protested Lisbeth. "He must air his ideas, however much we mayn't like them—and mind you, Julia, I don't like some of them any better than you do; but they're his, and he thinks they are grand."

"I know," said Julia. "I said it was only natural; but if he'd just think of something quite different—something that everybody really wants—it would be such a help to his chances. All the same, he'd make a much better bailie than the Tait creature, and therefore I'm keen for him to win. *I* want the best for Colmskirk, too! I'm frightfully fond of the old place, and your father has all the right principles, only they seem to work out wrong somehow. He's generous and he's enthusiastic, and he's stickatitive—there's no end to what he might do if you could only guide him along the right lines."

"You seem to think that's so easy," Lisbeth told her, "but I wish you would try to do it! I'm devoted to Daddy, as you know very well, but when he gets hold of a notion he goes head-on at it like a charging bull, and everything has to get out of the way. I don't know what will happen if Mr. Tait defeats him, because he's keener on getting on that Council than he has ever been about anything—even rebuilding Gallowgate Square."

"I wish I knew," said Julia irrelevantly, "what B.B.B.B. stands for."

Next day, with the rest of Colmskirk, she was assured by posters displayed all over the burgh that she would soon know. The posters were headed by the four Bs so familiar by now, and continued, "You want to discover what these letters signify, and before long you are going to be told. The full meaning will cause the town an unpleasant shock, but it may save you from making a grave mistake. Meanwhile it should interest you to learn that the first B stands for Bartle."

"Which we all know already, in the nature of things," remarked Merran, when Mrs. Stiles came into the shop with this latest bit of news. "It will be more interesting to hear the rest."

Mrs. Stiles assumed the expression of someone-who-knows-a-great-deal-more-than-she-cares-to-say, an expression which she was fond of assuming on all suitable occasions.

"More people than Mr. Bartle begin with B," she said mysteriously. "There are many Colmskirk folk who think Mr.

Binnie has been Provost quite long enough, and that a change would benefit the burgh—and that's two more Bs."

"But this election has nothing to do with the Provost," protested Merran heatedly, "so how could the posters possibly refer to him, especially as you say they admit the first letter stands for Bartle?"

"I didn't say they referred to the Provost," replied Mrs. Stiles with repressive dignity. "I merely said they might. Now, that amethyst clip, Merran, is much too dear. Otherwise I would have bought it for Violet's birthday. However, that wasn't what I came in about. I really wondered if you might have a pair of brass tongs among your antiques that would do for my lounge. Nothing expensive, you know, since of course they will be secondhand; but I should require something really handsome, as they are for the lounge."

"I'm afraid I've got nothing of the sort, Mrs. Stiles," Merran answered, "but you might find a pair at Gregor's."

"Very likely, but his would be new, and he would charge accordingly. I'm not prepared to pay Gregor's fancy prices. Quite sure you haven't got any put away at the back somewhere? Really, you know, Merran, my dear, you are somewhat lacking in enterprise. Brooches and geegaws aren't everything, and you'll never make a living out of articles like that. What's this about Perry Boyd coming home for good?"

The question was shot out with disconcerting suddenness, but Merran, who knew Mrs. Stiles, flattered herself that the lady was never able to catch her unawares.

"I'm sure I don't know what you have heard, Mrs. Stiles," she replied with composure. "The town is full of gossip nowadays."

The bailie's wife reddened.

"That is why I asked you," she answered loftily, "because I

never listen to idle chatter; but I thought that you, being so friendly with Perry, might know the truth of these rumours."

"I know he expects to be home soon," said Merran steadily. "But you will need to wait till he comes and ask him what his plans are. I'm afraid I don't know."

"Ah, well," responded the lady, with studied indifference, "I am naturally interested because he has paid such marked attention to my Mabel when he has been home on leave. Not last summer—Mabel was away then—but on all previous occasions. There was nothing definite between them, of course, but—well, if he is coming back I expect they will be glad to see each other. Good afternoon, Merran, my dear. I hope we shall meet at the Burgh Chambers this evening. These municipal gatherings are so important. I shall look out for you."

And she bustled out, leaving Merran to tidy her tray of small trinkets with a placid smile.

"Mrs. Stiles always hopes to take something away with her, even though she never makes a purchase," she thought, "but I'm afraid she finds me rather disappointing these days. I didn't even rise to the hint about Mabel and her understanding with Perry!"

CHAPTER XXIII

JULIA TAKES THE WRONG TRAIN

JULIA was monitress for the week in her form-room, and considered this a doubtful privilege, as it meant that she was the last to leave it in the afternoon, being responsible for the state in which it was left, and therefore more than likely to miss the train by which the Colmskirk girls usually travelled home. This entailed waiting nearly three-quarters of an hour for the return of the other part of the train, which was detached at Westharbour Town and ran down to the Harbour station to meet an incoming boat. Julia had no fancy for hanging about on a dull, deserted platform with no occupation and plenty of work to be done at home; so she contrived for the first part of the week, through judicious planning, to catch the train by its tail and tumble into the last compartment just as the guard's whistle blew. On Thursday, however, there had been more than the usual amount of tidying to do, so Julia had given up the train for lost, and was agreeably surprised on reaching the station to see it slowly getting under way.

It was a case for acting promptly or not at all, so Julia acted. With one bound she was across the platform and, despite the indignant porter's shouts, she sprang on the footboard of the last carriage, wrenched open the door, and hurled herself in, sprawling, across the seat. When she had recovered her balance, straightened her hat, and collected the scattered contents of her satchel, she discovered with astonishment that she was alone in the compartment usually so full of her schoolfellows. Not even Lisbeth was there—Lisbeth, who made a point of being at hand to pull her in on the last mad scramble.

Then, as the train gathered way, Julia understood this strange desertion. For instead of puffing steadily on towards Kirkarlie, the next place on the line, it swerved left abruptly and began to run down the long railway pier among a labyrinth of docks and iron sheds. This carriage, which she had boarded with so much haste and agility, was in the hinder part of the train—the part that had pulled into the platform after the departure of the first portion filled largely with Academy girls. Julia had missed it, after all.

"Oh, well," she thought philosophically, slumping into a corner, "I was too late anyhow, and I may as well spend the time trundling down to the harbour and back in a comfortable compartment as kicking my heels on that cold platform. And since it will be quite fifty minutes now before we get to Colmskirk, I may as well use them profitably by doing a spot of prep."

She took the book she wanted from her bag and was soon absorbed in translating Hugo's "Les Miserables," heedless of the long wait on the dockside for the Irish boat to make its way in and discharge its passengers. There were not many, and no one came as far as the end of the train where she was ensconced, though two people presently got in next door to her, with a good deal of laughter and loud chattering, in which Julia, disturbed at her studies, recognized with impatient disgust the familiar accents of Gracie Tait. The carriage was an old-fashioned one whose divisions did not quite reach the roof, and every word came plainly through to her reluctant ears, defying all hope of further concentration. Taters had evidently been sent to meet some relative arriving by the steamer, and was giving him all the latest family news with much gusto and enjoyment.

"You'll be here, too, when Pa's made a bailie," she informed him. “That’s going to be something to write home about, I can tell you! There’s another man standing against him. Quaint old bird, wallowing in wealth, and only asking for the chance to spill it over Colmskirk—to his own advantage, be it said! Oh, yes, what Sam Bartle does for the town is all in the nature of an investment, though he makes out he’s very generous. Well, it’s the kind of generosity that pays handsome cash profits.”

Julia abandoned the adventures of Jean Valjean, since it was now quite impossible to fix her mind on anything but Taters’ informative talk, and set herself shamelessly to eavesdrop. Indeed, it was quite impossible to avoid doing so, as the other girl’s excited chatter ran on behind the partition. The train had started off again, and one or two sentences were lost, but soon she heard her late classmate announcing triumphantly: “It’s the best stunt out, and I’m fearfully bucked that I’ve been the one to think of it. I believe in going about with my ears cocked, and that was how I picked it up—through a friend who works in a house-agent’s office. She knows for a fact that Sam Bartle is planning to put up bungalows on the Broomieknowes—a lot of common little shanties right on Colmskirk’s most select sea-front! He has bought the ground, so he can do what he likes with it; but he won’t—till after the election—not he!”

“But the townsfolk won’t stand for that,” a man’s voice protested. “The fellow won’t get a single vote if it leaks out before the election. Your father’s as good as a bailie already.”

“Of course—we know that,” returned Taters jubilantly. “But Bartle will keep it dark, and we shan’t give him away till the last moment—when it will be too late for him to make any counter-move or deny what he’s scheming to do. Then Pa’s coming down on him! But it’s the way he means to do it that’s such a scream!”

The man’s voice rumbled something which was evidently a query, but the train rattled over some points at that moment into

Westharbour Town, and Julia lost the first part of the reply. What she did hear, however, as they pulled up at the platform, was quite enough for her purpose.

"… B.B.B.B. all over the place in big coloured letters with spaces between, to be filled in the night before the poll … Oh! it's simple enough, but it'll make them all sit up, and he won't be able to say it isn't true. No, I shouldn't think he'll get a single vote once they see it—and it was all my idea! Pa was no end pleased when I suggested it. 'Bartle to Build Bungalows on the Broomieknowes'—that ought to fetch the municipal electors!"

The train had stopped by now, and a number of people got into Taters' compartment, putting a stop to all further confidences for the remainder of the short journey. Julia was relieved that no acquaintance got in beside her to strike up a conversation, for it was important that her own voice should not in turn be recognized by Gracie; it would never do for that young woman to realize how completely she had given away herself and her designs to Lisbeth Bartle's friend. Julia saw plainly now that she had underestimated Miss Tait's talent for low cunning, and if she knew this fine scheme had been discovered, she might think up another and more deadly one before next week.

"And what Sandy said about her previous little effort," thought Julia sagaciously, "is perfectly true—once a lie gets a start it's not so easy to overtake it. Why, if I hadn't chanced to overhear all this, that slogan would have been painted in during the eve of the poll, and before it could be contradicted half the town might have voted—all the early birds, anyhow!"

As they steamed into Colmskirk her brain was very busy—but not with French translation—and she sat on for a moment after they had reached the terminus to give Taters and her uncle time to pass the ticket barrier before she herself got to it; after which she hurried home by a detour that avoided Main Street.

"Safety first!" she thought. "If I ran into that little serpent suddenly round a corner I believe she'd see in my eye or somehow that I'd found her out. That's the worst of having such an expressive countenance—it lets you down at awkward moments."

It so happened that it was not Taters whom she ran into round a corner, but Lieutenant Peregrine Boyd, R.N. (retired)—and bearing his retirement writ large, not only in his dark glasses, but all through the inert listlessness of his figure. So different did he look from the vigorous, alert sailor who had come so often to the Serendipity Shop during the previous summer that Julia, her mind full of other things, was taken off her guard, and uttered a little cry of dismay before she could stop herself.

"What's the matter?" he asked with a faint grin. "Think you'd seen a ghost?"

"Not exactly," faltered Julia, "but—but I wasn't expecting you—didn't even know you were back—so it gave me a bit of a shock to trip over you like that."

"You're not half up to it," he assured her with a touch of bitterness. "Why not tell me, as Mrs. Stiles did just now, that my glasses are *so* distinguished-looking?"

"Because I don't think they are," replied Julia bluntly. "But as they're only temporary, of course, what does it matter?"

"How do you know they're only temporary?"

"Dark glasses always are. The truth is, Perry, that I'm burdened with a guilty secret, and I'm hurrying home to discuss it with Merran. Come back with me, and we'll all discuss it over tea. I'm frightfully late because I got into the boat part of the train by mistake at Westharbour—but on the whole, perhaps, it's just as well I did."

Perry fell into step with her, finding it unnecessary to remark that he had been bound for the Serendipity Shop in any case.

"What is this guilt which lies heavy on your soul?" he inquired, forcing a show of interest, his mind being really on the sort of welcome he might expect from Merran.

"It doesn't lie on my soul at all," replied Julia briskly, "because it isn't my guilt. But if I don't do something about it there's going to be a most unholy mess at the Burgh Council election next week, and what to do I don't quite know. That's what I want to talk over with Merran, and it is all very awkward. One mercy is that she must have shut the shop by now, so we'll have a little peace."

"I thought of that myself," admitted Perry simply. "I only got back last night, and I can't be bothered explaining myself to everybody. That's the worst of belonging to a small town where everyone knows you."

Julia nodded sympathetically.

"All the same, it was careless of you to run into Mrs. Stiles. Nobody in all Colmskirk is quite so curious, or troubles less to hide it. Let's go round here and in by the workroom. I expect Merran has got tea ready and waiting."

He followed her somewhat diffidently into the cosy, fire-lit kitchen, where, as she had predicted, the evening meal was laid and ready; but it was empty, Merran having gone upstairs on some errand.

Julia flicked on the light.

"Sit down and get warm," she said hospitably, "while I call Merran. I shan't be a moment. I don't think William of Orange will mind you, even though you are a man—he must remember you from last summer."

Upstairs in Merran's room, where she arrived a trifle breathless, she said, "Perry's downstairs—got back last night—but, oh, Merran, do be careful not to let him see you notice any difference. I came on him suddenly and squealed out because I was so taken aback. Somehow he looks almost shattered, and I don't know how to cope with it—you may."

Merran slipped a slide into her brown hair and powdered her nose carefully.

"I'll try," she said. "Thanks for warning me;" and while Julia went to wash her hands, she ran lightly down the narrow staircase and pushed open the door at the foot of it.

Perry was standing before the fire, one hand on the high mantelshelf, while with his foot he gently rubbed the tummy of the recumbent Bill. Merran swallowed hard at the sight of the dark glasses, then hastened forward to meet him, throwing all she knew of welcome into her eager voice.

"Why, Perry, how jolly to have you back! I'd no idea you were coming so soon. But you must have lots to plan and arrange, and it will all be so new and interesting. Sit down and tell me about it while I make the tea. Julia will be ready directly."

CHAPTER XXIV

JULIA BEARDS THE LION

PERRY, as he drank hot tea and ate soda scones spread liberally with bramble jelly, began to feel a slight glow of comfort arising from the homely atmosphere around him. He had known nothing so cheery since his calamity had first come upon him, and yet there was no open show of sympathy. Both girls, indeed, treated him as they had done before he had joined his ship—little knowing that it was for the last time—and showed a lively interest, which was plainly quite natural and sincere, in his plans for farming at Glenbruie; they behaved, he felt, as though he had left the Navy freely of his own accord, so that he might, for preference, take up the life of a landlubber.

Then suddenly Julia's agile mind switched back to its own problems, and she exclaimed, "This is all immensely absorbing, but I haven't told you yet what happened on my way back from school to-day; and I need your advice badly, because I'm afraid it's up to me to do something about it, and to do it quickly—and I don't quite know how."

"Is it that guilty secret of someone else's?" asked Perry encouragingly. "It should be interesting to listen to—but need you do anything about it if it isn't yours?"

"Well, somebody must," retorted Julia. "Merran, I've discovered what B.B.B.B. means," and she gave them a full account of her afternoon's adventures, to which Perry listened with growing amusement and Merran with dismay.

"But, Judy," she exclaimed when the tale was finished, "if that isn't stopped at once—if those Tait people are allowed to get away with it—it will ruin Mr. Bartle in Colmskirk—ruin him completely! He won't be able to live in the town, much less sit on its Council."

"I don't know why that should break your heart," remarked Perry. "Hasn't he done all he could to freeze you out so that he might buy up your premises when he'd driven you to bankruptcy?"

Both girls laughed.

"The Binnies call her 'Miss Naboth,'" said Julia, but Merran answered:

"It isn't as bad as all that, Perry. I admit he tries to undersell me in his own stores, and won't let me gather pebbles from his foreshore—oh, and he has tried to annoy me in a dozen ways, hoping that I may give up my work and be glad to let him buy the place; but I really believe it's because he doesn't take me seriously, nor realize that I am working for my bread and butter. He thinks it's just a whim or a hobby. If Daddy had been a porter on the pier instead of a doctor, Mr. Bartle would have treated me very differently."

"There's something in that," agreed Julia. "I've always said he wasn't a bad old thing at heart, or Lisbeth wouldn't think such a lot of him. He was probably spoilt as a child."

"After all," added Merran, "he hasn't done me much harm. The things I make attract far more customers than the stuff on his trinket counter, though I says it as shouldn't; and his beach hasn't got all the pebbles, though it has the prettiest, for some odd reason. Anyhow, Julia, there's nothing else for it—you must put on your coat again and go straight over to his house at once. He'll have to hear this whole story, just as you have told it to us.

He'll lose enough votes over Meadows and his other blunders, without having to suffer for that appalling lie about the Broomieknowes. Go at once, and you can sit up later to finish your prep. Perry will help me with the washing up, won't you, Perry?"

"I don't think Mrs. Stiles would like him to," murmured Julia demurely, "but that's neither here nor there. It's a mercy I did some of my French in the train."

She hurried out again into the gathering shadows and rising wind which was sweeping up-Firth from the south-west, driving herds of white horses before it. Along sheltered by-roads she sped until forced out on to the road-bridge over Robin Water and up the short steep brae beyond, where she met the full force of the breeze across the Broomieknowes, and had to push her way head on to it along the verge of the rough grass, till the road bent in a little at the gate of a grey, rambling house with big, rounded windows. Julia hastened up the short entry to the door and rang the bell. It was the first time she had been to Lisbeth's home, for there was a tacit understanding between the girls that Merran's sister could not go there while Sam Bartle continued his campaign against Merran, though Lisbeth herself was always welcome at the Serendipity Shop.

"Is Mr. Bartle in?" Julia asked the maid who answered the door. "Then do you think he would see me, please? Will you tell him Miss Julia Lendrum wants to speak to him about the Burgh election?"

The maid showed her into a small, rather bleak room, obviously used for business purposes, since it looked much more like an office than a study. In the distance she could hear Lisbeth practising, which was a cheery, reassuring sound; not that Julia at any time suffered from nervousness, but she was acutely conscious of Sam Bartle's unfriendliness towards anybody of the name of Lendrum, though Lisbeth might maintain, and with truth, that it was only because of their shop's situation.

Presently she heard a heavy tread in the hall outside, and at the same time Lisbeth's music stopped and her voice called to her father. The next minute they both entered together, and Sam Bartle announced gruffly, "I brought Lisbeth along, young lady, when I heard you were inquiring for me. Thought perhaps there might be some mistake. Oh, yes, the girl did say something about election business, but I doubted she hadn't got it right."

"But she had," confirmed Julia, who was standing where the light fell full on her dark, wind-tossed curls and eager, piquant face flushed from her struggle against the buffeting sou'wester. Lisbeth, knowing her well enough to scent her excitement, waited for more. "I've got news of the election which my sister and I felt you ought to know at once, so she sent me round to tell you. I've found out what the four Bs stand for, and you will probably want to take steps about it as soon as possible."

"Take steps about what?" She could see that his interest was roused. "I'm not a man who's keen on taking steps, if you mean starting up unnecessary rows among the townsfolk."

Lisbeth, who was holding on to his arm, gave it a reproving little shake.

"I've told you, Daddy, that for a hard-headed business man you've got the daftest ideas of running an election!"

"I pay an agent to take steps," he growled. "Lawson knows about this sort of thing, and I don't. Why should I take steps?"

"To stop lies being put about," said Julia clearly. "And this is a much worse lie than the one about Lisbeth being expelled, though it comes from the same quarter. 'B.B.B.B.' stands for 'Bartle to Build Bungalows on the Broomieknowes,' and the night before the polling they mean to fill in the blanks between the letters with those very words!"

She paused dramatically, and Lisbeth uttered a stifled exclamation of wrath; but to the surprise of both girls, Mr. Bartle threw back his head with a loud laugh.

"But that isn't a lie, young lady," he cried. "That's the truth, though maybe it's a bit premature. So they've got hold of that, have they, and they think it'll do me harm at the poll. Shows how little they know about it, or what's good for Colmskirk. Darned pretty bungalows of the most up-to-date type, and on the best situation in the town, too. Why, they'll be no end of a draw!"

Lisbeth dropped his arm, and the girls stared at him absolutely stunned, but Julia was the first to recover.

"I can see you're not joking, Mr. Bartle," she said slowly and gravely, "though for a moment I thought you must be. Do you actually believe the people of Colmskirk will stand for building on one of the place's beauty-spots? The Broomieknowes are unique—there's nothing like them up and down the coast. That stretch of greensward all golden with broom that can be seen from miles away on the Firth! And think of the people whose houses stand right along it, and whose view means so much to them—your own being one of them."

"I hope I shouldn't be so selfish as to hold on to my view at the expense of the burgh," growled Mr. Bartle; but she could see that he was a little less certain of himself. Her horror had startled him somewhat—had, perhaps, opened his eyes for the first time to what his fellow-townsfolk might think of this, his latest plan for benefiting them despite themselves.

Discussing it afterwards at home, Julia declared that that was the moment when she realized in a flash "what was missing in Mr. Bartle's make-up." The man had been created without any imagination, and it was this lack that lay at the bottom of all his blunders, turning his good intents and generous impulses to offences in the eyes of those whom he wished to please.

"And it was revealed to me, then and there," she informed Merran dramatically, "that I was meant to supply it to him—to deliver Colmskirk, once for all, from his bungling goodwill, and himself from having it go sour on him whenever he tries to undertake anything big and philanthropic. I felt so exactly like Joan of Arc that it almost turned me dizzy for a minute. *Now* I know what it means to receive a call to some special service—like nursing or the mission-field!"

And having received it, Julia (Julia-like) responded promptly and without hesitation.

"Mr. Bartle, do please listen to me!" she begged, so earnestly that his attention was arrested at once. "Nobody would be selfish who wanted to keep the Broomieknowes as they are, because they are a thing of beauty that belongs to everybody—not just to the people who live on them, but to all the townspeople who come to sit there in the evenings among the broom and the hawthorn—old bodies who can't climb the paths in the park and tired ones who haven't the energy to go any farther. Oh, and everyone who passes out yonder on the boats and sees how pleasant and homely it looks. All that power of giving pleasure belongs to you now, but if you destroy it with rows of bungalows, who will be the better for that?"

"Why, the families who come to live in 'em, of course, and the shops where they spend their money. Besides, look you here, Miss Julia. I'm not a mean man, and I'm out to give Colmskirk the best of everything. Those bungalows would bring me in a pretty penny, and I'm prepared to use the whole grand investment for the good and development of the burgh—plough it back, in fact. What do you think of that now?"

"I think," said Julia simply, "that it would be perfectly appalling!"

Sam Bartle glared at her more in sorrow than in anger.

"Well, I'm blest!" he ejaculated. "Yet you look like a lassie who has all her wits about her!"

Lisbeth smothered an irresistible desire to giggle. As the onlooker she saw most of the humour in this encounter.

"Oh, I can assure you she has, Daddy!" she interposed. "There are no flies on Julia! You'd better hear what she has to say about it. You're always out for ideas, and that's what Julia has got—heaps and heaps of them!"

"Then," retorted her parent, "I can only say they appear to be most peculiar!"

"But you haven't heard any of them," protested Julia. "I believe if you were to adopt some straight away you might win the election yet. There isn't too much time left, but it could be done."

"And you don't think I can win it without?"

"I'm not so conceited as that," said Julia seriously, "but I'm absolutely certain you'll lose every vote in the place if this business about the Broomieknowes gets out. You're going to make it into a Tom Tiddler's ground where you can pick gold and silver—oh, I know you mean to spend it on Colmskirk, but no one in Colmskirk will thank you for it. They'd rather have the gold and silver that grows there now—broom and hawthorn and daisies and birdsfoot trefoil. Why, the Burgh Council have always planned to keep the new bungalows at the back of the town where their newness can't spoil anything."

"Pack of nonsense!" snorted Mr. Bartle. "When I'm a bailie, now—"

"But that's what you never will be," interrupted Julia desperately, "if you insist on doing things and building things that nobody can bear! Believe it or not, Mr. Bartle, I'm frightfully keen that you should win, because you could do such lots for the town, and Mr. Tait never will. That's why I came here to-night to warn you about the four Bs. Can't you see that the other side are staking all their hopes on wrecking your chance by it? That ought to show you! We've got to put our wits in step and think of some way to circumvent them, or you'll never get on the Burgh Council."

"Well, I'm blest!" reiterated Mr. Bartle feebly. "I've never known anyone who talked so much, or used so many grand words for her age! But it was good of you to come—I will say that—it was good of you to come, under the circumstances, even if those ideas of yours that Leebie talks about are altogether out of the question. Sit down, now, and let's hear some of them. Tell me, for instance, how you'd set about becoming a bailie if it was up to you?"

CHAPTER XXV

"B.B.B.B.B."

Julia slipped into a chair beside the office table, paused for a minute to take breath, and then plunged straight into the programme which rose before her mind's eye.

"First of all," she declared, "I'd hold a public meeting—in the Burgh Chambers if I could get them, on the Esplanade if I couldn't—but I shouldn't put it off another minute! I'd call it for to-morrow night—Friday would be quite a good evening—and I'd tell everybody there and then exactly what I meant to do for the town."

"Hold hard a minute, young lady," interposed Mr. Bartle. "You can't call a public meeting without putting out posters to announce the place and hour. So you couldn't call it for to-morrow night because there wouldn't be time to get the posters up and showing. And you certainly wouldn't get the Burgh Chambers at such short notice. Even if you were to make it Monday—"

"Monday's much too late," interrupted Julia in her turn. "Tait's people are well away with it already, and we know they're quite unscrupulous. We've got to act quickly if we're to prevent them from circulating this B.B.B.B. lie, so the Esplanade will just have to do."

"But I've explained to you that it isn't a lie. It's gospel truth, and should be one of the best planks in my campaign."

Julia withered him with a glance.

Mr. Bartle

"There's not much gospel about it, and it can't continue to be truth unless you want to lose the election. Ask anybody or everybody, if you don't believe me; but if you take my advice you won't wait to ask at all—besides, it's most essential that no one should guess you were even thinking of such a thing. Safety first! That's why the meeting must be to-morrow night—so that you can come out into the open right away, and the voters will know where they are."

"But," demurred Mr. Bartle. "I'm not on in this. We're discussing what *you* would do if you were to stand for a bailie-ship."

"We can't afford to trifle about it," Julia told him firmly. "It's your affairs we're discussing, and I'm only offering a few suggestions. Oh, Mr. Bartle, we must get you in, and it's absolutely necessary to have that meeting not a minute later than to-morrow night—please say you'll call it!"

"But the posters can't—"

"I know they can't. We must do without posters, and I've thought of a much better plan—one that will catch everyone's attention. We must dress someone up as a town-crier and send him round all the streets and by-lanes with a megaphone, proclaiming that there's to be a meeting on the Esplanade opposite the church at seven-thirty p.m., and that everybody's invited."

For once Sam Bartle was struck dumb, but Lisbeth clapped her hands excitedly.

"What a marvellous idea! I told you she had them, Daddy. It'll be a tremendous draw—and you've got a good voice for open-air speaking."

Mr. Bartle settled himself farther back in his chair.

"Perhaps, when you're about it," he said grimly, "you might like to tell me what I'm to say. It's just possible you mightn't approve of any speech I planned to make."

"I'm afraid perhaps we mightn't," agreed Julia gently—"not if it was about those bungalows. You see, it's terribly important not to make any mistake now, with only a week and a day left before the polling."

"I should say!" he assented sarcastically. "But what am I to do with the Broomieknowes now I've bought 'em? Are they to be another bad investment, like Gallowgate Square?"

Julia coloured.

"I've been giving a great deal of thought to Gallowgate Square," she assured him earnestly. "My sister and I are both very worried about it, and she doesn't want to be an obstructionist; but I'll tell you about that presently, because it would be another excellent thing to put in your speech if it took your fancy. Meantime, we must decide at once what to do with the Broomieknowes, because they're a big opportunity which mustn't be wasted."

"I'm glad you think so," replied Mr. Bartle, still heavily sarcastic. "Personally, I know of only one thing to do with them; but you may have one of your ideas coming on."

"I think I have," said Julia slowly, and leaning her elbows on the table she propped her head on her hands. "You really did buy them for the good of Colmskirk, didn't you, not just as a business proposition?"

"Well, I kind of worked it out as being one and the same thing. Thought they might earn big money to be ploughed back into the burgh."

Julia sighed, finding herself once more up against this lack of imagination that was cramping all his generous impulses.

"But you do agree, don't you," she said persuasively, "that one can do good in other ways than with money? I'm quite sure you agree with me there?"

"Of course he does," broke in Lisbeth with promptitude. "You do, don't you, Daddy?"

"So you say, my dear—otherwise I mightn't be so sure of it myself. Money's a mighty big help if you're out to benefit anything or anybody."

Julia looked up, her eyes shining again, and Lisbeth knew that an inspiration had been born.

"Of course it is! Only money could have bought that bit of land and shore, but now you've got it, Mr. Bartle, wouldn't it be a gorgeous scheme if you gave it to Colmskirk as it stands? You could get Sandy—I mean, Lamond and Beith would draw up a deed of gift for you, something to show it was your donation to the Royal and Ancient Burgh—and then no one could ever take it away from them or spoil it in any way."

"By building bungalows?" suggested Sam Bartle drily.

"Yes, certainly. But if you like, there might be a few comfy seats dotted about for old stiff people who couldn't sit on the grass. Or even a drinking-fountain, if it wasn't too blatant. Oh, Mr. Bartle, can't you see how it would take all the wind out of the Taters' sails? And the townspeople would simply love it—you'd romp in with a thumping majority!"

Sam Bartle's small eyes suddenly glittered. At last Julia had managed to strike a spark from that dull imagination.

"By George!" he exclaimed in tones that were half awed, half surprised, "I believe there's something in that after all! And a concrete walk along that bank above the edge of the shore—and maybe a shelter or two."

"We could see about the details later," said Julia hastily. "The great thing is to fix up the meeting as fast as possible for to-morrow evening. Do you think you could get in touch with your agent at once, Mr. Bartle? I know it's latish, of course, but it's so urgent."

Mr. Bartle put out his hand to draw the telephone towards him across the table.

"It's never too late for what's necessary," he replied firmly. "If we can do that town-crier stunt we'll get a crowd all right, and I'll show 'em what B.B.B.B. means!"

It was Julia's turn to clap her hands.

"We'll put a fifth B on to them," she cried. "Leebie, we could go out and do it ourselves to-night when our prep's finished. Then *we* shall fill in the spaces on the posters the night before the poll, and in the morning they'll read, 'Bartle Buys the Broomieknowes to Benefit the Burgh.' Isn't that a grand idea?"

"One of your best!" exclaimed Lisbeth. "Daddy, what did I tell you? Oh, between us we'll get you in, never fear!"

"We'll see, we'll see," responded her father in his driest tones. "I allow there's something in it. And now I'll trouble you to let me 'phone Lawson. No, don't go, Miss Julia, if you can spare me a bit more of your valuable time. You said you'd another idea—about the square—and I've a fancy to hear it."

The girls waited in silence while he issued terse instructions to an astonished agent at the other end of the wire, and finished them with the information, "I'm trying out a new line at the eleventh hour, Lawson, and I'm expecting to win the election on it. But I'll explain it all to you when I come round to-morrow morning. What's that? Meadows? No, it's nothing to do with Meadows. Unpopular in the town? That's what you tell me, but they'll soon learn to think differently when I get it going. Yes—I'll have more chance and a bigger say when I'm on the Council. All right, then—you get cracking with those arrangements for to-morrow evening."

He hung up the receiver and turned back to the two girls.

"Chap's possessed with the idea that I'll lose on my plans for Meadows. Says the town's full of some silly-ass prejudice against having a fun-fair at all, let alone on that particular spot. Lot of ignorant fools! Site's perfect for it—all those grounds running right down to the front and a big house that can be adapted quite easily. I don't know why it is," added Mr. Bartle pathetically, "that whenever I try to do the place a good turn I'm up against it at once. Most disheartening—that's what it is!"

He looked so like a big disappointed child that all Julia's mother-instincts were at once aroused.

"Never you mind, Mr. Bartle," she said soothingly. "It's just a case of misunderstanding, that's all, and we can soon put it right if you'll listen to me. It really isn't much use trying to give them a fun-fair when they don't want it; but there are heaps of other things they do want, and they'll be tremendously grateful to you if you give them any of those."

"I seem to remember," he said slowly, "you making a suggestion to me about a hospital. I've turned it over in my mind, and there may be something in it. Not that I say I'm going to do anything about it—oh, no. That would mean buying another site, and sure as eggs are eggs they'd find something wrong with that. Unless, I suppose, I was to take you with me to choose it!"

Julia beamed upon him kindly, and ignored the sarcasm.

"I'll always be delighted to help you in any way I can," she replied, with becoming modesty. "But about Gallowgate Square, now—"

"You weren't thinking of advising me to put up a hospital there?"

"Oh dear, no! If you did it would back on to the old kirkyard and other unsuitable things. Besides, that wasn't what you bought it for. Didn't you say you wanted to move your store there?"

"I certainly did. Had it all planned out," he went on in aggrieved tones. "Sort of place that people would come from far and near to deal at. Something unique. Pillars running from pavement to roof, and plate-glass—I was preparing to spend a young fortune on plate-glass. Even thought of an escalator—just a short one, but it would have given the place a tone."

Julia sternly controlled her shudder, but it was Lisbeth who exclaimed, "But, Daddy, there would have been nothing unique in that. It's the type of store you'd find in any town. Nobody would look twice at it except to wonder what it was doing in a little place like Colmskirk."

Sam Bartle's jaw dropped a little.

"Eh?" he said. "Not unique? Well, I'm blest! What would you call unique, then?"

"I'll tell you," struck in Julia crisply. "At least, I've never heard of anything like this idea of mine, and if only you could bring it off, I'm sure people would come miles to see it just out of curiosity; and then when they got inside they'd buy—you would know how to make them. Don't pull down the cottages, Mr. Bartle. Leave their outsides just as they are, with fresh paint and whitewash, and new thatching; but take out all their insides and fit them up each as a different department of your store, with a connecting corridor running the length of the square behind. Keep the departments all in character, each like a separate village shop on its own and each with a separate sign hanging above its door; any artist would paint them for you—a crinoline lady over the haberdashery, a flock of sheep over the woollens—"

"Over the toy-shop a picture of tin soldiers marching to a band," added Lisbeth excitedly, "and a cosy fireside scene above the chair-covers and cretonnes—"

"A huge metal pot over the ironmongery," chimed in Bartle, rapidly kindling to the vision put before him, "and for the provisions, a fat prize pig! Couldn't do better. Gosh, Miss Julia, there's something in that! Do you think your sister would agree to come in on it under those conditions? Because, if so, Gallowgate Square needn't be wasted after all. Well, I'm blest! Lisbeth wasn't so far wrong when she talked about your ideas."

Julia rose to her feet with a glance at the clock.

"I'm very glad you like them, Mr. Bartle," she said demurely, "and I shall try to think up some more, if they're of any use to you. I can't answer for Merran, but I'm quite sure she'd work in with you in any way she could, even though she still kept her corner—and that wouldn't matter if you no longer wished to rebuild the square. I must go home now and get on with my prep, if Lisbeth and I are to go out later and stick on those additional Bs; but I'll be at your meeting to-morrow evening prepared to cheer like mad!"

CHAPTER XXVI

MR. BARTLE SEES THE GALLOWS-MOUND

It was Wednesday—early-closing day—and Merran, having closed a little earlier than usual, had eaten her midday meal with more speed than common sense, and appealed to Julia to wash up.

"You don't mind, do you? The days are so short now, and I'm going over to Inchmore to hunt for pebbles in that little cove where we found them before."

"I don't mind a scrap," responded Julia cheerfully, "but even so, you can't get across till the steamer takes you, and she won't be in for a good hour."

Merran looked a little self-conscious as she picked up the brown bag in which she usually brought back her finds.

"I'm not waiting for the boat," she replied with elaborate carelessness. "Perry said he'd take me over in *Fiammetta*. It will save a lot of time in every way, as he'll make straight for the cove, and I shan't have that long walk round from the pier."

"It's an excellent suggestion," Julia agreed with dancing eyes, "if you put on all the warmest clothes you've got. Remember it won't be exactly balmy if you're not back before sundown—but I expect you won't care much!"

"Not if I'm lucky with my stones," replied her sister innocently. "Sure you don't mind, Judy? Then I'll dash off at once. Perry said he'd have the boat waiting for me about two o'clock."

Julia waved good-bye to her from the door, and went back to clear the table.

"I don't suppose," she remarked confidentially to William of Orange, "many people are as keen on sailing as I am; but I'm hanged if I'd go out in an open sailing-boat on a November afternoon, with the temperature near freezing-point. To be in love must have a very exhilarating effect on one's circulation. I wish it was the same with public meetings, but I'm sadly afraid there won't be much of an audience at Mr. Bartle's this evening. It's quite true that people don't take enough interest in local politics to put themselves about, and they won't come out in a cold wind just to hear speeches."

She shook her head regretfully as she bent over the sink, for there was no doubt that her candidate had been gaining ground since she had taken him in hand five days before. The improvised town-crier had proved as great a success as Lisbeth had foreseen, and Mr. Bartle, inspired by the big attendance, had made an excellent speech at the impromptu meeting on the Esplanade. He had certainly not "come out into the open" with his plans, as Julia had urged, but he had admitted that he was ready to abandon his first scheme for Gallowgate Square, and had hinted at the possibility of providing a hospital for the burgh if someone else would provide the site—"choosing sites not being my long suit, apparently," he had finished, with a wry smile amid ironical applause. All this Julia had taken down in shorthand, leaning on the bonnet of Lisbeth's car, and had rushed it round to the office of the local paper that evening, where she cajoled the sub-editor into making room for it.

"I know you've practically gone to press," she told him kindly, "and it's frightfully inconvenient to squeeze in anything else at the eleventh hour—but think how urgent this is! It's really the first decent speech Mr. Bartle has made, and the *Colmskirk Herald* must print it. Above all things, a local paper should be right on the spot, and you won't be, this week, if you haven't got this."

"But, Miss Julia," protested the sub-editor, whose father had dispensed Dr. Lendrum's medicines, "I simply haven't allowed for it. Eleventh hour is right! If anyone had warned me it was likely to be coming in I might have saved half a column now—"

"I couldn't warn you, Tom, because I didn't know myself; but you must see how important it is. This speech shows a distinct change in Mr. Bartle's policy. I shouldn't wonder if he were to give up his previous notions and start benefiting the town according to its own ideas and not his."

"What?" demanded Tom Mason, suddenly awaking to the fact that he was being presented with something like a scoop. "If that's true, Miss Julia, you've got hold of something!"

"That's just what I've been trying to explain to you," she told him patiently. "Now, will you find room for my report?"

He took the paper from her and glanced down it with a practised eye.

"I might hold over that notice Mrs. Stiles sent in of her forthcoming 'Bring-and-Buy,'" he observed thoughtfully. "It doesn't come off anyhow, for another two weeks—but she won't be pleased."

"Probably not," agreed Julia. "Quite often she isn't, and I shouldn't think once more would make much difference. But it will matter a lot if the town makes any mistake in its voting next Saturday. Mr. Bartle is in a marvellous mood just now, and if only we make him bailie, I imagine he'd give us almost anything!"

"Do you think," asked the sub-editor, eyeing her keenly, "he'd give us a free library—with help from the Carnegie Grant, of course?"

"I believe it's just the sort of thing he'd love to give us," said

Julia promptly. "Would it affect the voting, do you think, if people heard he was considering an idea like that?"

"I'm quite sure it would. There's a crying need here for a good library, and so far nobody has bothered to do a thing. We keep on getting letters about it. If Sam Bartle's a friend of yours—"

"Well, his daughter is—and I am in touch with him. Get that report of mine in somehow, Tom, and I'll see what I can do. I might at least put the library into his head and leave it to simmer. One thing I can tell you—if you need to be told—Tait won't spend a brass farthing on the burgh if he gets in, for all his brollies! But if Mr. Bartle could be guided away from his mad-cat schemes for fun-fairs and glass-house polytechnics, there's no saying what he mightn't do; he's tremendously generous."

"I dare say," mused Tom, "I might re-write my leader—there's still time—and drop a hint or two about the advantages of having Sam Bartle on the Town Council. I don't mind telling you, Miss Julia, I'd do a lot for any chap who'd help us towards a library."

Julia chuckled to herself now as she dried the dishes, thinking of that leading article and the pleasure it had given Mr. Bartle, as described later by Lisbeth. The town, too, was agog over the fifth B which had appeared wherever there had hitherto been four. It was soon known that this, in some mysterious way, was Bartle's retort to Tait's equally cryptic slogan. Only two and a half days remained before the polling, and this evening was to see Sam Bartle's big meeting in the Burgh Chambers, which he had booked six weeks before. Julia was going there to practise her shorthand, though she knew that this time there would be a properly accredited reporter from the *Colmskirk Herald*.

"And I hope to goodness Mr. Bartle will make some sort of reference to a free library," she thought, as she put the last plate back into the rack. "He didn't exactly turn it down when I suggested it to him, but neither did he leap at it. So much depends on to-night, and I believe the wind is dropping, so we might get a good crowd after all. He must put his cards on the table and give them something to take away and vote about—something really tempting."

A loud knock sounded on the shop door, and she hurried through to answer it. Outside on the pavement stood the subject of her thoughts, broad and burly in his thick check overcoat.

"Is your sister in, Miss Julia?" he inquired, peering past her a trifle nervously into the shadows behind.

"No, Mr. Bartle; I'm sorry, but I'm afraid she won't be back just yet. She has gone across to Inchmore to hunt for pebbles."

He looked rather disconcerted.

"Surely that's a long distance for such an errand. Aren't there enough chuckies on this side of the water?"

"Not the sort she requires," replied Julia firmly, "except on your foreshore, and of course she can't go there now."

At this he seemed even more uncomfortable.

"Oh, come now, Miss Julia, there was no need to take me as seriously as all that, especially now when you are helping me so kindly with this canvassing business. Why, Lisbeth told me Miss Lendrum went round herself last night with that batch of circulars. You tell her she's very welcome to anything she finds on my beach in future. Truth of the matter is, that's what I've come across about just now—to—to thank her, and see if she'd let bygones be bygones, and give me her views on this scheme of yours about Gallowgate Square."

Julia's eyes twinkled.

"I thought so!" she exclaimed. "Won't you come in and talk about it beside the fire, Mr. Bartle? It isn't much warmer to-day, though the wind has gone down in the last half-hour."

"Thanks," he responded, removing his hat as he stepped down

into the shop and followed Julia through into the cosy kitchen, "though we can't get very far without Miss Lendrum. Still, maybe you'd be good enough to let me see over the place as far as is convenient. It's like this, Miss Julia—even if your sister won't sell, I was thinking she might let me rent your premises—No! wait a minute till I explain! I shouldn't disturb her business, or even the rooms you've got upstairs—though I'd certainly be glad enough to have them too—but I've got a notion, if I carried out your suggestion, to open up this corner as a restaurant, building on at the back, and running it right along behind the Esplanade houses, with an opening into Main Street at the other end."

"Take the big chair by the fire," said Julia. "Don't mind William of Orange—he thinks every man's a burglar except Perry Boyd. Even if Merran was ready to sell and clear out to-morrow, you couldn't build anything of the kind, you know—not just there, at any rate. To do so you'd have to desecrate the tomb of goodness knows how many people and destroy an Ancient Monument besides—and there's a Society for the protection of that sort of thing."

"Well, I'm blest!" he exclaimed in excusable surprise. "I'd no idea I'd be doing all that. Of course, I knew there might be difficulties about land-tenure, but—what on earth do you mean, Miss Julia?"

"If you'll come upstairs," said Julia impressively, "and look out of our bathroom window, you'll see exactly what I mean. Another place from which you can see it is the old kirkyard at the back of Main Street; but I don't suppose you go there much. Nobody does now, not even when they're dead, because it's closed for burials. I'm not sure it isn't another Ancient Monument."

"But of course," protested Mr. Bartle as she led him up the walled-in staircase, "I wasn't thinking of—I didn't mean to build a tea-room *there*."

"Well, it's just as bad where you did mean it," Julia assured him, throwing up the stained-glass window. "Now do you see why?"

Sam Bartle stared open-mouthed.

"However did that come there? A hillock right at your back windows!"

"This," said Julia grandly, "is not a genuine hillock. It's been—er—superinduced. You're looking at the old gallows-mound of Colmskirk, and nobody can build anything where that stands."

"I suppose not," he admitted stupidly. "If you were to blast that away you'd blast the square and half the front along with it."

"And a good deal more besides," Julia added, closing the window again. "You may have heard of the Battle of Colmskirk, when the Scots defeated the Northmen with stupendous slaughter? Well, before that mound was used for the gallows it was the cairn erected over the bodies of the slain—thousands of them! You can't go blowing up all that."

Sam Bartle's rubicund colour faded a little, and turning about he clattered hastily downstairs.

"Why did no one mention this before?" he asked unsteadily. "Not that old fool, Roberton, nor your sister—not even you! I'd never have thought of buying the place if I'd known. For you're right, Miss Julia—it would never do to go pulling down walls and laying new foundations round about here. Goodness knows what you might dig up! There's no end to that sort of thing once you get a spade into it. Thank you very much for showing me. After that my mind's quite made up about Gallowgate Square. Your plan is the right one—no rebuilding except internally. I've got the car outside, and I'm off to Twabrigs this very afternoon to see an architect chap about reconstructing the innards of these cottages."

"Don't be late for the meeting, then," Julia warned him, as

she showed him out. "You'll be able to tell them all about the scheme for the square, and they'll be immensely interested. They never quite took to the Crystal Palace idea, you know."

"It was a fine idea—a very fine one," he maintained with dignity as he swung himself into his car. "But yours is more original—I'll say that for it. Eh, it's looking misty out to sea. I hope we're not in for a fog to-night."

CHAPTER XXVII

THE LOST LUCK RESTORED

WITH a cold but useful breeze behind her, the *Fiammetta* ran swiftly over the cold, grey, heaving waters of the Firth, while Merran, a warm leather jerkin zipped up to her chin and a scarlet beret pulled tightly over her brown curls, steered her in obedience to her skipper's instructions.

"This is great!" she cried exultantly as the yacht rode the waves with a conquering lift in her action and the spindrift flew back in her face. "But it won't be so good going home, I expect."

"It won't," agreed Perry, considering the weather signs, which he had learnt to read during a life's experience of sailing on the Clyde estuary, "but not for the reasons you're thinking, my dear. This wind is going to drop presently, and it will take us all our time to get back when we are ready to go. Feel like doing a spot of rowing if that happens?"

"Rather!" she responded readily. "Nothing to beat it for keeping one warm, and we'll need it after dawdling about on the beach looking for stones. Run her in behind that jutting rock, Perry. That's where I made my best finds last time, and it gives us some shelter from the wind."

"Wherever you say," he consented obligingly. "The wind's beginning to veer already, however. I say, Merran, there's a cottage, up there to the right, where they might give us some hot tea before we start home again. They do that sort of thing in summer."

"This," said Merran unnecessarily, "is not summer, but we could try."

They sailed round the sheltering rock and made fast, after which Merran got to work at once upon her search, for already the afternoons were growing short. Perry hunted near at hand, bringing his discoveries to her to be approved or discarded, and soon began to learn which stones were likely to repay the cutting and which were quite impossible.

"You'll be very helpful in time," Merran told him encouragingly. "You wouldn't believe how much Judy knows now, simply from going about with me and watching what I like or leave. She throws herself so whole-heartedly into everything. Just now it's the municipal election. I'm growing quite keen myself, since she has persuaded Sam Bartle to give up the idea of rebuilding Gallowgate Square as a super-Selfridge's."

Perry chuckled. "Properly guided," he remarked, "the chap could do a lot for the town, and he seems to be submitting with surprising meekness to Julia's guidance. He's got the sense to realize that her ideas are good, and he knows, too, that your father's daughters cut quite a lot of ice in Colmskirk. You've been doing quite a bit of canvassing for him yourself, haven't you, the last few days?"

"Partly because Julia's so keen, but chiefly," confessed Merran, "because I don't like the Tait man, and I can't believe he'd be an asset to any town council. My goodness, Perry, look at the weather!"

During the hour in which they had been wandering along the shore the wind had fallen entirely, leaving behind a calm that was almost unnatural, though they had been too much absorbed in themselves and their occupation to notice it. Now they straightened up and looked around them, to discover that a soft blanket of fog was creeping towards them over the water, blotting out every vestige of the mainland hills and the red spires of Colmskirk. The waves on which *Fiammetta* had danced her way across such a short time before had vanished, and in their place stretched a smooth, grey, shifting plain.

"Well!" was Perry's only comment when he had recovered from his first surprise, "I didn't expect it so soon and so suddenly—but at least the rowing shouldn't be too heavy on that mill-pond with the tide in our favour."

Merran gazed out over it uneasily.

"I don't know that I'm all that keen on rowing about the fairway in a dense fog—there might be other boats, and bigger ones, wandering around too. Couldn't we, at any rate, go up to the cottage first and try for some tea?"

"By all means," replied Perry amiably. He was quite ready to prolong the expedition indefinitely. There was always the hope, moreover, that the fog's sudden descent was due to a change of wind, and that it might be blown away presently by a breeze from a more propitious quarter. With both wind and tide to help them, Perry felt that the sail back might be well worth waiting for; so he followed Merran up the rough little path leading to the cottage, where they were received with kindly hospitality.

"I'll no' say that we do teas this time o' the year," admitted the woman as she showed them into the cheery comfort of her kitchen, "but you're very welcome for all that, and we'll surely find you a bite and sup if you don't mind takin' it in here. Come ben to the fire and get yourselves toasted. I mind seein' the leddy doon on the shore yonder before noo, huntin' for shells."

"Not shells," Merran corrected her, smiling, as she warmed her chilled fingers at the blaze. "I come across now and again to look for pebbles. You have some very pretty ones over here that we can't find at Colmskirk."

The woman scanned her visitor's face more closely now as she settled the kettle on to boil.

"Colmskirk?" she exclaimed. "Why, you'll be the bit leddy that keeps yon wee bead-shop aff the Esplanade. Ay, I've keekit in afore noo at your windy and seen the bonnie show. That's never what you want the chuckies for?"

"But it is," nodded Merran. "I have tools to cut and shape them when I get the right kind without cracks or flaws. Next time you are over you must come inside, and I will show you how it's done, if that would interest you."

"Ay, thank you—I'd like that fine," replied the woman, spreading a clean cloth on the table. "To tell the truth, I was thinkin' I'd gie ye a cry in ane o' thae days when I was passin'—just to speir if ye'd care to tak a string o' beads I've had by me for twa-three year. They're no use to the likes o' me, but they're bonnie—ay, they're bonnie!—and I'm thinkin' they're no' just canny either. I pickit them up doon yonder amang the rocks, and whaur they cam' frae, or hoo they got there, dear kens, for I dinna!"

"On the rocks down below there?" Something in Perry's tone startled Merran as well as their hostess. "I wonder if you would let me look at them—now?"

She stared at him in mild surprise.

"Surely! I'll awa' and fetch them the minute I get your tea maskit. Eh! but I'm real sorry I've no cakes baked for you the day. Yon's blaeberry jam, though, gin ye can mak' dae wi't on the scones."

"We could make do with much less than that," Merran assured her graciously; and when the tea was ready, and the woman had left them to go in search of the beads, she asked in eager tones, "Perry! do you think it could possibly be your great-grandmother's necklace?"

"That occurred to me, too," he answered, trying to steady his agitation, "because it was round here that girl lost them. Gosh, Merran, if the luck were to come back to Drumbruie!"

"You believe in it, then?" she asked, half-incredulously, while reminding herself that sailors were notably superstitious.

"I only know everything has gone wrong with us since we lost it. Oh! I'm not such a mutt as to attribute our family tragedies to the disappearance of a string of beads. But there's the lesser bits of ill-luck that have dogged us ever since, including this last blow about my eyes. I'll tell you what, Merran—it's all undermining my self-confidence, somehow. There's something I want, but I haven't the nerve to try for it. If the beads came back—"

"Would they give you courage?" she asked, smiling at him in a warming, intimate way. "Oh, Perry, what a baby you are! No, of course I don't think you're a fool, but—I shouldn't like my fate to hang on a string of beads!"

He leaned across the table, bending on her a queer, penetrating glance.

"Wouldn't you?" he asked. "Wouldn't you, Merran? Tell me quick, before she comes back—would you trust it to a poor unlucky devil who hasn't much more than his love to offer you? Oh, lord! I've done it now! And if you say no—"

"But I'm not going to say no," she answered, with a little laugh of sheer happiness. "You see, I happen to believe in something higher than luck—something far better, that doesn't get lost or broken.—Oh, here she comes. Look, Perry, look! Are these the fairy beads?"

The woman came down the rickety stairs, holding out the necklace towards them, and Merran gave an involuntary gasp at the beauty and colours of the roughly cut crystals, for she had never before seen any quite so fine.

"I'm sorry to be so lang awa'," said the woman apologetically, "but I'd pit them in sic' a safe place that it was a wee while afore I could lay my hand on them. Ay, I thocht ye'd think them bonnie."

"They're so bonnie," responded Perry recklessly, "that I'll buy them from you, whatever you ask, and I'll show you where they'll look bonnier still."

Rising, he took them from her, and going round the table, he hung them on Merran's neck, where they shone and sparkled—most unsuitably—against her tawny suede jerkin.

"There!" he exclaimed. "The Luck of Drumbruie on the throat of Drumbruie's future lady! Could you see a lovelier sight than that anywhere? I ask you!"

Over on the mainland the fog had rolled down from the hills, enveloping the whole coast in a soft white blanket, which struck consternation to Julia's heart as she watched it thickening against the sitting-room window and eddying out to sea.

"I needn't worry about Merran," she thought. "They must have landed fully an hour before this came on, and even if she can't get back to-night, the Patersons will take her in at the Manse—Perry, too, if she asks them. She's sure to ring up from there and let me know what she's doing. It's the meeting I'm bothered about, for one can't expect people to go out in this. Yet, if they don't—why, it's Mr. Bartle's last chance, before they vote, to tell them what he means to do for the town!"

Possibly at this stage only Julia was quite sure of Mr. Bartle's intentions; nor did she guess, as she peered out into the fog, that he himself was by no means certain of anything now, except that he no longer had any desire to rebuild Gallowgate Square. True, he was impressed with her ideas and "inspirations," and was certainly beginning to share Lisbeth's respect for her friend's brains; but in his calmer moments he told himself it was quite unthinkable that he—the great Samuel Bartle of Bartle's Stores

(Edinburgh, Glasgow, Aberdeen and Dundee, besides dozens of smaller branches)—should let himself be guided in matters of policy by a mere chit of a schoolgirl not yet seventeen.

One thing was all-important to him at the moment—that he should be elected to the Council of this burgh in which he had settled, and be thereby in a position to patronize it to the extent of his wildest dreams—or so he hoped. Samuel Bartle wished to leave his mark on this place of his adoption, and make of it a lasting monument to the magnificence of his philanthropy; and yet—so mixed are all human motives—he was genuinely eager to set Colmskirk on high among the little towns of Clydeside as possessing every advantage that money could provide. But lately he had begun to grow doubtful whether he was really heading in the right direction. There was no disguising the fact of his unpopularity, and people would not vote for a bailie whom they disliked, however mistaken they might be in that dislike.

He was still divided in his purposes when he drove out of Twabrigs late in the afternoon and headed for home. His interview with the architect had been most satisfactory, and he could look forward to getting his plans for the adapting of the Gallowgate cottages within a few weeks; indeed, the man had been quite enthusiastic.

"A most original idea, sir, and one which it will be a great pleasure to quote for. The whole thing will be unique when finished—more like an exhibition than an ordinary store. You'll be having photographers down from all the papers—a tremendous advertisement! May I ask if you are thinking of doing the same thing at any of your other country-town branches? Of course the idea wouldn't work at the big city depots—wouldn't be suitable there—but I believe you are established in various smaller places—"

"Humph!" grunted Mr. Bartle. "Mightn't be able to find

anything so suitable in them. Not every town has got a Gallowgate Square ready to my hand. And remember, Colson, the whole thing's to be interior—no digging out foundations to build on at the back of the premises, or—or anything of that sort. I don't know if you'd call it architecture exactly, but the great thing is to preserve its character."

Mr. Colson quite understood and entirely agreed; in fact, it was a long time since Sam Bartle had found anyone who agreed with him so entirely, and he drove away from the office feeling wonderfully soothed. Moreover, if Julia was right, he should find the meeting equally in agreement with him that evening, when he told them what he had decided to do about Gallowgate Square; they had seemed pleased, too, on Friday, with his hints concerning a possible hospital. Surely, under these pleasant circumstances, they would also come round to his views regarding the fun-fair at Meadows. Mr. Bartle was very loath to abandon his fun-fair; nothing else, he felt, would give the town such standing.

Occupied with these musings, he was scarcely aware that the wind had gone down, and that the atmosphere was thickening about him, until, rounding a wooded bend in the road, he found himself enveloped in a dense, white, impenetrable fog.

CHAPTER XXVIII

JULIA SAVES THE SITUATION

DESPITE the untempting weather outside, the little town hall was filling up rapidly; for there was a spice of mystery about this Council election—the mysterious Bs, the rumours and counter-rumours—that had gripped the public and roused its curiosity. Julia, as she slipped into the corner which Mr. Bartle's agent had kept for her at the back of the platform, began to feel that she had been needlessly nervous. People were not staying at home because of the fog, which now was beginning to shift and lessen. In family parties and in solitary units the good burghers of Colmskirk were jostling in to hear what Sam Bartle had to say for himself, before they gave their votes at the end of the week. They had heard Brolly Tait, and knew that there were no sensations to be looked for there. Brolly Tait was sound and solid; if they put him in the vacant chair he would fill it as all the other bailies—good, honest men—had done before him. He had no desire to build a Blackpool on Scotland's green and pleasant coast. The wildest innovation at which he hinted was a possible lowering of the rates, and that, though startling and novel, was not unpleasing—and anyhow, nobody believed in it for one moment.

But Sam Bartle—past experience of his six years among them had served to show that goodness only knew what he would be up to next, but that at all costs he must be prevented from doing it.

The agent, a harassed-looking young man, came on for a moment from behind the scenes and surveyed the gathering crowd.

"They've come to ask questions," he complained in Julia's ear, "and how the dickens are we going to answer them?"

"We don't have to," she replied cheerfully. "Mr. Bartle will do all that himself. I believe he means to let them into some of his secrets to-night."

"Huh! does he?" said the agent sceptically. "What I say is, you never know with Mr. Bartle, and it keeps you in a state of nervous tension up to the last minute."

"I quite agree," answered Julia. "That's why all these people have turned up to-night."

"Yes, but," said the plaintive Mr. Lawson, "he hasn't turned up himself, and it's very nearly time to begin. I've been 'phoning in all directions—even Miss Bartle can't help—"

"What?" cried Julia, startled out of her complaisance. "Hasn't he arrived yet? Why, look at the clock! Where's Lisb—Miss Bartle!"

"I'm looking at it," said the agent gloomily. "Miss Bartle should be here any moment. She has been waiting for him at home till now, but when I rang through a minute ago they said she was on her way. She thinks he may come straight to the hall. It's that confounded fog, of course. It's got the chairman held up, too."

"But it's lifting now. A man who came in just now said there was a slight breeze springing up—a westerly breeze."

"It may be lifting here," replied the pessimistic Lawson, "but that's no guarantee it's clearing farther along on the Twabrigs road, and that's where Mr. Bartle is, or should be, at the present moment; for he ran over to Twabrigs early in the afternoon about—Oh, here's Miss Bartle!"

Lisbeth hurried up the short steps at the back of the platform, breathless and glowing, having run all the way from the Broomieknowes.

"Oh, there you are, Julia!" she cried. "This awful fog—but it's thinning now. Has Daddy arrived? Oh, gracious! I made sure he'd be here by this. Why, the meeting is due to start in five minutes!"

"If it starts in fifty-five we'll be lucky," stated the agent. "And how we're to keep that audience quiet till he comes is more than I can tell!"

"For goodness' sake, Lawson," snapped Lisbeth impatiently, "don't stand there wringing your hands and looking so lugubrious! We shall have to hold the people somehow till Daddy gets here, and you must think of a way. Where's the chairman?"

"Who is the chairman?" inquired Julia.

"A business friend of Daddy's who promised to come down from Glasgow for the meeting. He—he couldn't get anyone locally, so he asked this man."

"Exactly," said young Lawson, "and he's probably sitting in the train somewhere up the line. I 'phoned the station, and they told me all the trains are about an hour late."

Down below the audience was beginning to fidget and murmur. Some instinct told Julia that before very long they would rise in ones and twos and straggle out, taking with them the same opinion of Sam Bartle as they had brought in—the prevalent opinion that was going to spoil the voting for him on Saturday morning. Unless they were told they would never know how his ideas had altered of late, and how valuable he could be to Colmskirk. Her eye fell on Sandy Lamond sitting at the end of the front row, and she clutched Lisbeth's arm.

"Lisbeth," she urged, "we must have a chairman, and we must get going. I believe Sandy Lamond would take the chair if you asked him. I know you'd hardly call him a city father or anything weighty like that, but he's well known and he has plenty of sense. Shall I ask him?"

"Yes, do." Lisbeth accepted the suggestion with fervour. "He might do it for you, even if he isn't keen on all Daddy's ideas."

"He'll be keen enough when he knows what they are," Julia assured her stoutly, and slipped down into the hall, to return in a few seconds with Sandy, bewildered and protesting, in her train.

"He's a little shy about it," she informed Lisbeth, who was awaiting them at the head of the steps, the perspiring Lawson having withdrawn to telephone once more to the station, "but he'll do it just to help us out of a fix—at least, till the real chairman arrives. You will, won't you, Sandy?"

"My dear Julia, I'm willing to do anything I can in reason, but—"

"Thank you very much, Sandy! It's really awfully good of you, because this meeting is most important, and it would be appalling if it broke up and went home before Mr. Bartle had a chance of explaining what he means to do."

"Yes; but, Julia, hold hard a minute! It isn't enough to provide a temporary chairman for a meeting—you need speakers too, and where are they?"

"There was only Daddy," Lisbeth told him unhappily. "He had a good deal to say—and then he knew he would have to answer questions."

"And who will answer them now? Lawson?"

"Heaven forbid!" ejaculated Julia. "Lisbeth, you'll have to do it."

"But, Julia, I shan't know what to say!"

"Oh, yes, you will, more or less. If you leave it to Lawson he'll destroy every hope your father's got, and probably burst into tears as well. He should never have taken up this kind of work, for he goes to pieces in an emergency."

"Well, there's no time to argue," said Lisbeth in desperation. "Come along, Mr. Lamond, and let's do the best we can. If only this fog is fading out everywhere else down the coast, Daddy might be here at any moment."

Sandy Lamond's quiet exterior hid a freakish sense of humour, which stood him in good stead now as he moved to the front of the platform, followed falteringly by Lisbeth in her green woollen suit with its beaver collar and a beaver cap on her fair curls, looking very young and scared, and surreptitiously gripping Julia's hand to make sure that she did not stray beyond her reach. Lawson, just back from his fruitless errand, brought up the rear in melancholy trepidation.

"Thank heaven," he muttered, "somebody's going to do something!"

"Ladies and gentlemen," began Sandy in his pleasant, well-trained voice, "it's fortunate, perhaps, that you all know me well enough to dispense with an introduction, since there's no one here to perform such a ceremony. In fact, I must introduce myself as the chairman of this meeting, *pro tem.*, since the gentleman who was to do the job has gone astray in the fog, and so, too, has Mr. Bartle. Still, the weather is improving, so there's every hope that they may both be with us presently. Till then—I believe you have some questions to ask, and it is possible that Miss Bartle (who is here with us) may be able to answer some of them. She is ready when you are."

He sat down, and a murmur ran round the hall again, indistinct except for one voice louder than the rest which carried to the platform.

"A bit lassie like yon! What-like answers can she gie us? This meeting's naethin' but a wash-oot, and we maun just awa' hame!"

The speaker made a movement to rise—a movement that

would certainly have spread through the rest of the gathering—but before he had time to get to his feet a wholly unexpected figure in a brown frieze coat sprang to the edge of the dais, shaking back her mane of thick brown curls.

"You maun just do nothing of the kind, Willie Macdougal." Julia's tones rose clear and high in indignation. "The chairman has told you that Miss Bartle will answer all the questions she can, and I can think of nothing more unsporting than for you to go off without asking her even one. If you don't know any, at least you can sit still and listen to what other people have to say. I can see Mrs. Nisbet sitting over there at the back, and I know she's got something to ask."

And poor faithful Maggie, who had not had the faintest intention till that moment of opening her lips, bleated feebly without rising from her seat to which she appeared to be glued, "Ay, Miss Julia, ay! I'm no' just verra guid at speakin' in public, but there's ae thing we're a' wantin' tae ken wha live in Gallowgate Square—"

"Yes, Mrs. Nisbet?" said the chairman encouragingly. "Let's hear what it is?"

But Maggie had gone as far as she dared. Giving her husband a dig in the ribs, she said, "Dave—Dave 'ull dae the speirin'. Come on, Davie mon! Ye ken what it is we're a' wantin' tae ken." And Dave, thus urged, shambled to his feet.

"We'd like fine," he said deprecatingly, "gin the young leddy could tell us what her faither's thinkin' tae dae wi' the property he's bocht in oor Square?"

Lisbeth came forward, a flush of mingled nervousness and excitement on her face.

"Oh, yes!" she replied eagerly. "I can tell you about that, and it really is something marvellous which no one has ever thought of doing before. First of all, he means to see that those of you who live there are moved into new comfortable homes in another part of the town, which you'll choose for yourselves. And then he's going to re-thatch the cottages—"

"Is he no' going to pu' them a' doon, and build a grand shop?" called an incredulous voice from the left.

"No, he is not!" Lisbeth answered emphatically. "He's going to have their insides all re-done and convert them into one shop as they stand. They'll look like—like the clachan at the Glasgow Exhibition when you go into them, but outside they'll be just the same as ever."

This idea was so new and staggering to the majority of her listeners that, for the moment, it completely took their breath away. But there was no longer any fear of the audience going home, and presently a buxom lady in the front row called out, "We'd like an answer to a question that's been puzzling us all, Mr. Chairman, for long enough, and perhaps Miss Bartle can give it. What's the meaning of all those Bs about the town?"

Sandy looked across at Lisbeth and raised his brows.

"I can't tell you if Miss Bartle knows the answer to that one," he said. "If she does, she is in the minority. What about it, Miss Bartle?"

Lisbeth smiled and dimpled.

"I believe I do," she admitted, "but it's a secret till polling-day. Then the people who get up early in the morning will be the first to solve the mystery. I can only tell you that it stands for something you will all like very much."

The meeting had begun to settle down to a pleasant humour, but at this an angry, strident voice from the body of the hall shouted out tipsily, "That's an absolute lie, and you know it! There isn't a soul in Colmskirk who'll be pleased to hear what those four Bs stand for, and not a chance for Sam Bartle when they know. I dare you to speak the truth!"

So far Lisbeth had got on well in her very unaccustomed position, and was beginning to gain confidence from her kindly reception; but now she flinched and fell back a little, and her voice was not quite so steady, though she retorted with spirit:

"My father has nothing to do with the four Bs—he is only concerned with the five; and I am speaking the truth when I say that Colmskirk will be delighted with what they stand for."

"Then tell us what they are!" challenged Mr. Tait's supporter from the ranks below.

"Suppose," retorted someone else in sympathy with the rather scared little figure on the platform, "*you* was to tell us aboot the fower Bs, gin ye ken sic' a lot! We may as weel start wi' them, since they cam' first. That is if they've got ony meanin' at a', which is no' sae sure!"

The man's tone was irritating and aggressive, and suddenly the heckler's control, already somewhat undermined by drink, snapped altogether.

"Is it not?" he shouted. "I'll tell you, then, and see how you like it. The four Bs stand for this—'Bartle to Build Bungalows on the Broomieknowes.' How does that please you, Colmskirk folk?"

In an instant of temper the well-kept secret of the past weeks was out, and pandemonium was let loose in the Burgh Chambers. In vain Sandy Lamond tried to regain control of the meeting—in vain Lawson waved his arms and stamped his feet on the edge of the dais, while Lisbeth withdrew helplessly to the rear. Down below people were mobbing the alarmed heckler and demanding to hear more. It was quite plain that they believed the slogan from their past experience of Sam Bartle's activities, and were roused to a surprising pitch of fury.

There was a slight commotion round the door at the back of the platform, which only Lisbeth noticed. With a despairing sob she rushed to her father as he entered, and clung to his arm.

"Oh, Daddy," she cried, "we tried to keep the meeting going for you, but they have found out about those bungalows, and now they'll listen to nobody. What can we do about it?"

But for once Mr. Bartle's confidence had deserted him. This was so different from the meeting to which he had been looking forward, driving as fast as he dared through the fog. So this was what the public thought about the bungalows, and the girls had been right after all! For a moment his chances of a bailie-ship looked very dim.

Only for a moment, however—then Julia, still unaware of his arrival, reached the front of the platform again. Taking advantage of a second's lull in the hubbub below her, she called in a clear, ringing voice, "Please, everybody, will you listen to me for one minute? The cat's out of the bag now as regards the four Bs, but that's only Mr. Tait's cat—and, let me tell you, it's stuffed! The real animal isn't out yet, but I'm afraid it will have to come, and I'm ready to explain to you about the *five* Bs if you'll only let me."

It was plain at once that she had gained their attention and roused their curiosity. Nearly everybody there knew and liked "the doctor's lassies," and a man's voice called out, "Ay, we'll let ye! Gin onybody has the temeerity to interrupt, I'll sort him! Wheesht, noo, folk, and hear what Miss Julia's got to tell us."

CHAPTER XXIX

HAPPY ENDINGS

JULIA turned towards the chair with dancing eyes, and Sandy nodded permission for her first public speech. At this moment of crisis all her long words and grandiloquence fell from her, and she became a schoolgirl bent on seeing fair play.

"Thank you very much, Mr. Gregor," she called back gaily, "but I don't believe anyone's going to interrupt—they'll be far too much taken up with what I'm going to tell you all. If you'd waited till Saturday morning on your way to vote you would have seen the answer to the puzzle of the five Bs—'Bartle Buys the Broomieknowes to Benefit the Burgh.' That's the truth, the whole truth, and nothing but the truth, and I'll tell you what it means. Mr. Bartle has bought the Broomieknowes so that he can give them to Colmskirk for a public park, and nobody will ever be able to build there through generations yet unborn. He is putting seats there for the old people, and a drinking-fountain; but these are the only changes he will make. That's rather a different tale from Mr. Tait's, isn't it? No, don't clap yet—I haven't finished. Miss Bartle has told you about what her father means to do with Gallowgate Square, and last week you heard what he himself had to say about a hospital. Can't you see for yourselves he's a public benefactor, and ought to be on the Council if anybody ever did? Won't you all vote for him on Saturday, and give him a chance to help us?"

Above the burst of applause that answered her rose one sinister query. “Meadows! Can you tell what he’s going to do with Meadows?”

For a moment Julia wavered, and glanced back at Lisbeth to see her father standing beside her in the shadow of the heavy curtains, anxiety in every line of his face. At last Sam Bartle realized on how slight a thread his chances hung, and he was badly frightened. That glimpse gave Julia her cue, and like a flash she swung round again to the audience.

“Yes, I can tell you what Mr. Bartle is going to do with Meadows. Not a vulgar, blaring fun-fair, as everybody seems to expect, but a public library, with reading-rooms, writing-rooms, and reference-rooms. There may be other attractions, too, but he hasn’t had time yet to work out all the details—and anyhow, that should be enough to begin with!”

In the background her candidate was mopping his brow and protesting indignantly.

“I said nothing about a library with reading-rooms or any other trimmings. Stop her, Lamond—Leebie—or she’ll be promising them botanic gardens and a zoo! I hadn’t even made up my mind definitely about the Broomieknowes!”

“Never mind, Daddy!” said Lisbeth, laughing hysterically. “It’s been made up for you, and a good thing, too! You saw what they thought of your bungalows—but Julia has saved the election for you. Oh, you’re going to win, hands down, after all! I don’t believe Tait has the ghost of a chance from to-night, and it’s entirely thanks to Julia! Now, all you have to do is to go forward and confirm her promises. Look, they’ve seen you—they’re waiting.”

Sam Bartle braced his shoulders, pulled down his waistcoat with a jerk, and stepped out into the full blaze of the electric lights, where, to his astonishment, he was greeted by a loud burst of clapping, led by Julia ere she retreated to her place in the background beside Lisbeth.

"It's all right," she whispered rapidly and reassuringly as she passed him. "I don't know if you heard all I said, but just remember you're giving them a hospital, a library, and the Broomieknowes, besides reconditioning the Square. I shouldn't promise them anything more in the meantime. Just hang on to what I've said."

"And that's more than enough!" he replied ruefully. "It's a mercy I arrived before you'd completely ruined me!"

The applause was dying down now, and the audience settled back in their seats to hear what he had to say on his own behalf; but for once in his successful career Mr. Bartle had lost his self-assurance.

"Ladies and gentlemen," he began, and stopped to clear his throat. "Ladies and gentlemen, I owe you an apology, first of all, for coming late to my own meeting; but that was due to conditions over which I had no control. It seems you have been well entertained in my absence, however—so well that there appears to be very little left for me to say now that I'm here. I asked you to meet me to-night so that I might tell you what I hoped to do for Colmskirk, if you should see fit to vote me on to the Burgh Council. But I understand Miss Julia Lendrum has put my programme before you a good deal better than I could have done myself, so I have nothing to do but to endorse the promises she has given in my name. You now understand—in spite of the malicious stories put about by my opponent—what I intend to do with the Broomieknowes, and also with my property in Gallowgate Square. You know that I'm prepared to help you to a cottage hospital as soon as a site has been provided, because, between you and me, I begin to think I haven't got what the newspaper chaps call a flair for picking out sites in this locality.

You have also heard to-night that I am going to set about founding a free library and other items at Meadows. That scheme is perhaps a bit nebulous at present, but I'll need to get together a committee of townsfolk and work it out. Meantime, I don't think there's anything left for me to do except to thank Miss Julia and Mr. Lamond for handling the meeting so well in my unavoidable absence, and to ask you all if you'll kindly vote on Saturday for Bartle of Bartle's Stores."

A roar of cheering greeted him as he stepped back, mopping his forehead again with a large bandanna handkerchief, and left Sandy Lamond to declare the meeting closed. In the room behind the platform, however, he took Julia solemnly by the hand and said, "Young lady, I hear from Leebie yonder that you're training to take a secretarial post when you leave the Academy in spring. Well, if that's so I'll ask leave, here and now, to engage you as my secretary the minute you qualify. If I get on to that Council on Saturday it will be your doing, and yours alone."

Before the next week opened Sam Bartle had achieved his two ambitions—he was a bailie of the Royal and Ancient Burgh with a new popularity behind him that he found as sweet as it was unwonted; and on his desk lay a letter which ran as follows:—

"DEAR MR. BARTLE,

"I should like to be among the first to congratulate you on your great success at Saturday's polling, which gave both my sister and myself much pleasure; but I also wish to approach you on a matter of business. As I expect very shortly to marry Mr. Boyd of Drumbruie, I shall no longer require the whole of my present premises, and should therefore be willing to lease you all except the shop and workroom. Those I wish to retain, as I intend to carry on the business with my future husband to help me regarding the furniture and antiques.

"If this suggestion interests you, perhaps you will kindly let me know, and I am sure we shall be able to come to terms.

"Yours sincerely,

"MARION MARGARET LENDRUM."

APPENDIX: ERRORS IN THE FIRST EDITION

The first edition of *The Serendipity Shop* contains very few errors. Here are some notes on those we have found.

We have standardised the spellings of 'Drumbruie' (it appeared twice as 'Drumbuie'), 'workroom' (there were a few occurrences of 'work-room'), 'to-morrow' (there was one 'tomorrow'), 'good-bye' (there was one 'goodbye'), 'bailie' (there was one 'Bailie') and 'Brolly' (there was one 'Brolley'), and corrected 'Tater's compartment' on page 208 to 'Taters' compartment' for consistency with the usage in the rest of the book. On page 130 we have changed '"with than end in view"' to '"with that end in view"'.

We have not attempted to correct the punctuation, except as noted above and in a very few places where a comma or a quotation mark was obviously required and there was a gap for it in the typeset text, indicating that the omission must have been a typographical error. The following anomalies are possibly also typographical errors, but since we could not be sure of this, we have left them as we found them:

p46: '"... we little thought, when we went out this afternoon that we should come back to find ..."' (unbalanced comma)
p54: '"... one story above the shop."' (storey?)
p174: 'made her way down Clyde' (down *the* Clyde?)
p177: 'She broke off, slightly, alarmed by the concentrated scorn ...' (superfluous comma?)
p222: '"I'm not on in this."' (in on this?)
p231: '"It doesn't come off anyhow, for another two weeks ..."' (missing comma)
p232: '"... mad-cat schemes ..."' (mad-cap?)

The firm that is known as 'Beith and Lamond' at the start of the book becomes 'Lamond and Beith' after Chapter XVI.

On page 123 Jenty is Perry's great-great-grandmother, but on pages 153 and 240 she is his great-grandmother.

Occasionally an exclamation mark appears in the middle of a sentence, and is followed by a lower-case letter—we have not interfered with this, as it appears to be a feature of the author's style. Similarly, we have not altered the transcriptions of dialect speech, although they are inconsistent in places.

Sarah Woodall, with thanks to Ruth Ogden

Girls Gone By Publishers

Girls Gone By Publishers republish some of the most popular children's fiction from the 20th century, concentrating on those titles which are most sought after and difficult to find on the second-hand market. We aim to make them available at affordable prices, thus making ownership possible for both existing collectors and new ones so that the books continue to survive. Authors on our list include Margaret Biggs, Elinor Brent-Dyer, Dorita Fairlie Bruce, Gwendoline Courtney, Monica Edwards, Antonia Forest, Lorna Hill, Clare Mallory, Violet Needham, Elsie Jeanette Oxenham, Malcolm Saville and Geoffrey Trease. We also publish some new titles which continue the traditions of this genre.

Our series '**Fun in the Fourth—Outstanding Girls' School Stories**' has enabled us to broaden our range of authors, allowing our readers to discover a fascinating range of books long unobtainable. It features authors who only wrote one or two such books, a few of the best examples from more prolific authors (such as Dorothea Moore), and some very rare titles by authors whose other books are generally easy to find second-hand (such as Josephine Elder).

We also have a growing range of non-fiction: more general works about the genre and books on particular authors. These include *Island to Abbey* by Stella Waring and Sheila Ray (about Elsie Oxenham), *The Marlows and their Maker* by Anne Heazlewood (about Antonia Forest) and *The Monica Edwards Romney Marsh Companion* by Brian Parks. These are in a larger format than the fiction, and are lavishly illustrated in colour and black and white.

For details of availability and ordering (please do not order until titles are actually listed) go to www.ggbp.co.uk or write for a catalogue to Clarissa Cridland or Ann Mackie-Hunter, GGBP, 4 Rock Terrace, Coleford, Bath, BA3 5NF, UK.